"It's a girl," the doctor announced.

Eyes still closed, Lexie tried to catch her breath. A girl. She'd brought a little girl into the world. All by herself. Not exactly how she'd expected to deliver this baby.

Lexie returned her attention to the newborn in her arms. A surge of warmth flooded through her, tightening her throat, making it hard to breathe.

This child was depending on her. And Lexie wasn't going to let her down.

A wrinkled hand clasped the edge of the curtain and drew it back. Pappy leaned closer, peering down at the bundle in Lexie's arms. "Aw. Look at that sweet face. I think she looks like you."

"Really?" Lexie studied the infant she held.

"Yup. Definitely has your nose."

Huh. That was interesting. Considering the child wasn't hers.

Available in February 2006 from Silhouette Superromance

Whose Child?
by Susan Gable
(A Little Secret)

Two on the Run
by Margaret Watson
(Count on a Cop)

The Daughter Dilemma
by Ann Evans
(Heart of the Rockies)

To Save This Child
by Darlene Graham

Whose Child?
SUSAN GABLE

DID YOU PURCHASE THIS BOOK WITHOUT A COVER?
If you did, you should be aware it is **stolen property** as it was
reported *unsold and destroyed* by a retailer. Neither the author nor
the publisher has received any payment for this book.

All the characters in this book have no existence outside the imagination of the author, and have no relation whatsoever to anyone bearing the same name or names. They are not even distantly inspired by any individual known or unknown to the author, and all the incidents are pure invention.

All Rights Reserved including the right of reproduction in whole or in part in any form. This edition is published by arrangement with Harlequin Enterprises II B.V. The text of this publication or any part thereof may not be reproduced or transmitted in any form or by any means, electronic or mechanical, including photocopying, recording, storage in an information retrieval system, or otherwise, without the written permission of the publisher.

This book is sold subject to the condition that it shall not, by way of trade or otherwise, be lent, resold, hired out or otherwise circulated without the prior consent of the publisher in any form of binding or cover other than that in which it is published and without a similar condition including this condition being imposed on the subsequent purchaser.

Silhouette, Silhouette Superromance and Colophon are registered trademarks of Harlequin Books S.A., used under licence.

First published in Great Britain 2006
Silhouette Books, Eton House, 18-24 Paradise Road,
Richmond, Surrey TW9 1SR

© Susan Guadagno 2004

ISBN 0 373 71204 9

38-0206

Printed and bound in Spain
by Litografía Rosés S.A., Barcelona

Dear Reader,

I grew up reading a lot of science fiction, and it amazes me that some things imagined by authors long ago have become reality. Scientific progress has been amazing. But sometimes science raises more questions than answers.

Advances in fertility techniques have helped many people create the happy families they want. But occasionally I wonder about some of the ramifications. You read stories in the news about surrogates who changed their minds, or fertility clinics that made mistakes, or even about babies switched in the hospital and raised for years by people who love them, then the courts getting involved in deciding whose child is whose, breaking the hearts of parents and causing trauma for the children.

Situations like that are sparks for a writer's imagination—at least, they are for mine. That kind of question led to this story. What makes a parent? Is it DNA? Is it raising and caring for a child, being there when the child is sick, setting up day-to-day routines? Is it love so large that sacrificing everything for the sake of this child is first nature?

I hope you'll enjoy this story about two people who love a child so much they're willing to put that child first in their lives.

I'd love to hear from you! Visit my website, www.susangable.com, e-mail me at Susan@susangable.com, or send me a letter at PO Box 9313, Erie, PA 16505, USA.

Sincerely,

Susan Gable

To Tom, my personal hero, whose unwavering support and faith keep me going.
Thank you for putting up with the many pitfalls of life with a writer.

Special thanks to:

All the editors at Superromance, especially Zilla and Paula, who gave me a chance, and Johanna and Laura, who continue to give me a chance. To Lara, for answering all my questions. Also, to all of the other wonderful people who work for Silhouette! Thank you for helping make my dreams become reality.

Julie Jackman-Brink, my faithful Montana adviser. Go Grizzlies!

The town of Philipsburg, Montana, whose geographical location I have usurped for Mill Creek, and who provided some of the inspiration for my fictional Montana town. (To enjoy a trip to Philipsburg without leaving home, go to www.philipsburgmt.com.)

Heather Davis, from Northwest Plastic Surgery, who answered my questions about port wine birthmarks and laser treatments.

Lisa, for coming up with the perfect back story. I miss you.

Sus, for her eagle eyes in going over this manuscript, her encouragement and friendship.

Last, but definitely most, Jen, a true friend and great cp. I couldn't do it without you.

PROLOGUE

LEXIE JACOBS HAD NEVER felt more afraid or alone in her life.

That said a lot, since the two sensations had become near-constant companions in the past few months.

"I don't know how I'm going to pay you," she said for at least the eighth or ninth time. "I don't have any money." Yesterday she'd given her last twenty to the old man who'd offered her a room in his enormous old Victorian house. After her car had died just outside of town. In the snow. She had a total of $4.63 left in her pocket. "And I don't have any insurance—" Searing pain radiated through her body as her uterus contracted, transforming her semicoherent babbling into a twisted moan.

"I told you, don't worry about that. This baby is coming into the world *now,* whether you've got money and insurance or not. And since I'm not about to let you deliver on the sidewalk—good! The baby's head is crowning, Lexie. We're almost there," the young doctor said, looking up at her. "Push!"

The nurse, an older woman with black hair, propped her upright. "Come on, honey. Push hard!" She started counting.

Lexie scrunched her eyes shut and bore down with everything she had. Sweat trickled down the side of her face. Time blurred, measured in sets of ten-counts as she pushed and the unbelievably short minute-and-a-half rest periods between contractions.

Relief came as the child was pulled from her body.

"It's a girl," the doctor announced.

"Congratulations, honey," the nurse murmured as she lowered Lexie to the exam table.

Eyes still closed, she tried to catch her breath. A girl. She'd brought a little girl into the world.

All by herself.

The sharp, reedy wail of the newborn elicited cheers from the waiting room beyond the faded curtain of the tiny medical clinic in the equally small town of Mill Creek, Montana.

Not exactly where or how she'd expected to deliver this baby.

No, that was supposed to be Millcreek, Pennsylvania. And David was supposed to be at her side.

"Boy or girl?" someone shouted.

"A baby girl," the doctor answered.

Applause thundered back, and a chorus of "Happy Birthday" began from the other patients who'd been forced to wait when Lexie, clutching her enormous belly, had stumbled into the clinic on the arm of the old man who'd insisted she call him Pappy.

Warmed by the response from these people, she opened her eyes to see the doctor pass the squirming, squalling infant to the nurse. The nurse's smile faded, and her expression held a question as she looked down at him. He shook his head slightly.

"What? Is something wrong?" Lexie's voice caught as a sliver of panic swelled in her throat. "Can I see her?"

"Everything's fine," he said. "Let's just have Martha clean her up for you first, and then weigh and measure her. Besides, we're not finished here. We still have more work to do."

"Everything's there?" she asked, not reassured. Her prenatal care had been lacking recently. Being on the run would do that. "All the fingers and toes, and everything else?"

"Ten perfect little toes, ten long fingers—this one's going to play the piano," the nurse answered from the other side of the curtain where she'd disappeared with the baby.

Exhausted, Lexie closed her eyes again, barely registering the doctor's soft-spoken comments as he delivered the afterbirth and whatever else went on after a woman had a baby. She was too tired to care.

At least, about that. She had more important things to worry about.

A while later, a warm masculine voice penetrated the haze of drowsiness she couldn't seem to shake. "Lexie?"

"Hmm?"

The doctor—she kept thinking of him as the young doctor, even though he had to be several years older than she was, but then, she'd aged a heck of a lot in the past four months—stood beside her, a blanket-wrapped bundle in his arms. "Does she have a name?" he asked gently.

A name.

It wasn't supposed to be her responsibility to name this child. But now... An overwhelming flood of homesickness poured through her—the same empty ache that had driven her off the main highway onto the Pintler Scenic Route, in the direction of a tiny town that shared its name with her hometown. How she wished her own mother could be here. "Sarah," she choked out. "Her name is Sarah."

"That's pretty." He edged closer, his eyebrows drawing together. "Now, before I give her to you, I want to explain something."

Lexie's stomach did a double cartwheel. "Something *is* wrong." She rose up on her elbows, reached out one hand toward the baby. "What's the matter?"

"It's not serious. I just wanted to give you a little warning. She has a port-wine birthmark on her face."

"Let me see her." She accepted the wiggling bundle swaddled in a white blanket. Round, chubby cheeks, tiny button nose, wisps of dark hair—and the right side of her little face blotched with a deep purple mark, as though someone had spilled grape juice on her.

Lexie's lower lip trembled and tears welled up, blurring her vision. "It's my fault," she whispered. "Oh, baby, I'm so sorry."

"It's not your fault."

She looked at the doctor through a watery haze. "Is

it genetic?" Bad genes triggering the birthmark would go far to soothe her guilt.

He shook his head. "No. It's just something that happens."

"Then how do you know it's not my fault? I haven't seen a doctor in months, and—"

"It just happens," he repeated firmly. "No one's at fault."

Lexie returned her attention to the newborn in her arms. The tiny mouth stretched open in a yawn. She stroked the baby's unblemished cheek, causing the infant to turn her head. Soft pink lips pursed in a sucking motion.

A surge of warmth flamed across Lexie's chest, tightening her throat, making it hard to breathe. Despite the fact that her milk wouldn't come in for a few days, her breasts ached with the need to nurse the baby. This child was depending on her. Had been depending on her for some time. And Lexie wasn't going to let her down.

She'd protect her from everything and everyone.

"They're doing great work with new lasers on port-wine stains," the doctor was saying.

Borderline hysterical laughter bubbled from her. "I'm sure $4.63 will take care of that." The chuckling continued even as tears coursed along the line of her nose. "I don't even have a place to go."

A wrinkled hand clasped the edge of the curtain, and drew it back. A face deeply lined from too much sun, wind and numerous years appeared. "You and that baby can stay with me, Missy, for as long as you want. I told you that. I got me more room than I need in that big old place."

"Oh, Pappy." If angels really existed, Lexie knew they didn't have wings, but wore battered Montana Grizzlies baseball caps to cover snow-white hair. "Thank you."

"A few of the ladies are already putting together some stuff for you and the little one."

"Stuff?" Lexie sniffled. The doctor offered her a tissue, and she wiped at her nose one-handed.

"Old baby clothes, blankets, that kind of thing."

A tiny flicker of hope blossomed deep inside her. She wasn't alone anymore. A little girl now shared her life. And the town of Mill Creek had adopted them both.

Pappy leaned closer, peering down at the bundle in Lexie's arms. "Aw. Look at that sweet face."

Once again, she silently blessed this old man with the enormous heart for not mentioning the baby's obvious birthmark.

"I think she kinda looks like you, Missy."

"Really?" she blurted out, taking another long look at the infant she held.

"Yup. Definitely has your nose."

Huh. That was interesting.

Considering the child wasn't hers.

CHAPTER ONE

Almost four years later...

THE CARDBOARD coffee cup trembled in David Mitchell's hand. And he hadn't even taken a sip of the high-octane espresso yet. Few people lingered in the café area of the Barnes & Noble. The final Saturday of September had brought Indian summer with it, so everyone was probably enjoying a last hurrah down on the Peninsula or someplace else outdoors before the long Pennsylvania winter descended.

He glanced at his watch. Where the hell was she?

As if summoned by his thoughts, the fifth, and hopefully last, private investigator he'd hired appeared around the half wall that separated the rest of the store from the café. Short, stocky, with an olive complexion and hair more gray than black, she looked more like someone's Italian grandmother than a P.I. or ex-policewoman.

When she met his gaze, Betty Leicester's face lit up. A broad grin appeared as she hurried toward the table he'd claimed in the corner.

David hastily set the coffee down as the liquid sloshed toward the rim. Surely an expression like that meant good news, right?

She dropped into the chair across from him, laying a black leather briefcase on the table. "I told you my methods would work. I found her."

The muscle along the side of his jaw tensed. He sat up straighter. "Where? And? What's the story?"

"A small town out West." She reached over and patted the back of his hand. "Congratulations. You have a daughter."

A daughter.

For four years he'd wondered if the child he'd fathered had actually been born or not. Worried he or she was out there, living without him. Living without a father's guidance, support…

And now he knew.

He had a daughter.

His hand curled into a tight fist and he resisted the urge to cover his mouth with it—or smash it down into the wooden tabletop, torn between shouting with glee and venting his frustration at having four years of his child's life stolen from him. Torn between elation, and hanging his head with shame. "How is she? Are they together? Is she okay? How did you finally find them?"

Betty held up a hand with a chuckle. "Whoa, easy there. One thing at a time. Yes, they're together, and your daughter is being extremely well cared for. Lexie is an excellent mother, so there's nothing to worry about there."

David raised an eyebrow at Lexie Jacobs being referred to as his child's mother. He'd thought of Lexie as many things over the years, but mother of his child—that concept took enormous getting used to. It wasn't what they'd planned on. But after almost four years…his child surely thought of her as her mother.

He chugged back a swallow of the now-lukewarm coffee to prevent a sharp retort. He hadn't told this P.I. everything. It wasn't her business.

Besides, the full story sounded almost like something you'd read in one of those trashy tabloids from a grocery checkout counter—a tangled web of relationships, intrigue and…betrayal.

"How I found them…" Betty's face grew serious, and she shifted in the chair. "David, I found them through a temp receptionist who did some work for a plastic surgeon. It was the lucky break we needed. I knew those missing-persons posters and the Internet exposure would get you a better response."

"Plastic surgeon? Lexie went that far to hide from me?"

The older woman shook her head. "Not for her."

"I don't understand."

She reached into the briefcase. "Your daughter, whose name is Sarah, by the way—" she shot him a look that said he'd failed in some way by not asking "—is being treated for a birthmark on her face." She laid several three-by-five photographs across the table.

His fingers shook as he reached for them. *Definitely too much caffeine in the espresso.* The first picture, of a small girl with a tentative smile, sandy-brown curly hair and a purplish stain marring a large portion of her one cheek, made him suck in his breath.

His little girl.

A bizarre sensation struck, as though a giant had grabbed him and was squeezing his chest.

"Do you still want her?" Betty asked softly.

His head jerked up from the photo. "What kind of question is that? This is *my* child, for God's sake. You think a mark like that is going to make a difference to me? If anything, it makes me more determined to get her back."

The investigator smiled and reclined in her chair. "Good. Because the way that woman loves that sweet little girl, if you'd said anything less, I'd have been sorely tempted to return your retainer and keep their location to myself."

"How do you know so much about the relationship between my daughter and Lexie?"

"Lexie manages a bed-and-breakfast in a little town called Mill Creek, Montana." Betty's expression turned bemused. "Gotta give her that one. Who'd look for someone in a town with the same name as home? I spent three days with them last week. On your tab."

"And your evaluation of their relationship is based on…what? Your years as a cop?"

"No, it's based on raising three kids of my own and having five grandkids." Betty pulled out a manila folder. "My complete report is in here." She grinned. "Along with my bill." She held out her hand. "It's been a pleasure doing business with you, Mr. Mitchell. I wish you lots of luck in reuniting with your girlfriend and child."

He closed his fingers around her hand, pumped it a

few times. "One more question. Do you think she'll run again?"

"Only if you scare her. You take it nice and slow. Avoid making ultimatums. Get to know her again, and your daughter. Court her some."

He nodded. "Thanks, Betty. I can't tell you how much it means to me to find my little girl."

She rose, picking up the leather bag. "Send me an update. I want to know how it all works out."

So did he.

After she left, he dumped the folder's contents onto the table. A brochure for the Mill Creek Bed-and-Breakfast offered several images of the huge white Victorian house his daughter called home.

And knowing Lexie, it *was* a home. For him, the word conjured images not of the house he'd lived in as a child, but the house down the street where he'd spent countless hours. Lexie's home. With Lexie's two older brothers, her mother and father.

David picked up the stack of photographs. One showed Lexie, with Sarah cuddled up next to her on a burgundy leather couch, reading a book. No surprise since Lexie had been a children's librarian in Erie. Briefly.

Before she'd run.

She'd named his daughter after her own mother. A woman who'd been as much of a mother to him, as well, as his own had.

Guilt, mingled with anger, swirled over him.

Stuffing everything into the folder, he tucked it under his arm and strode from the bookstore, squinting against the bright afternoon sunshine. He tossed the package to the passenger's seat of his Toyota 4Runner. Settled inside, he pulled out his cell phone and stared at it awhile before dialing a number he hadn't called in quite some time.

He cleared his throat as a woman answered. "Mrs. J.? It's me…David."

"David! Oh, it's nice to hear from you. How are you?"

"Good. More than good. I—I have some news."

"News?" Her voice quivered. "About Lexie?"

"Yeah. I finally found her."

"Oh my." He could hear a chair scrape across the floor and visualized Mrs. J. sinking into it. "She's okay?"

"Yes. She seems to be doing quite well."

"And…the baby?"

"I have a daughter. Named Sarah."

A deep sob echoed through the phone, followed by muted crying.

Making him feel even worse for what he was about to do. What he'd done. They'd never openly blamed him for Lexie's taking off. Except for Marc, her older brother, who'd been David's best friend since second grade, the best man at his wedding. The guy who no longer spoke to him and gave him frosty glares when they happened to stumble into each other around town. At least the rest of them were civil to him. Kenny, the younger brother, still talked to him. David had even been invited to Kenny's wedding three years ago, but hadn't gone, not wanting to cause chaos on Kenny's special day. Marc had threatened him with bodily harm if he showed up.

"Where is she? I want to talk to her."

"Mrs. J., I'm sorry. I can't tell you that. I need some time first. I don't want to spook her so she runs again before I can get to her. I want my daughter home with me, where she belongs."

The soft sniffling sounds stopped. "And I want *my* daughter home with *me,* David Edward Mitchell. Don't you give me any lip. Where is my Lexie?"

"I can't risk it. I'm sorry. Really."

"Then you bring them both home. Wherever they are, whatever it takes, you bring them both back here to Erie."

Erie was the last place he wanted Lexie Jacobs. He wanted Sarah, but not the complication of Lexie. She'd betrayed him. Stolen his child.

"You tell her right off the bat about Angela, and I'm sure Lexie will come home. Do you hear me, David?"

"Yes, ma'am. I hear you." But he didn't want to think about Angela. Not now, not ever, if he could manage it. The ache it caused deep in his gut…talk about betrayal.

"Oh, I have to call Tim. He and Marc are fishing at Walnut Creek. They're both going to be so happy! Thank you for letting me know she's safe, David."

"You're welcome." At the very least, he owed them that much.

He'd already lost too much time. Missed too many things. Three birthdays and Christmases had happened without him, first steps and words, too many other things he didn't even want to consider. He needed to settle some details with his software-design company, but being the owner helped a lot with flextime and working out of the office.

He'd have his daughter back home long before the next round of holidays. She'd celebrate her fourth birthday with him.

"MOMMA, I want the mousie cupcakes for my birfday." Sarah's plaintive voice rose to overpower the rattle of the now-empty cookie trays in the wooden wagon as it *ka-chunked* along the cracks in the sidewalk. A cool breeze stirred the just-turning-gold leaves on the cottonwoods, but the bright sunshine warmed Lexie's face. Not bad for the first Saturday in October.

Lexie spared a quick glance over her shoulder at the little girl in the faded pink windbreaker who rode in the wagon. "They were cute, weren't they? Sure, honey, you can have those for your birthday."

"When is it again?"

"A little over a month."

"Oh. Okay. Is that, like, next week?"

She chuckled. "No, it's a lot longer."

"Oh. Okay." They traveled the next block in silence. Then Sarah piped up again. "Fallyn can't come to my party. She's mean."

Lexie stopped the wagon and turned to face her daughter. "Why? Did she say something to you at the bake sale?" The kids had played in the church's nursery while the women of the Mill Creek Ladies Auxiliary ran the bake/rummage sale to benefit the town's new fire engine fund.

Sarah clutched her love-worn Raggedy Ann doll to her chest and shook her head.

"Are you sure? You can tell me if she did."

"No."

"All right." Lexie resumed her trek back toward the house at the far end of Main Street that had been their home since just before Sarah's birth. Converting it into a bed-and-breakfast had given both her and Pappy a new lease on life—something to occupy their time and provide for them.

"Know what else I want for my birfday?"

"What's that, sweetie?"

"A daddy."

Lexie froze, then she coughed, choking on the saliva that suddenly didn't want to go down her throat. A shudder rippled over her despite the fact that the air had stilled. She turned once more to the child behind her. "Honey, it doesn't work like that. You can't just say you want a daddy for your birthday."

"Why not?" Sunlight glinted off the reddish-blond highlights in Sarah's brown curls. Her face tightened as she looked up at her mother.

"You just…can't."

"Do I not have a daddy 'cause of my mark?"

"What?" The metal handle clattered to the walkway as Lexie moved along the wagon's side and dropped to her knees, heedless of the tiny pebbles jabbing through the denim of her jeans. She wrapped her arms around the child who, as far as she was concerned, was the reason the sun rose every morning. "Absolutely not! Why would you even think such a thing?"

A soft sniffle emerged from the head crushed against Lexie's oversized University of Montana sweatshirt. "F-Fallyn said so."

Lexie sucked in a deep breath, then counted to ten before exhaling. Her nails dug into her palms, and she forced her hands open. Luckily, the monster… er…child in question wasn't within reach. She cuddled Sarah, rocking slightly, wishing she could draw the little one's pain into herself. "Fallyn doesn't know what she's talking about, baby."

"B-but—"

"No buts." She stroked the soft hair. The scent of generic baby shampoo rose with the breeze. Gently disengaging herself from the small arms wrapped around her neck, she put her finger beneath the sharply angled chin and lifted it until Sarah's eyes met hers. "You're beautiful, Sarah. Special."

"And—and, it's better, right?"

"With every treatment, baby, it's better." Lexie silently blessed the people at the Happy Face Foundation who made Sarah's laser treatments possible. It had been for exactly this reason that she'd wanted the port-wine stain lightened. Kids—and sometimes adults, too—could be cruel. But Lexie hadn't expected Sarah to be feeling the effects of it at not quite four. It didn't seem fair.

But then, little in life was.

"O-okay. But…"

"But what, baby?"

"If I can't get a daddy, can I have a pony?"

Lexie laughed, amazed at the resiliency of kids. Her kid in particular. "A pony? And just where would we keep a pony?"

"In Pappy's garage."

"And then where would Pappy keep his truck?"

Sarah shrugged.

"I don't think a pony is on the list of possible birthday gifts, either, sweetheart. Try to think smaller." *A lot smaller.* She sighed, hating to burst the little girl's fantasies, but determined that Sarah would be well grounded in reality. Hell, their *reality*—a patchwork family that barely made ends meet—determined that her daughter be well grounded. Practical. Pragmatic.

And that was for the best, Lexie told herself. She'd grown up with her head in the clouds—maybe head in a book was more accurate—a dreamer, living a comfy, cushy life, fed fairy tales and happily-ever-afters by her parents.

She'd been ill equipped when life had soured, and she'd been forced to flee with a baby in her belly, a baby she'd sworn to protect. Which was why she clung so fiercely and gratefully to Pappy and Mill Creek.

Despite her desire that Sarah be well grounded in reality, Lexie had already passed on her love of books to the child, whose advanced vocabulary and blossoming reading skills bore testament to the fact that reading aloud to kids made a big difference. "Ready to go home?"

Sarah nodded, clutching her rag doll tighter to her chest.

"All right." Lexie kissed her, then continued the journey home. When they reached the white picket fence running the front of the property, she lifted her hand to shade her eyes. On the opposite side of Main Street, in front of the medical clinic, Dr. Kegan Riley had one foot propped on the running board of a black pickup truck as he carried on a conversation with the driver, Bernie Kellerman.

"Morning, Kegan!" Lexie called.

He turned and waved. "Morning, Lexie! Sarah!"

Besides Pappy, Kegan had become one of her first friends in town. He'd delivered Sarah, and hadn't batted an eyelash in judgment when she'd shrugged in response to his question about what to fill out on the birth certificate under Father's Name.

"Don't know or aren't telling?" he'd asked, pen poised. She'd shrugged again, so he'd written Unknown in the space on the paper.

Unknown.

The guilt of that one word weighed heavily on Lexie's heart, knowing how it would break David's. But then she'd watch Sarah playing, or sleeping, and know without a doubt she'd done the right thing to protect her.

The tinted window of the truck Kegan leaned against slid lower. He turned toward the driver for a moment, then looked back at them. "Any of your cinnamon bread left at the bake sale?" he asked.

"No, sorry. It sold out in the first twenty minutes."

"Dang," said Bernie, the town pharmacist, who was probably hassling Kegan over his handwriting again. "I was hoping to get some," she called across the street.

"Sorry, Bernie!"

Lexie waved to both as she turned onto the dirt driveway. A dark blue Ford Explorer with Montana plates was parked in the guest area.

She picked up her pace. Maybe it was the mystery guest *Western Bed-and-Breakfast* magazine had been promising to send out. If she scored well, they'd do a four-page spread complete with color pictures of Mill Creek B&B, and that could mean a big jump in their bookings.

"Momma!" Sarah giggled and clutched the sides of the wagon. "Yeah, go faster!"

Lexie drew the wagon into the detached two-car garage, stowing it on the side littered with wooden sawhorses, old screens and other assorted junk. Sarah scrambled out as Lexie retrieved the cookie trays.

The little girl darted ahead of her, running to the back door on the enclosed porch. Lexie caught up with her as they entered the airy country kitchen. Sarah struggled with the zipper on her windbreaker, then sighed deeply. "Momma, it's stuck again."

Setting the trays on the floor, Lexie knelt down and worked the thrift-store-purchased windbreaker's flannel lining free of the zipper. "There you go. Sorry about that." She hung the jacket on one of the pegs by the back door.

"Annie needs a nap, Momma. I'm taking her upstairs."

"Okay, baby." Lexie picked up the cookie trays and crossed the enormous kitchen, dropping them into the sink. Sarah opened the door that concealed the back staircase and trotted upstairs.

Washing the dishes from the morning's hurried baking projects would have to wait. She wanted to be sure their new guest had settled in and was comfortable. Especially if it was the mystery guest.

Leaving the kitchen, she strolled down the center hallway, passing the dining room and first-floor bathroom, then Pappy's room. His knees demanded a bedroom on the first floor, so they'd converted the old parlor. Finally she emerged in the foyer, where the front stairs boasted a massive banister, and there were entrances to the library on one side of the house and the living room on the other. A small mahogany table near the front door held their guest book. She peered down at it, but there was no new entry. The loud roar of a televised football game came from the living room.

"Pappy?" she called.

"In here," he answered. "Flag on the play! What in tarnation was that?"

Inside the spacious living room, Pappy lounged in his faux-leather recliner, his sock-clad feet propped up, the tip of his big toe visible through a tiny hole. "Whose car is that outside?" she asked him. "Do we have an unexpected new guest?"

"Yup. I think he's in the library. Wanted to locate

how to hook up his computer or something. I told him about the phone-jack thingamabob in there." He leaned forward to yell at the TV. "Damn it, boy, catch the ball!"

Lexie chuckled. "Pap, how many times have you watched the video of this Grizzlies game? It doesn't change, no matter how many times you yell at them."

He offered her a sheepish grin. "I know. Hey, they won, and I'll watch it till I get to see the next game."

She just shook her head at him. "I'll go and welcome our new guest. What's his name?"

"David something-or-other. Didn't catch the last name."

"And did you catch how he was paying?"

"Nope. Not my job. I just own the place, Missy. You run it." He reached into the bowl of red pistachios on the end table and grabbed a handful.

With a soft sigh, she turned and crossed the foyer to the library, lingering in the archway. Several large woven rugs covered the varnished floor. Dark leather sofas and chairs, old books, rich wooden surfaces. Bright sunshine streamed through the picture windows that looked out onto the wide wraparound porch.

On the far side of the room, a set of sturdy shoulders and a head of wavy brown hair showed over the back of the wooden chair in front of the huge antique rolltop desk. Lexie pasted a welcoming smile on her face as she crossed the room. "Hi, I'm Lexie, I'm the manager. And you are…?"

The wheels on the chair squeaked as he pushed away from the notebook computer on the desk. He rose somewhat stiffly and turned to face her. "Has it been that long, Lexie?"

Her smile faltered. Recognition seared every circuit in her brain, like a glass of water poured over his laptop. The muscles in her legs tightened, as did the ones along the back of her neck and shoulders. Moving—shoot, even breathing seemed to be an optional activity. And Sarah's innocent birthday wish came back to her.

Be careful what you wish for…

"Nothing to say to me after all these years?" David asked.

Numerous possibilities occurred to her, like how had he found them and what did he want and go to hell…yeah, that was a good one.

But then something more solid, more horrifying, occurred to her.

He was here.

Sarah was upstairs.

And Angela…

"Ohmigod! Sarah!" Her knees started to shake and every muscle in her body screamed awake. "Where's your wife?"

CHAPTER TWO

HE'D FORGOTTEN HOW sensitive she was. Her dark hair was now shoulder length instead of the short pixie cut she'd always sported. The small bit of color on her face drained from her porcelain complexion, making her look terrified and almost…fragile.

He was not, repeat, *not* going to feel sorry for her.

She was a kidnapper, for God's sake.

Not his best friend's little sister. Not the tagalong who'd followed them everywhere until she'd learned how to read and chosen adventure through books.

Not the woman who'd tried to give him his dream of a child. The woman who'd *stolen* that child.

"Where is she?" Lexie asked again, her voice rising, a note of panic lacing the quivering words. "Sarah!" She whirled toward the library's doorway.

David grabbed her by the forearm. "Angela isn't here." He wasn't going to get into the details of his divorce and the rest of his ex-wife's sudden psychotic behavior, not now. "Sarah is safe, calm down."

She turned back to face him, yanking on her wrist. He tightened his grip. "Calm down?" she shrieked. "Calm down? I'll give you calm down!" They fought a minor tug-of-war with her arm, then she kicked him in the shin.

He released her, bending over to rub the throbbing spot. "Ow, damn it, Lexie, that hurt."

"Really? Imagine that. Too bad I'm not wearing something with a pointed toe. Now get out of my house!"

"Or?" He straightened to his full height, which at six feet gave him at least a five-inch advantage over her. He squared his shoulders, setting his jaw. If she thought he was going to march out of his daughter's life just because she said so, she was in for a rude awakening that would stand Miss Manners's hair on end.

"Or, or...I'll call the sheriff."

David crossed his arms and nodded. "Good. You do that. Saves me from having to. I had hoped we could do this in a civilized manner for my daughter's sake, but, hey, if you want to go to jail for kidnapping, dial away. And maybe we can end up in the middle of a media circus, too. Won't that be fun? Can't you just see the headlines?"

He swept his hand across the air as though spreading out a paper. Surrogate Mother Kidnaps Child In Utero, Father Regains Custody Four Years Later with Help of Small-town Sheriff. He'd avoided the media during his search for Lexie with the passion he usually reserved for a particularly nasty software virus. He'd had enough headlines when Angela had been arrested the year after their divorce. He knew how the vultures could be. It wasn't something he wanted for his daughter. Or himself.

"Kid—kidnapper?" The spark of outrage faded

from her green eyes, and they widened. "Jail?" Her mouth formed a little O but not a sound came out for several seconds. Then she said, "I—I need to sit down."

And she did. Right in the middle of the library floor.

She crossed her legs, and her fingers picked at the seam of her faded jeans. She hung her head.

David exhaled loudly, ignoring the softening in his gut, the urge to tell her he wasn't going to send her to jail. Let *her* worry for a change. He'd done enough of it. He recrossed his arms and waited for her to pull herself together.

The sounds of a ball game drifted in from the other side of the house, the old man cheering on his team. At least his attention had stayed focused on that. The last thing David needed was an overprotective friend of Lexie's butting into the middle of this mess.

A soft sniffle made him look back down at the woman on the floor. She lifted her head. Tears shimmered, as yet unshed, in her eyes.

"Oh, no," he said. "No." He pointed at her. "Don't you dare cry. Don't do it."

Her bottom lip trembled and the floodgates opened, sending the tears cascading down her cheeks. "S-sorry," she choked out.

"Aw, shit!" If there was one thing he couldn't stand, it was the sight of a woman in tears. Genuine tears. The fake, manipulating ones he could resist, but real ones…hell. They made him feel like a helpless little boy again, watching his mother cry over a man not worth the salt she shed for him. "I'm not going to send you to jail."

"That's not why I'm crying." She ran the back of her hand across her face.

"Then what, for pity's sake?"

"You're going to take her away from me," she whispered. "Aren't you?"

"She's not yours. She never was yours."

"She's been mine in every way that counts for more than four years. You gave up your rights to her when you refused to listen to me. And stop talking about her like that. She's a little girl, not a piece of personal property." Lexie rose to her feet, hands balled on her hips. "And her name is Sarah!"

"I did not give up my rights to her, and I know damn well what her name is—the name you gave her. You stole from me, you stole from her. Four years she could have had a father in her life, but you thought you knew better." A niggle of guilt twisted inside him, guilt because she *had* known better than him.

Lexie shook her head, only partially amazed at his audacity in telling her off. After all, this was David, a man she'd known all her life. A man who'd wanted a family so badly that when she'd found out his wife couldn't carry a child, she'd impulsively volunteered to act as their surrogate. Still, who did he think he was? "I was worried about her *life,* something you seemed perfectly willing to risk at the time."

A small scuffling sound came from the doorway. David's glance darted over her shoulder, and his face shifted. The lines of anger and hurt melted away, changing into an expression of wonder she'd never forget.

Darn, if it wasn't just like a man to go and wreck a woman's perfectly good mad. She knew without turning that David Mitchell had just gotten his first glimpse of his daughter.

Her hand curled into a fist. If that expression turned to revulsion when he got a good look at the birthmark, she was going to coldcock him.

"Momma?"

Lexie forced her fingers open, smoothing them along the leg of her jeans. She turned and held her hand out. "Come here, baby. There's someone I want you to meet."

Sarah ran over, wrapping her arms around Lexie's legs, pressing her face against the faded blue denim.

Lexie stroked the soft curls on her daughter's small head, then looked over at the man who'd come to claim the child who meant the world to her. Though she felt hollow inside, she met his questioning gaze straight on. "She's a little shy."

He nodded, then got down on one knee. "Hi, Sarah. My name's David."

Sarah tightened her hold on Lexie's legs. She pried her loose and squatted, nearly falling over when the little girl threw her arms around her neck. "Sarah," she said, regaining her balance, "David is... He's..."

"I'm your father, honey."

The child stopped shifting in her arms. Lexie glared at him. *So much for tact or giving us time to adjust.* Sarah risked a peek at him. Then she shook her head, sending her curls into a bounce. "No. My daddy has black hair and a crown. He's a king."

David laughed. "Quite an imagination. But it's true. I'm your father."

"No!" Sarah wiggled in Lexie's embrace, shoving at her chest. "Momma said it don't work that way. And it's not my birfday yet!"

David looked at Lexie. She shook her head, not wanting to explain the whole birthday-wish conversation. He reached out toward Sarah's hair.

"No!"

The next thing Lexie knew, Sarah was leaning in David's direction. He yelped and yanked his hand back in a hurry, shaking it.

"What?"

"She bit me."

"She what?" Lexie released her. "Sarah! You don't bite people. What were you thinking?"

"I'm not Sarah, I'm a dog. Woof, woof."

David arched an eyebrow at her.

"Well, you're a bad dog, and you're going to your bed. We don't tolerate biting around here from anyone." Lexie stood, picked up Sarah and headed for the foyer, ignoring the child's protests.

Halfway up the staircase, she realized David was practically stepping on her heels. She stopped on the landing and glared at him over her shoulder.

"What? I want to see my daughter's room. Is that some kind of a crime?" He lifted his hand, showing her the row of tiny teeth marks. "Not to mention I'd better wash this."

"I'm sorry about that," Lexie said as she started to climb again. "Although she pretends to be a dog a lot, she's never bitten anyone before." But it served him right.

He grunted. "Just my luck. Miss out on plenty of my kid's firsts, but manage to make first bite. Great fun. So far, fatherhood exceeds my expectations."

ABOUT TWENTY MINUTES later—he'd wanted to give them all, himself included, a little time to calm down—David propped his shoulder on the doorjamb of his daughter's room. Lexie sat at Sarah's side on a white twin canopy bed, stroking the little girl's arm. She raised her other hand and lifted her index finger to her mouth.

He nodded. To his right, a door opened onto another bedroom— Lexie's, he presumed.

Sunshine streamed in from the windows on either side of the bed. A low bookshelf, filled to nearly overflowing, dominated the left wall of the bedroom. A tall chest of drawers, painted white with emerald-green pulls stood beside it. A mural decorated the hallway wall. Dorothy, the Tinman, Scarecrow and Cowardly Lion stood on the Yellow Brick Road, which rose into the background, then circled the room just below the ceiling, serving as a vibrant border on the light green walls.

He remembered the summer he and Marc had been…thirteen? Which would have made Lexie nine. And she'd read volume after volume of the Oz books, driving them crazy with nonsense about the magical kingdom.

Then she'd moved on to the Narnia books, and in typical big-brother fashion, Marc had locked Lexie in a closet one Saturday afternoon. Armed with a flashlight and *The Lion, the Witch and the Wardrobe,* she hadn't even made a peep, until her frantic parents had proclaimed her missing and run about the house, calling for her.

If only she'd been as easy to find this time, he wouldn't have lost so many years with his daughter.

"David."

He glanced back at Lexie. She crooked her finger at him. He crossed the wooden floor to stand on the braided-rag rug alongside the bed.

Lexie smoothed back Sarah's hair. "I want you to take a good long look at her," she whispered. "Now, while she's napping." Her fingertips brushed lightly over the birthmark and the child's breathing shifted, then eased into the relaxed pattern of sleep. "Look your fill of this now, when she doesn't know you're staring." Lexie turned to him, a challenge in her eyes. "What do you think?"

"I think she's beautiful," he murmured. He reached out to complete the caress she'd denied him while awake, stroking the brown curls, delighted to discover the same reddish-blond highlights he had.

His daughter.

The corners of his mouth pulled upward. His baby girl. He turned back to Lexie, whose expression had softened. "She's wonderful. Amazing."

"She is that," Lexie said. Then she sighed. "But what is your wife going to think about having a child who—" her fingers fluttered over the birthmark again "—who, uh, isn't exactly what she expected?"

David knew what she meant. Wasn't perfect. Damaged. Lexie's eyes grew large and panic filled them. He swore silently. He hadn't wanted to tell her about Angela right away, but she'd run once to protect the child from Angela, and the fear on her face said she'd do it again.

"I don't want to talk about it in front of Sarah, even if she is asleep," he said quietly. "Can we go someplace else?"

She nodded. "Just let me turn this on." She leaned over the night table and switched on a baby monitor. Then she brushed a tender kiss across Sarah's forehead and rose from the bed.

He lingered a moment longer, letting his own fingers stroke the side of his little girl's face. Lexie's instincts were right. Angela would have turned her back on this child in a heartbeat.

Much as it galled him to admit it, the surrogate mother had saved his child's life by running away.

David followed her down the long upstairs hallway toward the back of the house. Just before the final bedroom, they turned to the right and descended a narrow staircase, emerging in the large kitchen.

He nudged the door closed, noting how it vanished into the white paneling along the wall.

"I could use a drink," Lexie muttered, turning on the monitor's counterpart on the windowsill. "But since it's only—'' she glanced at the large black-rimmed clock over the sink ''—11:32, and since I don't drink anyway, I think I'll have some herbal tea.'' She gave a sharp laugh. ''Caffeine is the last thing my body needs right now.'' She took a yellow teapot from the stove, filled it with water and replaced it. ''What about you?''

''You know I'm a caffeine junkie. If you've got coffee, I'll take it.''

''I've got all kinds of coffee. Do you still take it black?'' She opened a cupboard to the left of the sink.

''Yeah, straight up. The stronger, the better.''

She flitted about the kitchen like a hummingbird, hands in constant motion. The scent of fresh-ground coffee beans filled the air, then she set the pot to brew. ''There. That'll take a few minutes.''

''Good. Why don't we sit down then.'' He motioned at the table. ''This time, in a chair?'' He pulled two back, dropped into the one on the end.

''I can listen and work at the same time.'' She pointed at some cookie trays in the double sink. ''I need to—''

''You need to sit down.'' He patted the table near the chair he'd drawn out for her. ''Come on.''

She draped a towel over her shoulder and hesitantly approached him. She sank into the chair, propped her chin in one palm, and the fingers on her other hand began to drum on the oak surface.

If she were wound any tighter, she'd give the Energizer Bunny a run for his money. He reached out, covered her tapping fingers with his hand. "Relax, Lexie."

"Easy for you to say."

"Not really. I'm just as apprehensive about all this as you. Maybe more. So far, my daughter doesn't seem to even like me."

"What did you expect, David? Surely you didn't think you'd walk in here and have her rush into your open arms?" She stared at him for a moment, peeling away his layers of defense until he shifted uncomfortably in the chair, letting go of her hand. "Oh, David. You did. She's shy and you're a stranger to her."

"And whose fault is that? Not mine."

Her mouth tightened into a thin line. "I ran to keep her safe. You know that."

He cleared his throat. "Yeah, well, you don't have to worry about Angela anymore."

"I don't?" Her eyes had matured since the last time he'd seen her. Though still sparkling with an innocence he found appealing, they were older somehow. Like she'd aged more than four and a half years since she'd come to him with her fears about his wife.

"No, you don't."

"How can you guarantee it? You didn't believe me back then, wouldn't even listen to the possibility—"

"Angela is dead." He pushed his chair from the table and rose, walking to the window that looked out onto the back porch.

"Oh." Silence ruled the kitchen for several long seconds, broken only by the hum of the refrigerator.

Then her chair scraped on the floor. "I'd say I'm sorry, but...I'm not. For Sarah's sake."

"Yeah, well..." A tentative touch on his shoulder triggered a surge of warmth in his chest to go with the ache deep in his stomach, the acid pain brought on by thinking about Angela and how everything had unraveled in their lives like a computer program with a bad line of code.

"I guess I am sorry for you, though," Lexie said softly. "It's not easy to lose someone you care about."

He tried to control the dismissive noise that rumbled deep in his throat. Once upon a time, he'd cared for Angela, loved her more than he'd ever thought possible. What a fool he'd been. But then, love was for fools.

Angela, on the other hand, had loved only herself. And he'd been too blind to see it. But she'd seemed normal then. Fun-loving, if a little high-maintenance. It had been the pressure of his wanting children, of Lexie's pregnancy, that started the messy, downward spiral that ended with Angela's death. A death he didn't want to talk about.

"Don't sweat it," he said. "It was almost two years ago. And we were already divorced."

Lexie struggled to make sense of it. *His wife—no, his ex-wife—was dead.* Had been dead for some time.

The threat to Sarah was gone.

And so was Lexie's reason for keeping her. But how could she ever give her up, after loving her, caring for her for all this time?

She let her hand fall to her side. The refrigerator clicked off, leaving the kitchen silent.

He turned around to face her. "Lexie?"

"What?" She didn't look at him. Couldn't.

"I want to make this as easy as possible on Sarah. I don't want to traumatize her any more than I already have."

And what about me? she wanted to scream. But the whistle of the teakettle pierced the air, and she moved to get a mug, drop in a tea bag and fill the cup with water.

"I shouldn't have rushed so fast to tell her who I am. I scared her, and that was stupid on my part. Lexie?"

"What?" Her spoon tinged against the sides of the mug.

"Will you help me get to know my daughter? Help me make this easier on her?"

Why don't you ask me cut out my own heart? The tinging got louder, and the tea sloshed over the rim of the cup. "Yes. I will." For Sarah's sake. "I guess you'll be taking her back to Erie."

"Eventually. Once she's comfortable with me."

"How long do you intend to stay?" She gripped the hot beverage, but didn't trust herself to pick it up.

"I'm not sure. However long it takes, I guess. That's sort of up to Sarah. A few days?"

A few days.

Lexie blinked back the moisture gathering in her eyes. She had a few days to come up with a way to stay part of Sarah's life.

And what about Pappy? It wasn't as if Lexie could just go back to Erie herself and walk out on the old man who'd given her and Sarah a home and a family where they'd had none. He needed her.

What was she going to do?

CHAPTER THREE

JOHN NONNEMACHER rolled over and stared at the clock's big red numbers: 3:26 a.m. And the scent of fresh-baked bread was wafting from the kitchen. What in tarnation was that girl thinking?

'Course, she'd been walking around the whole afternoon and evening like a cat with its fur rubbed the wrong way. All prickly and stiff. And Sarah. The little one had been pretending she was a dog again. Why, he'd even heard her growl at the new guest, and Lexie had said Sarah had bitten him. Something was going on. He wasn't sure he liked the way his old mind was putting one and one together and getting three.

He rose from his bed, shrugged into the plaid bathrobe Sarah and Lexie had given him for Christmas the year before. His slippers scuffed against the floor as he shuffled out of his room and into the kitchen. The dim light over the sink showed Lexie turning out two loaves of bread onto wire cooling racks. Several dozen freshly baked German cookies also sat on the island, and numerous mixing bowls and measuring spoons littered the rest of the surfaces.

"Can't sleep, huh?"

She gasped and fumbled with the loaf of bread.

"Jeez, Pappy, you scared me. What are you doing up at this hour?"

"I asked you first." He trudged across the kitchen, snagging two of the little rolled pastries on the way. Sinking into a chair, he bit a cookie in half. "Mmm. Girl, you are a talent in the kitchen. No wonder these are Sarah's favorites."

A tin clattered onto the floor. He glanced up to see Lexie just staring at it. "Missy? You gonna tell me what's wrong, or you gonna make me guess?"

She bent down and picked up the metal container.

"All right, lemme see. Everything seemed fine until lunchtime today. What was different about lunchtime today? Oh, I know. That's when that young man showed up. You know, he reminds me of someone, but I just can't quite figger it out."

Lexie gathered all the utensils and dishes and placed them in the sink. Then, with a long exhale, she picked up a cup of tea along with a rack of the cookies and came to sit next to him. She pushed the nut-and-brown-sugar cookies in his direction.

He accepted one and ate it in a single bite this time. She'd never been big on telling him the hard things. Stuff about her past. And he could tell, this was gonna be a doozy. He waited. After all, it wasn't like an eighty-two-year-old man had much else to do.

"I'm going to lose her, Pap," she finally whispered.

"Lose who? What are you talking about?"

"Sarah. David's her father. And he's going to take her away, back home to Pennsylvania with him."

He let loose with some well-chosen curses, words

his wife, God rest her soul, woulda given him grief over. "What do you mean, he's going to take her away? The hell he is! We'll get us a lawyer, Missy, don't you worry. We'll just see about that. You're her mother."

"But that's just it, Pap. I'm not."

He grabbed her mug of tea and held it beneath his nose, inhaling deeply. "What kind of herbal crap are you drinking, girl? I told you this stuff would do weird things to your head. Of course you're her mother. I was there when you whelped the young'un. Not her mother." He hmmphed.

Lexie accepted the cup he thrust back at her. The warmth from the mug soothed her fingers but did little to quell the cold that went right through her like a sharp Montana winter wind. "Pap, if I tell you something, promise not to tell anyone else? Not even your coffee buddies?"

"You know better than to even ask."

She nodded. Of all people in Mill Creek, Pappy was the one least likely to judge her, too. "I'm not sure where to start."

"The beginning usually works best."

"I just don't know where it began. Was it with David growing up like another big brother in my house?" Lexie chuckled. "Although he was a lot nicer to me than my real brothers. Guess he didn't think his status with the family extended to abusing the kid sister." She tapped her fingers on the rim of the cup. "Or did it start with our broken dreams?"

"Yours or his?"

"Both." She told Pappy about the night David had sought refuge in her parent's supposedly empty house, only to discover her there, mourning her own broken dreams: a severed relationship when she'd expected Andrew to propose, a lost job due to budget cuts at the library in Pittsburgh and having to come home and live with her parents again.

Lexie's chest tightened. "But my wounds were nothing compared to his. For three years, his wife had managed to conceal from him the fact that she couldn't have children. And David really wanted children. He always said he'd have a family just like mine one day. He was devastated."

His pain had touched her. David had always been her hero, from the time she was small and he'd buffered some of her brothers' actions, to the time he'd taken her to her junior prom when her klutzy, geeky date had broken his leg two days before the big event. David hadn't cared how uncool it was for a twenty-year-old college guy to escort a sixteen-year-old high schooler, and he'd suffered plenty of razzing about it from Marc and Kenny.

She couldn't stand the empty ache in his eyes.

"Late that night I heard him blowing his nose. The man who can't stand to see someone in tears was crying, Pappy," Lexie said. "After some thinking, I came up with the idea of carrying a child for them. I figured one of us might as well have our dreams."

"Seems like quite a favor, Missy. Not something you do for just anybody."

"No. But for David…" She shrugged, not wanting

to delve deeply into the emotions that had led her to act as his surrogate. "It took a while to get all the testing done. The first procedure didn't take. David was crushed. But the second time, I got pregnant with Sarah."

"So, what happened? Why did you run away?"

The mug had cooled in her hands and her voice faltered as Lexie continued. "Oh, Pap. I was about four months pregnant when we discovered Angela had been keeping more secrets. Turns out she had no uterus because she'd given birth at nineteen, and complications from the delivery forced her to have a partial hysterectomy."

"That's tough. But that's not all, is it?"

"Her first child—" the words caught in her throat "—died. SIDS, they claimed. But Angela's first husband went to David when he found out they had a surrogate carrying a child for them. He told David Angela had…murdered their baby."

"She killed her first baby?" Pappy asked. "What kind of mother kills her own child?"

Lexie shook her head. "I don't know, Pappy. Her ex said she went a little crazy after the surgery. But I was scared. She hadn't shown much interest in Sarah at that point. Only David came to the ultrasound appointments and talked to me about the pregnancy." Lexie shuddered. "The father of that baby came to me, Pappy, after David wouldn't believe him."

"Didn't the police check it out?"

"The coroner ruled it SIDs. They thought her ex was making up the accusation because their relationship was sometimes volatile. But he seemed honest and genuine to me. Frantically worried about the baby I carried."

Lexie set the mug on the table and slumped back in the chair. "I tried to talk to David about it. He didn't believe what I saw. Couldn't imagine his wife would do anything like that. I think he loved her a lot."

"So, you ran." Pappy shook his head. "I knew you'd run away from something, Missy, knew it probably had to do with the little one's father, but I never imagined it was anything like this."

"I had to run," she whispered. "I had to protect her."

"'Course you did." His rough hand closed over hers. "You did the right thing."

"Tell that to him." She jerked her head toward the ceiling.

"Don't think I won't, 'cause I will." He squeezed her hand. "Where's his wife now? Surely he doesn't think you're going to let Sarah go anywhere near a woman like that?"

"She's dead." Lexie puffed her cheeks and blew out a slow breath. "And God forgive me, but I can't be sorry for that."

"Don't think there's anything you need to be asking God's forgiveness for. I'm sure he understands." He squeezed her hand one more time, then let go. "Don't you fret. Things have a way of working themselves out."

"Oh, Pap. I wish I could believe you. But we both know life doesn't work like that. I mean, look at me.

I ended up a single mom, struggling to support myself and my little girl. A woman with a master's degree in library science, but not able to use it. Hiding. It sure wasn't what I had in mind."

"You've done a helluva job, Missy. Don't you ever forget that."

"I couldn't have done it without you." She offered him a tremulous smile.

He hmmphed again. "What kind of man is he?"

"Well, except for not listening to me, not wanting to believe what I said about his wife, which really annoyed the heck out of me, David is a good man. Why?"

"If he's a good man, then everything's gonna be jest fine." He grabbed another cookie and pushed back his chair. "Leave the dishes till morning, Missy, and go get some sleep. My old bones need some more rest, too. Things'll look better in the morning light." He brushed his palm against her shoulder as he moved past, leaving her alone in the kitchen with only the hum of the fridge and her thoughts for company.

If only she could be as sure as he was.

Lexie carried her mug to the sink, then moved to bag the bread and put all the cookies away in tins. She switched off the baby monitor then slowly climbed the stairs. She went into Sarah's room and stood by the bed. In sleep, the little girl always looked so peaceful. So calm. Even now she slept as though all was right in the world.

But Lexie knew that the world—her world—would never be the same again. Bending over, she kissed the child, then entered her own room through the connecting door. The bed frame creaked as she perched on the edge of the mattress. In the dim light that crept in from Sarah's Emerald City night-light, the telephone gleamed. She reached for it, then glanced at the clock on the chest of drawers across the room: 4:17. Which meant that back home, in Pennsylvania, it was 6:17. Early, but not too early. She picked up the receiver and pecked out a pattern that she hadn't used in four and a half years.

A familiar voice answered. Warmth and blessed relief spread through her.

"Mom?" She heard a sharp intake of breath on the other end. "Mom, it's me. Lexie."

"Lexie! Oh my!" Her mother coughed, then began to sob.

Lexie blinked back her own tears, struggled to speak around the volume of *War and Peace* suddenly stuck in her throat. "Don't cry, Mom. I'm sorry I haven't been in touch... Oh, I've missed you so much!"

It took a few moments for her mother to regain enough composure to speak. When she did, her voice was laced with sniffles. "Oh, sweetheart, we've missed you, too. You're okay? Is David with you?"

"I'm fine. Well...except for the fact that yes, David's with me."

"But honey, that's good news! When are you all coming home? I can't wait to meet my namesake." Another sob choked her mom.

Lexie brushed away the moisture on her cheeks.

How did her mother know she'd named the baby after her? "Oh, Mom. I can't come back to Erie."

"But—but, why not? David told you about Angela, right? Honey, the baby is safe now."

"I know, Mom, but…" How could she explain to her mother that she had a new home now? And another "family" member who depended on her? Pappy wasn't a blood relation, but Lexie loved him and couldn't just abandon him any more than he'd abandoned Sarah and her in their moment of need.

Besides, at home, she'd always been the one taken care of. As the baby of the family, and the only girl, she'd been spoiled.

It was nice to be needed.

"Right now we're focusing on letting Sarah get to know David in her own environment. Finding out David is her father has been kind of a shock to her." Lexie stifled an ill-timed chuckle as she recalled Sarah's response. It hadn't been funny at the time, but in hindsight, it was. Sort of.

"Don't you think it would be better to get it all over with at once? You know, rip the bandages off in a hurry, then let her heal? Honey, we haven't seen you in more than four years!"

Her mom had always advocated jumping into the cold water in one big leap, whereas Lexie preferred the one-toe-at-a-time method. "I want to see you, too, but Sarah's a very sensitive child."

"Bring her here and we'll all help her deal with the changes."

"Mom, I don't know that David's going to want

me—or any of us—anywhere near Sarah when he brings her to Erie. He's pretty ticked at me.''

''I know, honey. And believe me, I can understand how he feels. He lost time with his daughter just like we lost time with you. Only he lost the really special beginning stuff, like seeing her born, watching her grow from an infant into a child. But we're as much family to David as you are to Sarah. Give him time, honey.''

Guilt prodded her. She'd conveniently forgotten how much David had missed out in his daughter's life—because of her. ''Time is what we all need right now, Mom. Time to sort things out. If it's this confusing for us grown-ups, imagine how Sarah feels.''

''All right, honey. Well, when you get her accustomed to David, we'll have a big party to welcome you all back home.''

''Oh, Mom.'' Lexie's voice dropped to a whisper. ''How can I come home and watch him raise her without me after I've been her mother this long? She's mine, Mom.'' Fresh tears welled up in her eyes. ''I love her.''

''Of course you do.'' A heavy sigh echoed across the country via the long-distance line. ''I tried to warn you about that before you became David's surrogate, honey.''

''I would have been fine if things went the way they were supposed to.'' Right? Would she have felt this strongly for Sarah if she'd given up the baby at birth like she was supposed to, had played the doting honorary auntie to the little girl instead of becoming her mother?

Giving her up now was going to be the hardest thing she'd ever done in her life.

CHAPTER FOUR

DAVID CLUTCHED a gift bag in one hand and the railing in the other as he descended the narrow stairs to the kitchen. Opening the door, the scents of cinnamon and fresh coffee assailed him. Lexie bustled around the island wearing a full apron over a beige dress with little pink flowers.

He cleared his throat. "Good morning."

She turned to him. Her eyes were puffy and red-rimmed, as though she'd spent the whole night crying.

He ignored the tug that created in his gut.

"I hope you slept well?" she said.

Better than you, apparently didn't seem like a wise thing to say. "Yes, thanks."

"Well, since this is a bed-and-breakfast, and you've had the bed, let me get your breakfast for you." She poured a mug of coffee. "Usually I set breakfast for guests in the dining room. This way." She moved toward the doorway.

"I'd just as soon eat in here, if that's okay."

She shrugged. "Suit yourself." She handed him the coffee. "Breakfast on Sundays is homemade cinnamon buns. Or, if you prefer, whole wheat toast or bagels, and eggs. I make a mean omelette."

"Cinnamon rolls sound—and smell—delicious." He looked her over again. The dress exposed well-shaped calves. Her figure had changed since carrying Sarah. Matured. Gotten curvier, more feminine. In places he shouldn't have noticed. Her brothers would beat the snot out of him for it if they knew, but hell, he'd have to be dead not to.

The way she filled out an apron...

She wore stockings, but no shoes. A pair of battered pink slippers covered her feet.

"Where you off to?" he asked as she set a china plate in front of him. White icing dripped off the edges of the pastry, and his stomach gurgled as the aroma drifted upward.

"Church. Sunday school starts at nine-thirty. I thought you'd end up sleeping clear past breakfast. Breakfast hours are posted in the rooms."

"I saw them. No need to fuss about me, I can take care of myself." He cut off a piece of the bun and lifted it to his mouth. Damn. He hadn't tasted something that good, that sweet, since...well, her drown-your-sorrows sundaes that night at her parents' house came to mind.

"Sarah?" Lexie called up the stairs. "Hurry up, honey."

David's head jerked up from the plate. "You're taking Sarah to church? What church?"

"The Methodist church a couple blocks away."

He set the fork on the table. Time to make some things clear to her. "No."

"No, what?"

"No, you're not taking her. I was raised Catholic, and if that was good enough for me, it's good enough for *my* daughter."

"It's part of her routine. What she's used to."

"Well, I guess she's going to have to get used to a new routine, isn't she?"

Her face flushed. "Don't you think you're rushing things? She wouldn't even look at you yesterday."

"No, I don't. Get it through your head that she is *my* child. You've taken care of her for four years, but she's my responsibility now. I'll make the decisions regarding her." The church issue in and of itself mattered little to him. The control issue, however...

The door creaked, then popped open, and Sarah came through it. Wearing a black dress with sunflowers on it, she carried a pair of black shoes in her hand. "I can't do them," she said to Lexie.

"Hey there, sport," he said.

She glanced in his direction, then quickly ran behind the island.

"Baby, I'm not feeling so well this morning." Lexie removed the apron and tossed it on the counter. "I think we're going to have to miss church this week."

"But Momma, I need to see the puppets!"

"I'm sorry, baby. Not today." Lexie knelt down, disappearing from his view. "You did a great job of getting yourself dressed. But now, why don't you go put on some regular clothes, okay? Then you don't have to worry about the shoes, either."

"You gonna change, too?"

David figured that as long as Sarah couldn't see him, she didn't have to acknowledge him. Well, he wasn't going to put up with that. He rose from the table, scooped up the bag he'd set on the floor.

"Sarah? I have something for you. A present. I meant to give it to you yesterday, but I guess I forgot." He held out the pink and purple bag.

She turned in his direction, but stepped away from him, closer to Lexie.

"The lady at the store said most little girls love these. I have to admit, I don't know much about little girls." He let the tissue paper rustle enticingly. "But—" he got down on one knee again "—I really want to learn. Here, sport. Take it."

Lexie's chest ached at the hopeful expression on his face. He wanted so much to connect with his child. Despite her own misgivings, she nudged Sarah. "Go ahead, baby. Isn't it nice that David brought you a present?"

She could see how torn Sarah was. Presents were rare things in her life. The B&B provided for all their needs, yes, but extras were few and far between.

Sarah darted forward, grabbed the bag from his fingers and retreated back to Lexie's side. She set the bag on the floor and shoved both hands into it, pulling out the gift. Her brown eyes widened, and her mouth opened in silent awe. Finally, she said, "Look, Momma," and turned the box in Lexie's direction. A bridal Barbie, complete with satin wedding gown, veil and a tiny white-and-pink bouquet, stared back. "She's pretty!"

"Yes, she is, baby." Lexie swallowed the bitter taste in her mouth. The doll had been on Sarah's wish list for her birthday, one of the "think small" items that ran between fifty and a hundred dollars. Lexie had been squirreling money away, a smidge here and there, wondering if she'd manage to have enough by the time the little girl's birthday rolled around. Sometimes a hundred bucks might as well have been a thousand for her, when Sarah needed other things like new shoes and clothes, winter boots, a coat...

Now it didn't matter.

For two reasons.

One, her father had already provided it for her. And two, Sarah would be gone long before her birthday came.

She ignored the stab of pain so intense it made it hard to breathe. She prodded the little girl with her elbow. "What do you say?"

Sarah turned slowly to face David. "Woof, woof."

"Sarah," Lexie admonished.

"That's how dogs say thank you," she whispered.

A broad grin stretched David's mouth. Enormous, deep dimples—heck, they were craters—appeared around his lips and his eyes brightened. He was absolutely adorable when he smiled like that. Irresistible. She'd seen the same expression when he'd realized she was serious about carrying his child, and at the ultrasound appointment, when the doctor had pointed out Sarah's beating heart, arms and legs. She'd been sucking her thumb. His joy was so amazing.

His joy...

In finding his daughter.

Her pain...

In losing her.

"I'm gonna put her away," Sarah said. She darted around David, giving him wide berth, and ran up the stairs.

Lexie climbed to her feet, as did David.

"Thank you for not making a big issue over the church thing," he said.

"Get over it. I did it for her, not you. I'm trying to help her get used to you. Just like you asked."

"Still." He reached out and took her hand. "Thanks."

Her fingers trembled. "Don't mention it." She disengaged their clasped hands, unnerved by the tenderness he displayed. She had to remember he was taking away the child she loved, breaking her heart into pieces.

"I have to go change," she murmured. "Help yourself to more coffee and cinnamon rolls.

"Nooo!"

Clattering footsteps on the stairs outside his bedroom followed the drawn-out wail, jolting David awake the next morning.

Across the hall, a door slammed. Another set of footsteps climbed the steps, this set firmer, slower. Determined.

He pried one eye open. Bright sunlight assaulted him. He glared at the bedside clock: 10:35.

How was he supposed to sleep in with that kind of

racket going on? He'd spent too many hours during the night debugging glitches in a software project, then e-mailing the new file out to the office. He hadn't gone to bed until just about sunup. Beneath the brocade quilt, he rolled onto his back, draped his arm across his face to block out the light.

"Sarah, I know you don't want to go, but we have to." Lexie's voice drifted from the hallway, along with scuffling sounds.

"Nooo! I don't wanna go, Momma!" Sarah's voice was louder, closer now.

"I'm sorry, Sarah, we have to go. Shush now, or you'll wake up...your father."

Only one set of footsteps, this time heavier, went down the stairs. She had to be carrying his daughter.

Her words finally clicked in his fried brain.

Go? Go where? Holy crap. Was she about to bolt on him?

A blast of adrenaline surged through his body.

He threw back the covers and sat up, scanning the room. His jeans were in a crumpled heap on the floor alongside the four-poster bed. He yanked them over his boxer briefs as more squeals of protest, fainter this time, filtered upstairs.

Then he heard the heavy front door close.

He barreled out of his room. "Oh no you don't." Starting down the stairs, he skidded to a stop on the landing, narrowly missing knocking the old man ass over teakettle.

"Easy there, boy. These stairs can be slick. Take it from someone who knows." A gnarled hand grasped the banister, and the man drew himself up another step.

David tried to dodge around him. "Did she put you up to stalling me?"

"Who? Lexie? She don't know I come up here, and I sure hope you don't tell her. I gotta hide my pipe from her someplace she don't think to look."

"I'm in a hurry, Pops. Excuse me." He squeezed past the old guy, then bounded down the rest of the stairs. "Your secret's safe with me!" He raced to the front door and yanked it open, ignoring the cool breeze that triggered goose bumps across his chest and down his arms.

He hurtled onto the wide porch and off the steps. The pair had already crossed the road in front of the house and were entering a building on the opposite side. The rough surface of the sidewalk bit into his bare feet. The gate in the white picket fence swung behind him as he passed through it, squeaking, but not shutting. "Lexie!" he yelled. She didn't seem to hear him as the glass door closed behind her. At least she wasn't leaving town, as he'd first feared. Shivering against the cold again, he turned and ran back into the house and up the stairs. He grabbed a T-shirt from his suitcase and crammed his sockless feet into his still-tied sneakers, then charged back down the stairs, pulling the shirt over his head on the way.

He crossed the street at a jog and stormed into the building, noting the gold lettering on the glass door: Mill Creek Medical Clinic. Was his daughter ill?

Lexie stood at the reception desk, Sarah propped on

her hip, when he finally caught up to her. Breathing slightly hard, he wrinkled his nose at the scent of new carpet that overpowered any medical smells in the building.

Sarah squirmed. "Lemme go."

Lexie set the child on the reception desk. "Sit still so you don't fall." She kept one hand on the child's leg as she filled out a form with the other.

"What in the hell are you doing?" he demanded. "Is Sarah sick? Don't you think that's something I ought to know as her father?"

"You are not my daddy!" Sarah said.

The young blonde behind the desk turned to stare at him. The murmurs from the other waiting patients dropped off as they also looked at him, leaving only some morning talk show yapping on the television.

Lexie's face pinkened as she gaped at him.

"What?" he asked.

Her gaze trailed a path down his chest toward his jeans, then quickly jerked back up to his eyes. He wouldn't have believed it possible, but the color in her face deepened. "That T-shirt fits like a second skin," she hissed at him. "Did your housekeeper shrink it or what?"

"Hallelujah," muttered one of the ladies in the waiting area. "That's one fine-looking creation."

Amen, Lexie wanted to shout. Broad shoulders. Well-muscled arms and chest...she could even make out his sculpted abs. He'd filled out a lot since the last time she'd seen him in such a shirt, playing football in her backyard with Marc and Kenny. He looked more like a construction worker than a guy who programmed computers for a living.

The body-hugging white T-shirt drew down to a pair of well-worn jeans that also fit him intimately, like a lover's caress. Her cheeks warmed and she jerked her gaze back up to his face. Again. This time there was a hint of smugness in his eyes.

"I said, is there a problem here, Lexie?"

She whirled to find Kegan standing behind her. "Uh, well, I don't know if I'd call it a problem."

A catastrophe, maybe.

A plague? Yes, that was it. David Mitchell was a plague on her life.

"Why don't we move this little party to someplace more private, like an exam room." Kegan gestured down the newly created hallway. The remodeled clinic was a far cry from the curtained cubbies she'd birthed Sarah in.

"Yes. That's a good idea." She lifted Sarah off the counter, ignoring the fact that Sue Ann, the receptionist, was staring at the man behind her. The hunky one who'd proclaimed himself Sarah's father in front of everyone.

Great, that ought to be all over town by lunchtime.

Kegan held a chart tucked under his arm. Lexie followed him to the small exam room. She lowered Sarah onto the table and propped her hip, leaning her body firmly against the little girl, offering—and drawing—comfort from the contact.

"I'm Dr. Kegan Riley." Kegan offered David his right hand as he shut the door.

"David Mitchell."

Kegan set Sarah's chart on the counter and opened it, flipping through the pages nonchalantly, as though pretending the tension in the room didn't exist. "You brought Sarah in for that chicken pox vaccine we discussed, right?"

"I don't need a shot!" Sarah yelled.

Lexie wrapped her arm around the tiny waist. "Shh. Everything's going to be just fine, baby. If you're a good girl, later I'll take you to Jo's diner for an ice-cream sundae, okay?"

"Hold it," David said. "What kind of side effects does this vaccination have? Is it really necessary? I mean, we didn't have a chicken pox vaccine when we were kids, and we managed just fine."

"I discussed all that with Lexie, Mr. Mitchell."

"Well, since I'm Sarah's father, perhaps you should just discuss it with me. I'm the one making the decisions for her now."

"Oh really?" Kegan leaned against the counter and folded his arms across his white lab coat. "I don't think so. According to the state of Montana, Lexie is Sarah's sole parent. I know. I filled out the birth certificate."

"You didn't list me as the father on the birth certificate?" An accusatory glint sparked in his eyes.

She shook her head.

"What the hell did you put?"

"Uh...um..."

His eyebrows drew down and his jaw tightened. No irresistible smile-craters apparent today. No, now he looked seriously pissed. "Lexie, what does it say on my daughter's birth certificate?"

She swallowed hard, then murmured, "Father Unknown."

"Son of a—" David took a step in her direction, but Kegan quickly moved between them.

"Take it easy," the physician soothed. "I'm sure you and Lexie can work all this out. But only if you both act calmly and rationally."

"She is not Sarah's mother." David's voice held a barely contained note of fury.

"Yes, she is!" Sarah shouted. Lexie was beginning to suspect the normally complacent little girl had inherited a streak of temper from her father. And that only her father could trigger it.

Kegan laughed. "That argument isn't going to work with me. I delivered Sarah."

"She was a gestational surrogate. Period. Sarah doesn't belong to her any more than any other child in this town does."

Lexie closed her eyes as Kegan spun to face her. She lowered her head, resting her chin on the top of Sarah's. Sarah's sweet scent rose to fill her nose…and tug hard on her heart. Losing this child would be the hardest thing she'd ever faced, surpassing even the pain of leaving her family and dreams behind to become a single parent on the lam.

"Lexie?" Kegan's deep voice demanded she look at him.

She opened her eyes, blinking against the harsh glare of the florescent lights—and reality.

"Is that true?"

The muscles in her neck protested as she nodded. "I'm afraid so," she whispered.

"Momma?"

Lexie's heart clenched at the word. Five years from now, would Sarah still call her that? Would Sarah recognize her? Remember her?

Sarah wiggled against her side. "What's a sirie-gate?"

"Nothing you need to worry about right now, sport," David said.

Lexie fought against the trembling sensation that seemed to wrack her whole body. She didn't want Sarah upset any further. Hopefully the discussion was far above her comprehension.

"What's it going to take for me to get the birth certificate changed?" David asked.

Kegan's puzzled glance left Lexie and went back to David. "DNA tests, for one thing. You'll need proof to back up your claim."

"Fine. Can you do that?"

Kegan nodded. "I can handle the collection, and I have a lab I can send the samples to for processing."

"Good. Let's do that while we're here, too. No point in wasting any time." David glared at Lexie, and she shivered. "I've lost enough of that already."

"Will it—" Lexie hugged the child closer "—you know, h-u-r-t?" She spelled out the letters carefully.

"No. A swab from inside the cheek is all we need," Kegan said.

"From me, too?" Lexie asked.

"Might as well. Rule out any and all possibilities, right?" Kegan gathered some long paper-coated objects from a drawer, laying them on the counter.

An irrational hope flared deep inside her chest. Was there any possibility the fertility clinic had made a mistake? Probably not.

But...love wasn't always logical.

And if David wasn't Sarah's biological father, then he had no more rights to the little girl than she did.

CHAPTER FIVE

DAVID STRUGGLED to contain the thrashing child on his lap. "Sarah, hold still. It won't hurt as much if you relax."

"Nooo! I don't wanna shot!"

"This is just cotton and alcohol, Sarah," the doctor said, swabbing her arm.

The little girl shrieked so loud David feared permanent hearing loss. And he silently cursed Lexie for bailing on him as soon as the painless cheek swabs for the DNA tests had been completed.

"You can start the job of being a father right now," she'd said on the way out the door.

They'd have words over that—along with the fact she'd left him off Sarah's birth certificate—later. How could she have done that to him? She knew that he'd been kept in the dark about his own father's identity until he was thirteen. Even though Lexie had only been nine, he was pretty sure she remembered how he'd run away to her house and the nighttime "peace summits" held by the Jacobses to mediate between him and his mother.

Dr. Riley approached with the vaccination.

"Shh, Sarah. It's going to be okay." David tried to

soothe her. She screamed again as the needle struck home, and his stomach tumbled. He glared at the doctor as though it were his fault for causing his child pain, and wished there was actually something he could do to make it better.

"There, that wasn't so bad, was it?" Dr. Riley said.

"I want Momma." Tears wet David's shirt as Sarah sobbed. "I want my momma! Lemme go!" She wiggled from his embrace in a move that would have made Houdini proud, jumped off his lap and wrestled with the doorknob.

The physician's lab coat fluttered as he grabbed her and lifted her into his arms. "Easy there, sweetie." He pulled a tissue from a box on the counter and wiped her cheeks. "Let's dry those tears. Do you want Sue Ann to give you a sticker?"

Sarah nodded, bottom lip quivering.

Dr. Riley opened the door and then set Sarah on her feet outside the door. "Sue Ann?" he called down the corridor. "Would you please come take Sarah and let her pick out a sticker? Maybe two?"

"Sure, Doc." The blond woman from behind the front desk appeared in the hall, craning her neck to see around the doctor and into the exam room. She smiled at David, letting an appreciative glance linger on his torso before she took his daughter's hand and led her off to wherever the stickers were kept.

He fought the urge to cross his arms over his chest.

Dr. Riley closed the door with a sigh.

"Was there something else?" David slid off the table.

"I wanted to let you know it'll take two to three weeks for the DNA test results."

"Two to three weeks?" That seemed far too long. "On the news, the results are ready in a few days."

"In the high-profile cases, they also have politicians riding their butts to make them move faster, and seemingly unlimited taxpayer money to throw at the lab. Sorry, but this is going to take longer."

David sighed. He knew, deep inside, that Sarah *was* his daughter. The tests were just a formality that bureaucracy required so he could claim his own child. Two to three weeks, though. That was longer than he'd planned to be here. Longer than he wanted to be near Lexie. Her latest betrayal burned like a twenty-thousand-volt electrical surge through a circuit board.

When would he learn?

At least the time would be put to good use, building a relationship with his daughter, who didn't seem to want a father. Not him, anyway.

"Okay, thanks, Doc. Get the results to me as soon as you can." David reclaimed Sarah at the reception desk, accepting the bill thrust at him, and trying to look nonchalant about the gawks, tsks and shaking heads from the waiting-room inhabitants as well as the women behind the front desk. He quietly explained that his checkbook was across the street and he'd have to pay up later. Picking up his daughter despite her protests, he carried her outside and crossed the street again.

Once inside the bed-and-breakfast, he set her on her feet. "There you go, kiddo."

"Momma?" Sarah yelled. "Where are you?"

Lexie appeared from the dining room at the end of the hallway. "In here, baby."

Sarah's sneakers pounded against the wooden floor as she raced to Lexie, who opened her arms wide and lifted the child off the ground, kissing her on the head and murmuring something he couldn't quite catch. The pair vanished through the dining-room archway.

Damn, he'd give anything for Sarah to run to him like that. He sighed and headed upstairs, wanting to cool off a bit before he confronted Lexie about the birth certificate.

He toed off his sneakers, which were already chewing a blister into his bare heel, then dipped into his open suitcase, fished out a navy blue polo shirt and a pair of socks. He'd had no idea a tight T-shirt could cause such a stir. Either that or the town was simply inhabited by a bunch of sex-starved women, judging from the reactions in the medical clinic.

A few minutes later, he propped his shoulder against the dining-room doorway, watching as Sarah imitated Lexie, who was dusting the massive cherry table. "We have to talk," he said to her. He looked pointedly at the child running an old sock around the arms of a chair. "Alone."

"I'm helping Momma," Sarah said proudly, shaking the rag and causing the dust to dance in the sunbeams coming through the window.

"Yes, you sure are. I don't know what I'd do without you." Lexie's words sounded strange, strangled, as if she couldn't quite get them out. She cleared her throat. "But maybe Pappy needs some help, too. I think he's in the backyard. Maybe he's planting those bulbs we bought the other day. Why don't you run out there and see if you can help with the flower beds, okay?"

"Can I get dirty?" Sarah dropped the dust rag onto the seat of the chair.

"Well, planting flowers can be dirty work." Lexie smiled. "Don't forget to put your coat on."

"Yipppiee!" The little girl half skipped toward the doorway, turned sideways and edged past him, a scowl on her face that seemed to indicate she didn't trust him not to grab her and subject her to more pain. Great. Now the kid really didn't trust him.

She inched past, then turned and ran toward the kitchen. "Pappy! I'm helping you!"

Once the back door closed with a bang, Lexie set down the yellow can of furniture polish, then folded her arms across her chest. "Okay, and you want to say…?"

"I cannot believe that you put 'Father Unknown' on her birth certificate! What were you thinking?" He ran his hand over his hair. "You knew damn well who her father was."

"Yes, and I didn't want her father finding us, either. If I had put your name on the birth certificate, you might have used that information to track us down, and I couldn't risk that, David. I know how that must cut, since you didn't know who your own father was for so long, but I didn't do it to intentionally hurt you. I did it to protect her."

His anger eased just a bit. No matter what, he couldn't fault her motivation. His shoulders sagged, some of the tension draining from them. "It stings, Lexie. You know I always vowed my kid would know who her father was, I'd raise her myself, be a real dad, like yours. And you stole that from me."

"No, David. Angela stole that from you. Look, I don't know with one-hundred-percent certainty that Angela would have hurt Sarah. But it wasn't worth the risk, was it?"

David did know with one-hundred-percent certainty. Or at least ninety-nine point nine. After Angela had remarried a wealthy old man, her new stepdaughter had given birth and left the child with his "grandparents" frequently. Angela had been arrested following the baby's death under suspicious circumstances, and had been awaiting her trial for the baby's murder when she'd been killed by another inmate. But he sure as hell didn't want Lexie knowing how right she'd been. He owed her for carrying his child in the first place, for saving Sarah's life and caring for her for four years. And he knew Lexie. She could take that and twist it into something that would suit her. He didn't want her knowing how indebted to her he really was.

"I understand why you ran, Lex."

"And do you understand exactly what it cost me? My family, my job at the Erie library? I couldn't even work as a librarian, 'cause I didn't want a job on the books, or to have anyone access my college records or things like that. Knowing your computer skills, I figured you'd have a way to trace that kind of stuff.

Shoot, I don't even own a car anymore, and I'm driving on my expired Pennsylvania license. We use Pappy's truck when we need to go anywhere."

He wasn't sure how to respond to that, since he would have found her if there'd been any public—or not-so-public—records of her.

"David, I need to know your intentions."

"Huh?" Intentions? She sounded like a parent grilling him before a first date.

"If the DNA tests prove that you're her father—"

"I'm her father, Lex. We both know it."

"*If* you are, do I get anything? Visitation? Pictures once a year? Do I get to be involved in her life in any way? Or am I going to be totally cut out?"

Hellfire and damnation. Leave it to her to ask questions he didn't even want to think about, let alone answer. "I don't know, Lex. I hadn't really thought about it."

"Well, you need to think about it. I believe you owe me something." She sighed and retrieved the can of polish, then moved to the sideboard, turning her back on him. She didn't want him to see how much that question hurt, to see how willing she was to settle for just about any crumb he wanted to toss her.

"Okay."

"How did she make out with the shot? Did she give you a hard time?"

He snorted. "She didn't bite anybody. Me, especially. For which I was very grateful."

Lexie pressed her lips together to stifle a chuckle.

"That's a step in the right direction, I suppose. And how did you feel?"

"Mad. And...helpless."

She glanced over her shoulder at him. Frustration and pain filled his eyes. "Welcome to parenthood," she said quietly, "where you'll do anything you can to ease your child's pain and protect her, but often can only stand by and comfort after the pain's been inflicted."

"Does it get easier?"

She shook her head. "From what I understand, it only gets harder."

"I can hardly wait." He pushed off the doorway and approached her. "Lexie, I want Sarah to start depending on me, turning to me instead of you. She and I are never going to bond if you don't take a step back." He cleared his throat. "Although I think we could have done without me holding her down for the shot. I don't think that helped my case any."

Step back? Didn't she just explain to him how much it hurt to love a child, but to sit by helplessly?

On the other hand, maybe David had no idea how tough being a parent was. Maybe... "All right. You want me to step back, I will. You want to make the decisions, be my guest." She offered him her best angelic smile as she sprayed the china cabinet and ran the dust rag over it. "Happy parenting."

"LEXIE! I need a hand here," David shouted up the back staircase, over the sound of his daughter's uncontrollable sobbing. He turned back to Sarah, who was keeping the kitchen island between them. Water trickled from the ends of half her curls—the half he'd managed to wet down before she'd escaped his attempt to wash her hair. "Hey, sport, you're dripping all over the floor and your nice clean pajamas. How about you let me finish up and then dry your hair?"

Her lower lip trembled, and more moisture, tears this time, tracked down her unhappy face. She shook her head violently, flinging droplets across the counter.

He should have known three days ago when Lexie had flashed him that Cheshire-cat grin of hers that he was in for trouble. "Sweetheart, we have to wash your hair. I promise, I won't get any soap in your eyes."

Sarah shook her head. "That's not how Momma does it."

A chuckle, covered up with a cough, escaped the old man at the table. Pappy ducked his head lower behind the newspaper.

"What are you laughing at?"

"Nothin'. Just got a tickle in my throat, is all."

"Maybe it's that thing you've got stashed upstairs making you cough, huh?"

The old man dropped the paper and stared at him. "Now, you mind your manners, boy. You gotta admit, there's a certain humor in you trying to take Lexie's place with the young'un. Ain't working too good, is it?"

David blew out a long sigh. "No, it's not."

"Patience. That and you're trying too hard, boy. Not to mention the fact that there's just certain things women are better at than men."

"Don't let Lexie hear you say that. She'll be all over you for being chauvinistic." He glanced across the center island at his daughter's miserable little face, and his heart clenched. Would they ever connect? Seemed like all he did was screw things up with her. Lexie had covered bath duty again, which, to his surprise, didn't include hair washing because apparently Sarah had a major thing about getting her hair washed. Sarah had refused to let him give her a bath. That didn't bode well. What was he going to have to do, hire a live-in nanny just so his kid would be clean?

He balled up the towel in his hands and tossed it to the countertop, locking eyes with Sarah. "Maybe she'll show me how she washes your hair. Would that be okay?"

She nodded, then drew her arm across her nose. Pappy chuckled again as he left the room.

David turned his head back toward the stairs. "Lexie!" he yelled again.

Upstairs, Lexie forced a smile and ignored the bellow echoing up the stairwell. "As you can see, you've got a private bath, your own balcony and a king-size canopy bed. If you fill out this card and hang it on your door tonight, in the morning I'll bring up a tray with your breakfast."

The young bride blushed an adorable shade of pink that matched the blouse she wore. "Thank you."

"If you need anything, don't hesitate to ask. I hope you'll enjoy your stay with us." Lexie paused in the doorway as the groom held the knob, eager to usher

her out. "Oh, and don't forget to blow out the candles before you fall asleep."

"No, ma'am, we won't forget that. Wouldn't want to burn down the place. Leastways, I think we've got other heat sources to worry about for that."

"Ronnie!" The woman blushed deeper, sounding slightly scandalized.

Lexie chuckled as the door closed behind her. The pair had married a few days earlier in a little town about forty-five minutes away. Small-town economies being what they were, Mill Creek B&B did a strong honeymoon business for local couples.

Ah, young love. They'd held hands the entire time Lexie'd shown them the house and all the amenities they wouldn't be taking advantage of. Past experience with honeymooners had taught her the bed and the bath would be all they really needed.

Descending the back staircase, she brushed aside a twinge of jealousy. Someday there would be a man who looked at her the way the red-haired freckle-faced groom had watched his young bride. The way her father had always watched her mother.

With total adoration.

The dream of being married to a man who loved her so completely was the one dream she wasn't fully ready to let go of. The one she still believed could—would—come true someday.

"Lex—"

Lexie clamped a hand over David's mouth from the final stair. "Must you bellow like that? I was trying to get my newlyweds settled into the honeymoon suite, which happens to be right above this kitchen, thank you very much. I'm sure they're not going to appreciate hearing you holler like an enraged elk, or whatever the heck that was supposed to be.'' She removed her hand and pushed past him into the kitchen.

"Being honeymooners, I'm sure they've got much more important things on their minds than my yelling." He followed her, picking up the bottle of baby shampoo from the counter and thrusting it at her. "I need some help here." He jerked his chin in Sarah's direction. "Apparently in my bumbling maleness, I don't know how to wash hair the way Momma does it." A slow sigh escaped him. "Just like I don't know how to make a peanut butter and *elderberry* jelly sandwich, or 'tuckle' a child into bed or read a story."

"Oh. And here I thought it was something important with all that hollering."

"Momma, it *is* 'portant." Sarah sniffled. "I need you!"

"I wasn't talking about you, baby. I meant David." Lexie smiled at the little girl, then retrieved a dry washcloth from the drawer next to the sink. Part of her—a small part—felt badly for David's discomfort. Most of her, however, felt vindicated. The man had apparently never given a moment's thought to how he was going to care for his daughter once he'd gotten her back, and Lexie adored every incident when he discovered just how difficult parenting could be and how complex a child Sarah was.

She wasn't the blank slate that some philosophers—unquestionably male philosophers—had proclaimed children to be. No, Sarah definitely had her own opinions. And though shy with strangers, at home she wasn't bashful about making those opinions known.

"He don't listen to me!" Sarah proclaimed as Lexie dragged the step stool in front of the sink. "I told him that's not how Momma does it, but he did it wrong anyway." She sniffled again, though her tears had stopped when Lexie had arrived.

"Well, come on. Let's get this over with, okay? The sooner we start..."

"The sooner we're done!" Sarah finished as she climbed up onto the stool.

Lexie wrapped a bath towel around the little girl like a cape, then helped her press a dry washcloth over her eyes. "Hold that tight. Tip your head back as far as you can." She reached for the sprayer. As she worked, David watched intently. If nothing else, he was an eager student.

Twenty minutes later, she'd washed and dried Sarah's hair, and the three of them had gone upstairs. Lexie helped Sarah into a dry pajama top, which the child insisted be done in Lexie's room so David couldn't see. When they returned David reached for the bedcovers and drew them back. Sarah scowled at him.

"Sarah," Lexie admonished, torn between her desire to prolong her own time with Sarah and wanting the child to connect with David. "I don't think you're being fair to David. I think you need to give him a chance to show you what he learned last night about how to read stories and tuckle you in."

"But, Momma—"

"Don't 'but Momma' me. Do I give you a chance to practice new things?"

She bobbed her head, the freshly washed curls bouncing.

"Okay, then. You give David a chance. I'll be back in a little while to kiss you good night."

David's eyes widened, and he offered her a tentative grin. "Thank you," he mouthed silently. He accepted the book *If You Give a Mouse a Cookie,* which Sarah thrust into his hand, then settled onto her bed. Lexie nodded at him, and left via the connecting door to her bedroom.

She opened the window about an inch, causing the curtains to flutter with the cool night breeze, and caught the scent of wood smoke from someone's fireplace. Perfect early-fall night for a fire. Across the street, several lights gleamed in the clinic—Kegan probably dealing with some minor medical crisis that could range from a child's upset stomach to someone needing stitches...to delivering a baby.

The low murmur of David's voice as he read to Sarah floated into the room. He had a deep voice, strong. Lexie was glad that he and Sarah were getting to know one another. Especially since she no longer had to worry about Angela, or Sarah's safety.

So why did she feel morose? This was a good thing. *Right?*

To forestall the feelings, she grabbed a book from her nightstand and flopped down on her bed, immersing herself in fiction, a place where good always triumphed and happy endings were possible—at least in the books she chose.

A few chapters later, David appeared in the doorway. "She wants you to kiss her good night now. I think you'd better hurry, she's fading fast."

The room reflected the green glow from Sarah's night-light. Lexie sat on the edge of the little girl's bed, smoothed the curls from Sarah's forehead and placed a kiss in the middle. Then she kissed each cheek, finishing with the one with the birthmark, a ritual she'd begun the day she'd brought Sarah into the world, one designed to remind her that love made everything beautiful, even the birthmark. "I love you, baby."

"Love you, too. Sing me." Sarah rolled onto her side and snuggled deeper under the covers.

"What do you want me to sing?"

"The sunshine song."

Self-conscious with David standing in the doorway, Lexie very softly began to sing "You Are My Sunshine." When she got to the part about not taking that sunshine away, she glanced over at him. He shuffled his feet and looked at the floor.

Lexie finished the song and moved into humming the same tune as she rose from the bed, tucked the covers around the now-sleeping child and dropped another kiss on her forehead. After turning on the monitor, she locked the door leading to the hallway then crooked her finger at David, motioning for him to follow her out through her bedroom.

"I keep the hallway door locked at night when there

are guests in the house," she explained in a near whisper.

"Good idea. You never know what kind of kooks you could get."

Kooks like Angela? Lexie could tell by the way David's eyebrows drew together that she didn't have to say it, he was already thinking the same thing. She moved to her nightstand and picked up the other half of the baby monitor, which she extended to him. "Here. You can have night-call duty. Might as well get used to it."

"Okay. But how do I get in there if she needs me?"

"I guess you'll have to come through here. I'm a light sleeper. If she calls, I guarantee, I'll be awake before you are. So, don't make either of us wait."

"You don't keep your own door locked? What if some kook decided he was more interested in you than Sarah?" He took the device from her.

She shrugged. "Nah. I'm a big girl, I can take care of myself."

"So I can see. And her, as well. Little Princess Lexie is all grown up. You've changed a lot. For the better." He reached out and tucked a strand of her hair behind her ear, then brushed the back of his fingers across her cheek. "You're really good with her, Lex."

She held her breath as warmth spread beneath his gentle caress. Tilting her face upward, she silently urged him not to break the spell that seemed to have the night standing still around them. Even the breeze had stopped blowing the curtains.

But his eyes widened, and he dropped his hand, shattering the illusion.

Which she should have expected. After all, this was David. Despite her being "all grown up," she doubted he was ready to see her for what she really was—a woman. A woman who'd had a crush on him forever.

But if he followed through with a kiss on her forehead, like the night of the prom, or like she gave Sarah, she was going to slug him.

He backed away, raising the monitor in the air and gesturing toward the door with the antenna. "I, uh, I guess I should go. I…have some programming to get done tonight. I'll listen for Sarah."

She nodded. "Okay. Good night."

"Oh, one more thing. I won't be around tomorrow morning for Dad duty. I have an appointment in Missoula with a lawyer to talk about getting Sarah's birth certificate changed. 'Night." He turned and hustled out of the room, leaving her staring at his back as he retreated.

Okay. It was definite.

She was going to slug him.

CHAPTER SIX

FRIDAY MORNING, David strode from the lawyer's office, legalese bouncing around in his head: this code and that code, and pursuant to this subsection, proof of paternity...

Damn, he hated lawyers.

After climbing into the rented Blazer, he reluctantly hauled out his cell phone. He spent a few minutes staring at the keypad, then finally forced his fingers to move, dialing a number at the federal courthouse in Erie. "Judge Wysocki, please. If he's available. Tell him it's David Mitchell."

Canned classical music, horrible stuff designed to soothe but that actually irritated the crap out of him, savaged his ear for several minutes before it cut off and a deep voice said, "David! This is quite a surprise."

"Yeah, I'm sure," David muttered.

"How are things going with your little girl? You know, you should call your mother. She's concerned about you and that whole situation."

"I didn't call for a lecture on familial duties, especially not from *you*. I called because I need a favor, and I figure you owe me, oh, at least several hundred at this point." Though it was costing him to call in the man's marker, for Sarah, he'd do just about anything. Including swallow his pride.

"You know I'll do whatever I can to help you, David. What's the problem?"

"I need you to help decipher some legalese for me, and maybe cut through the red tape necessary for me to get my daughter's birth certificate changed. You see, unlike you, *Dad,* I actually want my name on my kid's birth certificate."

"You're never going to forgive me for that, are you?" Papers rustled in the background, which didn't surprise David. He had never been given his father's undivided attention.

"Probably not." Not for that, or for the fact that he'd missed out on having a dad growing up, or for the times his mother had shed tears over the Judge's broken promises. "I've heard enough times about the marriage, the sick wife, the career. Whatever. Right now, your excuses don't matter. What matters is my child. Mine. And I want the legal documents to back that up. Who do you know in Montana? Can you help me, or am I just wasting my breath with you, as usual?"

"I'll do what I can. You have the surrogacy agreement? You want Angela listed as the mother, and you as the father, right?"

An image of Lexie's face appeared, as she'd looked last night, singing to Sarah. Her eyes had been laced with a deep pain when she'd stumbled over the words about her sunshine being taken away. He banged his fist against the steering wheel. "Yes. No. I don't know." He sighed. "This is so complicated."

"Not really. Legally Lexie Jacobs has no rights to the child at all. She's not the child's biological mother."

"I know that. But Sarah calls her Momma, and she's only known Lexie in that capacity. I have to figure out what's best for my little girl." It sure didn't matter to Angela anymore. Hell, it hadn't mattered to Angela in the first place, but he'd been too preoccupied with getting what he wanted to see it.

"They may want proof of paternity."

"Already covered. DNA tests in process as we speak."

"Excellent. Fax the report to my office as soon as you have it. I'd say you have until then to decide how you want the revised certificate to read. Although legally it should read you and Angela."

"Legally I suppose it didn't matter that mine had a blank space on it. Morally you ditched your responsibilities."

The scratching of a pen against paper stopped, and a long silence followed. "Sometimes a man makes a mistake."

"Is that what I am?" David tightened his hand around the steering wheel until his knuckles went white.

"That's not what I said."

"Yeah. Look, I have to go. I'll fax that stuff to you as soon as possible." He flipped the phone shut, ending the conversation before the old man had a chance to say anything else. He turned the key and eased the truck into Drive, exiting the parking lot.

What a mess he'd created. Not a mistake. Never in a million years would he refer to his sweet little girl or the process that had created her as a mistake. But the situation was a lot more complicated than he'd ever imagined. When Lexie had offered him a chance at a child of his own, he'd jumped at it, not wanting to adopt because he'd spent too much time on the receiving end of his stepfather's disparaging remarks, how he wasn't good enough because he wasn't blood bound to the man. He hadn't considered the fact that he didn't give two shits about the blood-bond he did share with the Judge.

What made a parent? Was it the strand of DNA he shared with Sarah?

The DNA Sarah shared with Angela? God, now that was a scary thought. Almost made him wish for the DNA results to somehow reveal that he was the father, and somehow, Lexie was truly her mother. Which was totally impossible.

But it seemed more comforting than the idea of his sweet child sharing genetic code with a woman like Angela.

Even if that meant he'd have to share Sarah with Lexie for the rest of their lives.

He shook his head, as if it would do some good in clearing his thoughts. He pulled onto the highway that would take him back toward Mill Creek, back to the daughter who was reluctantly giving him a chance to try to get to know her.

Back to Lexie...

This whole suddenly-a-dad thing had knocked him for way more of a loop than he'd expected. What else could explain the impulse that had damn near overwhelmed him last night, when he'd brushed his hand over the smooth skin of Lexie's cheek and almost given in to the temptation to kiss her?

JOHN LEANED AGAINST the post at the bottom of the stairs, easing the dull ache in his knee while absorbing all the bustle of the house. From the library, Lexie's warm voice flowed as she read to the circle of children around her. Sarah snuggled against her side on the leather couch, and Connor, the little boy from next door, sat on the other side. A small flock of kids fanned out in a half circle on the rug in front of her.

The scents of homemade cinnamon rolls and coffee along with the chatter and laughter of the kids' moms came from the kitchen, where the women held a book swap, trading paperbacks. Lexie held story hour twice a month on Saturday mornings, another way she helped raise money for the town's new fire engine fund. The parents dropped donations into a basket in the library—never a set amount, and always on the honor system. Lexie never kept tabs. He knew she did it just as much, if not more, for the kids themselves.

Today's participation was a record. Even some of the women John knew hadn't read a book in years were there. Probably 'cause every busybody in town wanted to catch a glimpse of their latest visitor. Gossip spread faster in Mill Creek than mange through a cattle herd. Ever since David's adventure in Doc Riley's office, people stopped John everywhere—Jo's diner, the hardware store, Al's Market...wanting to know what was going on with Lexie and the handsome out-of-towner.

And so did he.

More loud laughter came from the far end of the hallway, and the kids broke into applause and cheers in the library. The house was alive with people...and Lexie had made it that way.

John sighed softly. The thought of losing her and Sarah cut deep. If they left, they'd take the spark that had made his life worth living for the last four years. Before that, he'd been biding his time in the huge empty house that once had belonged to his wife's family, a hollow shell of a home, like he'd been a hollow shell of a man.

But Missy and the little one had changed that.

Not normally a praying man, he offered up a silent plea as some of the children ran shrieking from the library down the hallway. *Please, God, don't take them away from me. I lost one family. I know I can't stand to go through it again.*

Lexie paused in the archway. "Pap? What's up?"

"Nothin'. Just stopped here to listen to you finish the story. I like that one."

"*The Giving Tree?* Me, too." She glanced over her shoulder at some of the kids still in the room. "Do me a favor? Keep an eye on Sarah and Fallyn? I have to go check on things in the kitchen."

"Sure."

"I'll make you a cup of coffee. Just bring Sarah with you when you come to get it." She cocked her head to the side and studied him for a minute. "You sure you're okay?"

"'Course," he said gruffly. "What could possibly be wrong with me?"

She shrugged, then lifted her hand, lightly caressing his cheek. With a quick smile, she whirled and strode down the hall.

You are such a liar, John Nonnemacher, said a voice in his head that sounded remarkably like Doris, his wife. 'Course, ever since she'd passed on, his conscience always sounded like her. Not that he listened any better now than he had when she'd been alive.

"Missy loves it here," he muttered. "She's not going anywhere."

Or so he hoped, anyway.

DAVID HEADED down the back staircase. Yesterday's conversation with his father still had him reeling, and even hours of tedious programming—made more tedious by the fact that he couldn't concentrate—hadn't been able to keep his mind from wandering to Sarah, fatherhood and Lexie.

Especially Lexie.

The well-worn treads in the middle of the steps were smooth beneath his bare feet. His mouth watered as the smell of fresh cinnamon rolls came through the gaps around the door. And it wasn't even Sunday. Maybe she'd make them again tomorrow. At this rate he was going to gain ten pounds before he went back to Erie.

The volume of noise in the kitchen crescendoed as he opened the doorway, then abruptly died as he stepped through. At least a dozen pairs of female eyes stared at him. He hesitated, one hand on the glass knob. "Am I interrupting something?"

"No."

"Absolutely not."

"Oh, not at all." The women rushed to reassure him.

"Okay." He closed the door and crossed to the island's counter, helping himself to a cinnamon roll. Icing dripped as he picked it up, and he caught it with his finger, popping it into his mouth.

The silence was so complete in the room he could hear the hum from the old refrigerator. Removing his finger with an audible pop, he shook it at Lexie, who stood near the table with several other young women. "Lex, if I'm interrupting your women's meeting or something, just say so. I'll take my roll and some java back upstairs."

Sarah ran into the kitchen, followed by another, bigger girl. Behind him, the old man's low chuckle broke the silence. "Shoot, boy, you're the main attraction."

"Huh?"

That brought the women back to life, and they talked over one another.

The little girl who'd followed Sarah into the kitchen propped her fists on her hips and tilted her head back, giving him a look that said she was sizing him up. "Are you really Sarah's dad?" she asked.

The women got quiet again. Lexie's face reddened.

"Yes, I am. Why?"

"'Cause you don't look like her. You don't got a mark like she does. And her mom don't. So where'd it come from?"

"Where'd it come from?" David fought the surge of heat igniting in his gut. Some of the women shook their heads at the kid's audacity. Was this what Sarah put up with on a regular basis? No wonder Lexie had risked being found in order to get the port-wine stain treated.

As soon as he got back upstairs, he was getting on the Internet and finding the best plastic surgeon in Erie. And somehow he'd make sure Sarah understood it wasn't because he didn't love her the way she was, but that he wanted to spare her these kinds of remarks, wanted the best for her.

Lexie briskly strode across the room, stopping at his side. Tension and barely controlled anger radiated from her. She pointed her index finger at the back door. "Fallyn, why don't you go outside with all the other children and—"

"Besides, everybody knows—" the kid rolled her eyes, implying that everybody didn't include him, and he was stupid for not knowing whatever tidbit of wisdom she was about to impart "—that moms and dads who haven't seen each other in a long time always kiss a lot. And Sarah says you never kiss her mom."

Lexie's hand curled into a fist even while her arm

sagged to her side. Her mouth opened and she gaped at the girl. Then she glanced over at the women gathered around the kitchen table and the small group standing near the door to the back porch. Eager, hopeful expressions filled most of their faces, while one or two of them looked...jealous?

When she returned her gaze to him, he could see the panic rising in the green depths of her eyes. She didn't want these people, her friends and neighbors, knowing she wasn't Sarah's mother. That was one thing she'd made him promise after the DNA swabs had been taken—that in Mill Creek, Montana, the truth of her relationship to Sarah would remain between them and Dr. Riley.

David had given his word.

His daughter watched as expectantly as the rest of them.

So he set the pastry back on the counter and gripped Lexie's shoulders. Her eyes widened as she realized his intent. He smiled, pleased at catching her off guard and being presented with the perfect opportunity to do what he'd wanted to so badly ever since the other night in her room—with an excuse to salve his guilt for wanting it.

He leaned forward, bending his neck. A fleeting brush of his lips against hers brought the faint taste of vanilla-almond coffee. A renowned java junkie, he needed to experience it—her—better, so he stroked deeper, coaxing her to respond, to open to him...

And she did.

Her hands fluttered to rest on his chest, then gripped the points of his shirt collar.

Vaguely David registered a woman's voice, something about the kids going outside now. Some other chatter. But nothing mattered other than the warmth of Lexie's mouth against his.

Until that warmth sparked life elsewhere. And he realized he was going to have to face a roomful of women with an embarrassing bulge along the fly of his jeans if he didn't pull back now.

Shaken by his body's response—this was Lexie, for God's sake—he tore his mouth from hers, disengaged her hands from his shirt and stepped away from her.

Her eyes flashed open, filled with a dazed, smoldering expression that did little to cool his own desire. Her hand trembled when she lifted it to smooth back a piece of her dark hair from her face.

Smug male satisfaction coursed through him. Good, the kiss had rattled her as much as it had him.

"I don't care, Fallyn, get outside with the other kids. It'll be winter soon enough and you'll all be stuck indoors most of the time." One of the women gently pushed Sarah and the obnoxious kid out the back door.

David retrieved his cinnamon roll, then saluted the room at large with it. "Ladies. I have work to do." He turned and swiftly retreated toward the staircase door, neglecting to get his morning coffee, but not needing a jolt of caffeine.

No, he'd had a jolt of Lexie.

And every nerve ending in his body jangled, wide awake, because of it.

The old man glared at him, eyes narrow, as he opened the hidden doorway. David shrugged one shoulder and quickly headed for his computer...at least logic ruled there.

And he needed some logic right now. 'Cause kissing Lexie...

Hadn't been a bright move at all.

"Earth to Lex, come in, Lexie." Nola waved her hand in front of Lexie's face.

She flushed, realizing she was staring at David's backside as he fled up the stairs. "Huh?"

"Jeez, girl, you've been holding out on me," Nola said in a low tone. "Not only is the man a hunk and a half, but the two of you together...it's a good thing it's not fire season around here." Her best friend grinned at her. "And in front of half the women in town, too."

"Oh my..." Lexie couldn't bear to turn around, but she picked up smatterings of excited female voices.

"Did you get a load of those shoulders?"

"Forget the shoulders, that man has a butt to die for."

A heavy sigh was followed by, "I had no idea a man's bare feet could be so sexy."

"Yeah, and did you see how big they are? You know what they say about men and the size of their feet, right? Holy moly." The women dissolved into a fit of laughter.

"Shoot me now," Lexie whispered to Nola. "Just shoot me now and put me out of my misery."

Nola giggled. "Come on, it's not that bad. The gossip will die down…oh, sometime next spring. Probably."

"Thanks for the reassurance." Lexie fought to calm the pounding of her heart. David had kissed her. Not an on-the-forehead-good-night-little-girl kiss, heck, no. This was an open-mouth-let-me-introduce-you-to-my-tongue kiss.

Her legs trembled as she recalled every mind-blowing stroke that tongue had provided. She'd waited years for him to kiss her like that. And he'd tasted as sweet as she'd always suspected. Of course, the icing from the cinnamon rolls had contributed to that.

What had possessed him? A challenge from a seven-year-old didn't seem enough. Had he seen her fear that the women would suspect something wasn't completely on the up-and-up?

Chairs scraped the floor as the women rose from the table. Lexie pasted a smile on her face and turned to offer goodbyes, bracing herself for the comments. "Thanks, Lexie," Martha said. Then she leaned closer and whispered, "That one's a keeper, dear."

"If you do decide to toss him back, I'll take him." Sue Ellen offered her a wink. "Looks like a good kisser. Wooieee." She fanned herself with her hand and grinned.

Lexie sighed, bidding everyone goodbye, smiling through their comments about David, until only she and Nola were left in the kitchen. Then she sank into a chair at the table and covered her face with her hands, groaning. "I am going to be the talk of the town for the next century."

Nola patted her shoulder. "We all get our turns. I'd much rather be the talk of the town 'cause a handsome hunk kissed me in front of half the women's auxiliary than because my rat-fink husband up and left without a word."

Lexie laid her hands on the table and looked over at her friend, whose wry smile did little to hide the fact that Duncan's betrayal still hurt. "Nola, I'm sorry. I wasn't thinking."

"'S okay. It's nice to have someone else in the hot seat." Nola lived next door, and three years ago, without warning, her husband had left a terse "Dear Nola" note and basically vanished. She and her seven-year-old, Connor, still struggled with it. "Judging from the heat you two generated, I'm thinking you'll soon not be needing the one birthday present I gave you this year, and needing the others instead." She laughed.

Lexie's cheeks warmed again. "Nola! I don't need either at the moment, thank you very much." The purple vibrator hadn't been her style. Her crazy friend had known that but the gag gift had been a blatant attempt to encourage Lexie to seek out a "real" man. The box had also been filled with a wide assortment of condoms in all colors, flavors, textures and shapes—in case Lexie ever found that man.

David Mitchell was *not* that man. Although he'd fed her fantasies on more than one occasion.

"That's the first time he's kissed you since he's come to town, isn't it?"

"Yeah, first time." First time ever. But Lexie wasn't admitting that, not even to Nola.

Just like she wasn't admitting how much the experience had shaken her.

LATER THAT AFTERNOON, Lexie hesitated outside Sarah's bedroom door, pausing to listen to the voices from within.

"Here's another piece," David said. "Where do you think that one goes?"

There was a long silence. Then Connor piped up. "I'll give it to her. Here, Sarah."

Lexie peeked around the corner. David sat cross-legged on the rug on the floor beside Sarah's bed. Connor practically leaned against him. Lexie knew the poor kid was starved for a man's attention. Sarah sat well away from both of them, leaning over a chunky-pieced jigsaw puzzle. David extended another section toward his daughter.

She eyed him warily, as if he was trying to sabotage her efforts. "Momma says look for outsides first."

"She does, huh? Well, I usually match the colors and shapes, instead."

"No, not there." Sarah grabbed it from David's hand. "Over here, see?"

David chuckled. "Yeah, I see."

Lexie's throat tightened, and she rapped on the edge of the door, feeling like an intruder on Sarah's life for the very first time. *I guess I'll have to get used to that feeling.* "Hey. What's going on in here?"

David looked up at her, that infectious grin activating his dimples. "We're doing a puzzle."

"That's 'cause *he*—" the venom in the word made it clear Sarah didn't mean Connor "—didn't want to play Barbies." She scowled and jumped up, rushing over to wrap her arms around Lexie's legs.

"I don't know how to play Barbies. Puzzles I know how to do."

Absentmindedly, Lexie stroked Sarah's hair. "You'll have to show him how to play Barbies, baby. I don't think David ever played with dolls. Although I think I recall one time…"

He shifted uneasily on the rug, his mouth turning down. "No, I'm sure you don't."

"Yes, that one time with Marc and Kenny," she said. "Remember? They stole my Cabbage Patch Kid and tied it to the tree in the backyard?"

Sarah whirled around, propping her fists on her hips. "That's mean!"

"Hey, I didn't do it." David held up his hands in mock surrender. "Her brothers did."

"Yes, it was mean," Lexie said. "But I also recall someone pretending to be James Bond and rescuing her. He cut her loose when my brothers weren't looking, and gave that doll back to me."

"I do remember that. Marc and Kenny ganged up on me afterward. Wrestled me to the ground and sat on me for an hour." David laughed.

The rich sound warmed her like mulled cider on a

frosty autumn evening. Their eyes locked. His dimples slowly faded and his expression became serious, searching.

A quivering sensation spread from the pit of her stomach. How could he make her feel so unstable just by looking at her? "I hope it was worth it," she said. "I loved that doll."

"Where is she now, Momma?"

"I'm not sure what happened to her." The doll's image—curly black hair and a purple dress—brought back too many memories of home, of her parents and brothers... She missed them all so much, even more now that she'd spoken to them on the phone several times. Kenny's wife was expecting their first baby any moment. She blinked hard to chase away the moisture fogging her vision.

David climbed to his feet. "Hey, you know what I was thinking? Let's go out to dinner. My treat."

"To Jo's?" Sarah asked.

"Actually, I was thinking about driving to Missoula. I passed this place the other day called Danny Dino's Pizza Playplace. Looked like fun."

"Oh, yeah! That place is great," Connor said. "I went to a birthday party there once. It has games you play and win prizes, and it has rides and this cool ball pit you can crawl around in."

Sarah's eyebrows drew together and she looked skeptical. "I like Jo's."

Connor leaped up, carefully picking his way around the puzzle, coming to stand beside Sarah. "It's really fun, Sarah. Would I lie to you?"

Lexie struggled to control the chuckle, clearing her throat. Connor was great with Sarah. The pair had a mutual-admiration society.

Sarah shook her head solemnly.

"So, you should go. You'll have fun, I promise." He patted her on the shoulder.

"Can Connor come, too?" Sarah looked up at Lexie.

"I'm not the one you need to ask, baby."

Sarah turned to David, folding her arms across her chest. "I don't wanna go without Connor."

"Fine by me," David said. "As long as it's okay with his parents."

"I only have a mom now," Connor murmured. Then he smiled. "She'll say I can go."

David rumpled the boy's hair. "Okay, you go ask her, and we'll wait for you."

"Waa-hooo!" Connor charged out the doorway, tossing "Be right back" over his shoulder.

"We're not going to the doctor's, right?" Sarah asked Lexie.

"No, honey. No treatments today."

"Okay. I'll go."

A half hour later they'd put Sarah's booster seat into the Blazer and buckled everybody in. Connor yammered nonstop once he discovered that he and David shared a passion for computer and video games.

The noise level at the Pizza PlayPlace was just a few decibels short of deafening. Kids shrieked, games buzzed and pinged and music blasted from speakers Lexie suspected were placed every two feet around the entire place. Sarah's small hand tightened around hers, and the child pressed herself against Lexie's leg.

David winced. "Don't they have to be careful with kids' sensitive, developing ears?"

"What? I can't hear you."

"Cute, very cute," he mumbled.

"Welcome to the Pizza Playplace." The young hostess greeted them. "I just have to stamp your hands."

"Why?" David asked, though he held out the back of his left hand for her.

"Because we check the numbers when you leave to make sure you all match."

"Oh. Good idea. Nobody takes out a kid that doesn't belong to them. I like that."

Lexie cringed inwardly as the teenager pressed the stamp to her.

"I don't want my hand marked," Sarah whispered.

"It's okay, Sarah." Connor got his stamp. "Look how cool this is. You can't see it unless you put it under the special light."

Lexie blessed the good-natured little boy when Sarah hesitantly held out her hand. The hostess smiled at Sarah, earning her a silent thanks, too.

After ordering pepperoni pizza at the counter, they filled their cups with pop from the fountain. David carried the tray as they searched for an empty booth. "This place is really hopping for a Friday night."

As they made their way through the place, he couldn't help but notice how people's gazes lingered over Sarah's face. Or how most people quickly looked away when he caught them. Sarah seemed oblivious to most of the stares, though she clung to Lexie, acting far more quiet and cautious than she did at home. He could sense Lexie bristle at some of the looks the little girl received.

Throughout the course of the next hour, he watched Lexie and Sarah carefully, learning his daughter liked her pizza cut into small pieces, wouldn't eat the crust and preferred orange soda. He envied Lexie's easy way of dealing with his daughter. Would he ever be able to relate to her like that? How long would it take before she trusted him enough to let him take care of her?

After the meal, David doled out game tokens to the children. Connor smiled. "Will you play a game with me?"

"Sure. What do you want to play?"

"That one." The boy pointed to a game that resembled a Jeep. A gruesome-looking T. Rex was painted on it.

"All right. Let's go shoot some dinosaurs."

Lexie shook her head. "Men. I think Sarah and I will find something a little more sedate to play."

"We'll catch up to you as soon as we put Rex in his place," David said, climbing onto the bench seat.

The girls wandered off. Connor slipped two tokens into the machine and laughed delightedly as it lurched to life beneath them. David smiled at the little boy and grabbed his mock gun from the holster.

After getting sidetracked into a round of air hockey, pod-racing and shooting hoops, David gently redirected Connor toward Lexie and Sarah. After all, he'd come here intending to make some progress with his daughter. Sarah was playing alone in a big container filled with multicolored balls as Lexie looked on from a nearby table.

"Cool, I love the ball pit!" Connor jumped into the play area and "swam" toward Sarah. "Watch this, Sarah!"

David perched on the edge.

Sarah hesitantly emulated Connor's submerging-beneath-the-balls trick, popping back up with a huge grin. "Momma, look at me!" She vanished again beneath the sea of purple, blue and red spheres.

"That's awesome, baby."

A pair of towheaded boys wearing SpongeBob SquarePants T-shirts leaped into the far end of the box, shouting to one another and laughing. Sarah scooted closer to Connor. The smaller of the two boys watched her, eyes wide. After a minute, he waded to her side. He pointed at her cheek. "Did somebody hurt you?" he asked.

"It's just a birthmark. Leave her alone." Connor climbed to his feet and stood chest to chest with the curious little boy.

"Easy there, buddy," David called to his daughter's protector. "He's not being mean. I think he just wants to know what happened to Sarah's cheek. Right?"

The little boy nodded.

"Well, if you come over here—" he let his voice drop to barely audible above the clanging and music of the place "—I'll tell you a secret."

Balls churned in all directions as they came closer to him. Sarah hung back, letting the boys, Connor included, gather practically on his knees. "Well?" demanded the taller of the brothers, "What happened? What's the secret?"

"Okay, just before Sarah was born, when she was up in heaven—"

"Babies are in their moms' stomachs before they're born," scoffed the boy.

"Before they get in their moms' stomachs they're in heaven, dummy," Connor said, folding his arms.

"No name-calling," David said. "It's not nice." He cleared his throat. "Anyway, like I said, Sarah was still in heaven and about to come down here. The angels were sad that she was leaving because they all loved her so much."

Sarah's eyes widened and she inched closer. David resisted the temptation to hold his breath, afraid to spook her with any type of a reaction at all. Instead, he looked at the smaller of the two boys. "They all kissed her goodbye on her cheek. So, now you know what that color is on her face."

"What?" the older boy asked.

"Angel lipstick." David nodded solemnly, thinking of the sticky lip-prints his aunt Sophie had bestowed on him as a child. "It's darn near impossible to get off."

Sarah's eyes grew even bigger and she reverently brushed her fingertips over the birthmark. A slow smile tugged the corners of her mouth upward and dimples appeared in her cheeks.

Dimples just like mine. The thought thrilled him beyond anything he could have ever imagined possible.

His daughter was smiling at him. "Angels," she whispered.

"Yeah, right," said the older boy, bounding away. "That's no secret. I knew it all along."

"Cool." The younger one grinned at Sarah before rushing to follow his brother, scrambling over the side of the ball pit and disappearing into the maze of games and rides.

"Angels kissed me?" Sarah asked. "Really?"

"Absolutely." David X-ed his fingers across his chest. "Cross my heart." He leaned forward and reached for her, pulse hammering madly as he lightly caressed her cheek. "Angel lipstick."

She turned her head toward his hand, and he fought the impulse to snatch it back. "Once bitten twice shy" definitely applied here. But the trust between them had to start somewhere—and since he was the grown-up…

She pursed her lips and feathered a kiss so light across his fingertips he thought he'd imagined it. Then she giggled and threw herself down into the balls, leaving him staring at his hand.

A warm tingling traveled up his arm and shot straight to the center of the X he'd drawn only seconds before.

Who knew a nearly nonexistent kiss from a little girl could melt a grown man? He was on top of the world.

Until he looked for Lexie to share the magical moment, and found her standing right behind him, mouth pressed together in a way that meant she was seriously ticked off.

Not the reaction he'd expected.

CHAPTER SEVEN

KISS HIM.

Or kick him. From one side of Montana to the other. Then back again.

Lexie'd waffled between both impulses since David had come up with the angel-lipstick story back in the restaurant. First, she'd wanted to thank him for the incredibly sweet tale. Then she'd realized exactly what kind of impact it could have on Sarah. And ever since, the kick-him impulse had been winning.

David peered in the rearview mirror. "Looks like they both finally gave out."

"Mm-hmm."

"That boy sure can talk."

"Mm-hmm."

"Unlike you, who hasn't said much of anything lately. What's the problem?"

"No problem." She turned and glanced into the back. Sarah slumped against the edge of her car seat. Connor leaned against the same side. Both kids were sound asleep, which figured, given the fact that they were almost home.

"Bull. You've been acting weird ever since Sarah kissed my hand. If I didn't know any better, I'd say you were jealous."

"Jealous? Of what? Sarah kisses me all the time."

He exhaled slowly. "Okay, so if it's not that, it must have been the story. Did you think you're the only person with an imagination? Personally, I thought the story was inspired. A stroke of pure genius."

"Yeah, great going, genius. Now how are you going to explain to her why she needs to go to the plastic surgeon and get the 'angel lipstick' removed from her face?"

A long silence filled the Blazer before he cleared his throat. "Damn it. I hadn't thought of that."

Lexie folded her arms. "Exactly. It was a pretty story, David. It made her happy, made her feel special, which is wonderful. But how do you reconcile the reality of the birthmark, needing to lighten it to make it easier on her in this world, and the dream of angel kisses?"

"I don't know. Maybe I'll have you plant a lipstick kiss on my cheek and show her that I can't walk around like that no matter how special it makes me feel."

A kiss from her made him feel special? A tingly sensation grew deep in her belly, and she fought to ignore it. David was a dream as well, a fairy-tale hero she'd longed for as a young woman. She needed to stay grounded in reality, just like she'd tried to be realistic and matter-of-fact with Sarah. She'd always told Sarah exactly what Kegan had said at her birth. The mark was just something that happened, and they dealt with it. "Well, you'd better figure it out, because she's going to ask, I can promise you that. A pretty fantasy isn't going to help her."

The lights along Main Street illuminated him as he shook his head. "What happened to you, Lex? You were the biggest dreamer I ever knew."

"Reality happened to me. Trying to take care of Sarah by myself, without benefit of my education or my identity. Hiding from you—from Angela. Realizing that life doesn't have the rosy ending I'd always imagined."

He made a low, gurgling sort of sound deep in his throat, then said nothing more as they pulled in to the driveway of the bed-and-breakfast. When he shut off the engine, she reached for the door handle, but he stopped her by grasping her elbow. She turned back to him. "What?"

For a moment, he just looked at her, then, puffing out his lips, he exhaled slowly. "I'm sorry, Lexie. This isn't how I imagined life would turn out, either."

"No kidding."

"No. No kidding." His lifted his hand, cupped her cheek. "I wouldn't have hurt you for anything, Lex. But I have to say, this has changed you. This new you seems so much stronger, so much more in control."

She snorted. "I didn't have much choice. There wasn't anybody to help me like at home. Besides, Sarah needed me."

His fingers slipped away. "Yeah. She did." He glanced into the back seat. "She still needs you."

"And that bothers you?"

"Yeah, it bothers me. I want her to need *me*. She does—she just doesn't know it. Or act it. Yet."

Yet. That tiny word tore at Lexie. It made her feel as if she'd soon be discarded, like a book taken out of circulation. No longer necessary. Out of date.

She moved again for the door, sliding from the vehicle. Climbing into the back seat, she unfastened Sarah's restraints. "Come on, baby." She nudged Connor. "Wake up, big guy. We're home."

Sarah murmured sleepily, then latched her arms around Lexie's neck, her legs around her waist, clinging like a little monkey. Slamming the door, Lexie rounded the vehicle to find David assisting Connor out. "Sarah and I will just walk Connor home, then we'll be upstairs."

David held out his arms. "I'll take Sarah and get her into bed."

"But I wanted to show you my computer games," Connor said.

"Not tonight, buddy. Maybe one day soon, okay?" David gripped Sarah's torso, just below the armpits, and pulled.

"Want Momma." Sarah's tired muscles didn't have the strength to resist, and her arms slipped from Lexie's neck.

David turned her around and hefted her against his shoulder.

"Momma," she protested again.

"It's okay, sport, Dad's got you." David nodded in Lexie's direction. "You go ahead and get Connor home. I can handle this."

"Whatever you say, *Dad.*" Lexie hoped he caught the sarcasm in her voice. How dare he?

He dares because he is Sarah's father, nagged a voice in the back of Lexie's mind. *That's what the DNA results will prove, and you already know it. You'll be left alone.*

Shut up. Lexie reached for Connor's hand as David headed for the porch. "You want to take the sidewalk, or should we cut through the backyard fence?"

Connor grasped her fingers. "Sidewalk. It's too dark for the shortcut."

They set off down the driveway. Once next door, Lexie had to confirm the little boy's recounting of the evening to Nola, including the story of the angel lipstick, which made both women roll their eyes. By the time she headed back home, a good half hour had passed.

Opening the front door, expecting the quiet evening routine of the B&B, Lexie wasn't prepared for all the noise coming from upstairs. Pounding, raised voices— Pappy? What was he doing on the second floor? Lexie rushed up the staircase.

Pappy, clad in his plaid bathrobe and slippers, banged on the door to Sarah's room. "Open this door now!"

"What's going on?"

"Ask him." The white head inclined toward the room.

"David?" Lexie slapped her palm flat against the door. "Let me in."

His muffled voice slipped through the cracks near the hinges. "I can handle this."

Sarah's crying said otherwise.

The young groom, red hair tousled, face flushed, stuck his head out the door at the far end of the corridor. "Is everything all right?"

"Fine. Just a little family thing." Lexie offered what she hoped would pass as a reassuring smile, and waved him off. The young couple certainly had better things to do on their last night at the B&B than worry about her problems. "Sorry to disturb you."

"Okay, ma'am." The honeymoon-suite door swung closed.

Lexie grabbed the glass knob in front of her and rattled it. "David..."

"Lex, I need to do this. Don't interfere." Footsteps moved away from the door.

"Momma!"

Lexie dashed into her own bedroom, Pappy one step behind her. "Tried that already. That one's locked, too."

"Not a problem." She yanked open the top drawer on the tall chest of drawers, pushed aside some socks, grabbed the key. She brandished it like a weapon. "If he thinks he can keep me out, I've got news for him."

"No! I don't want you! I want Momma!"

Lexie's pulse kicked into high gear. Her fingers trembled as she fumbled with the key in the lock. She knew David would never hurt Sarah, not physically, but the man obviously didn't have a clue.

Barging into the room, she found David perched on

the edge of Sarah's bed, practically wrestling with the little girl, whose arms and legs flailed. "Just what are you trying to do?"

"Momma!"

David turned to look at her, his hands trying to contain the thrashing child on the bed. Sarah's sneaker-enclosed foot sliced through the air and connected with David's cheek.

"Ow! Damn it!" He released Sarah, rubbing at his face.

"Momma says don't swear!"

He mumbled a few more things under his breath, fortunately below Sarah's ability to decipher them. But Lexie knew they were additional words on her "do not say" list. Arching an eyebrow and shooting her Montana winter glare—the below-zero-windchill one, the one designed to cause frostbite—at him, she moved to the bed.

One sleeve of her shirt dangling empty at her side, Sarah clambered to her feet, the mattress rocking beneath her. Then she jumped into Lexie's arms. "Momma!" The little girl pressed her face into the crook of Lexie's neck.

"Shh, it's okay." Lexie swayed back and forth, a motion she'd used to soothe her daughter since the day she'd brought her into the world.

David stood and stared at her, challenge clear in his eyes. The boards beneath Lexie's feet squeaked as she shuffled in place, gently shaking Sarah in her arms.

Slowly, the spark faded. He lifted his hands toward

the ceiling, then let them drop. "Fine. I give up. You deal with it."

David spun on his heel. He unlocked the door and stormed across the hall to his own room. Not bothering with a light—plenty came in from the hallway and from Sarah's room—he flung himself down on the bed, making the springs protest. He draped his arm over his eyes and bit back a yelp as he pulled it off. Gingerly, he explored his cheek with his fingers.

Of course, it figured Sarah had kicked him with the one shoe he hadn't managed to get off.

All he'd wanted to do was get his daughter settled in bed. She'd been almost asleep, for God's sake. Until he'd started to undress her. Then the kid had come wide awake and protested with a vengeance.

Okay, so maybe he hadn't been all that skillful about it. He sighed. He'd wager his entire company Lexie could undress the child and get her into pajamas without ever causing her to stir.

He'd never master this daddy stuff.

Maybe being an inept father was genetic. Something else to thank his old man for.

Note to self: Daddy Lesson #1— Let sleeping children, like dogs, lie.

#1B: And let them sleep in their clothes.

The lyrical rise and fall of Lexie's voice filled his room. After a moment's pause, he realized the sound came from the baby monitor she'd given him. He'd left it on, plugged in and sitting on the night table.

"Everything's all right, Pappy. I'll just get this

munchkin into her pj's and bed. Do you need help getting back downstairs?"

"No. Land's sakes, girl, what do you take me for, a feeble old woman?"

Lexie chuckled. "Of course not. 'Night, Pappy."

"'Night, Missy. Give me a kiss, squirt."

David ignored the pain that shot across his chest as he listened to his daughter give another man a goodnight kiss.

A kiss that should have been his.

The streetlight cast a four-paned outline through the window onto the bed. He wiggled his fingers in the glow, glanced down at the hand where Sarah had brushed her lips earlier.

He'd been that close...and had scared her off again. Damn.

He lay there listening to Lexie speak calm, soothing words as she changed his little girl for bed and tucked her in. Despite the knot in his stomach and pain still lodged in the center of his chest, her soft, melodic singing lulled him into a peaceful state as well.

"David?"

"Hmm?"

"David."

Her voice seemed louder, clearer. He opened his eyes to find her standing over him.

"I brought you an ice pack. For your face." She held out a white object.

"Oh." He took the chilled rectangle from her. "Thanks. But are you sure you don't want to pop me on the other cheek, instead?"

"Don't tempt me." The light streaming in from outside silhouetted her, accentuating the tuck of her waist, the curve of her hips.

Tempt *her?* He was the one feeling tempted. By his friend's little sister.

"What were you thinking?"

"Uh... I wasn't?" *And still not, apparently.*

"That much is obvious. Don't you ever try to manhandle her like that again. She's a person, David, not some little thing for you to boss around and subjugate. Not a blank computer to be programmed." Her lips pressed together and she wagged her finger at him.

"So how do you get her to do what you want if she doesn't want to cooperate? I'm betting spanking is out, huh?"

"Damn straight! Don't you ever raise a hand to her!"

"Don't swear." He suppressed a grin, knowing she'd get even more ticked if she knew he was tweaking her for fun. "And I was just kidding. Spanking. Not on the list of parenting tools I'd like to have."

"Good. Because she's never been spanked. She's a great kid, David."

No, he hadn't figured Lexie had ever felt it necessary to physically discipline Sarah. She was a natural mother. While he...wasn't a natural. He shifted the ice pack on his cheek and sighed. "I really blew it, didn't I?" He draped his arm carefully over his eyes, keeping the pack in place.

"Yes, stupid man, you did."

"Don't hold back, tell me what you really think."

"I think you've been spending too much time with computers lately. Your interpersonal skills aren't as good as I remember." The bed shifted as she sat down.

"Computers are so much easier to...fix when something goes wrong." Through the monitor, he heard Sarah shift and giggle in her sleep. A tight band encircled his lungs, making it difficult to breathe. The giant was back, squeezing him again, just as he had when the P.I. had shown him the pictures of his daughter for the first time. "I don't just want her to need me, Lex. I want her to…"

He let the comment dangle. Silence filled the room.

"Oh, David." Her fingers found his hand. Warmth passed into his arm as she intertwined her hand with his. "You want her to love you."

Love him? Well…yeah, he did. The love of a child wasn't the same thing as the love of a woman. That kind of love he could handle. He already loved Sarah so much it scared him silly.

But that didn't even come close to the terror he felt when he contemplated loving another woman.

"How—" he cleared his throat "—how do I do that?"

"You treat her like a person, silly. Even though she's only little, she's also a female. Woo her."

"Woo her? How do you woo a four-year-old?" Hell, he didn't understand the adult version of a female, let alone a miniature one.

"You were on the right track tonight. You listen to

her, and tell her stories and do things with her. Learn to play Barbies."

He removed his arm and the ice pack from his face, then looked at her. "Barbies?"

"Yes, Barbies. David, think about it this way. How would you have felt if your stepfather, when you'd first met him, tried something like you did with her tonight?"

"First of all, I was a lot older than Sarah when my stepfather came onto the scene. And second, I'm not her stepfather. I'm her *real* father."

"You're still a stranger to her." She released his fingers, stroked his cheek tenderly. "Be more patient."

He couldn't think with her touching him. "I have been patient. I planned on being back in Erie already."

She flinched and withdrew her hand. Taking a deep breath, she straightened her back. The corners of her mouth drooped, and he cursed himself for inflicting more pain on her. "Lex—"

"I'm grateful that you didn't just grab her and take her away. I... I always knew that you'd be a good dad. That's why I...wanted to give you a child."

"Do you still think I'll make a good dad?"

"Yes," she whispered, closing her eyes and nodding. "You will." Her teeth gnawed on her bottom lip.

A bottom lip lush, full and lovely; one he wanted to nibble on himself.

"Barbies, huh?" He heaved an exaggerated sigh, desperate to lighten the mood again. "I suppose if I have to, I have to. Can't she play with G.I. Joes, instead? How about if Barbie gets kidnapped, and we get Sarah some G.I. Joes and they can be the…"

Her eyes opened. A thin sheen of moisture glimmered in them. She offered him a tiny chuckle and placed her fingers over his lips, shaking her head. "Barbies."

His mouth went dry, as if someone had used canned air to remove every trace of moisture. "Lexie," he managed to croak against her hand.

"What?"

"There's something I need to do. It's crazy, but earlier today, it was under duress. I need to know. I have to do this."

"Do what?"

He reached up, cupping the back of her neck. "This."

Applying gentle pressure, he urged her forward and down. Her muscles tightened, resisting him. Then they relaxed, and she let him guide her closer, bracing her palms against his pecs. Her eyes closed, signaling she understood his intent.

The faintest wisp of cinnamon reached him, further addling his senses. His heart hammered faster. She was warmth and home and…forbidden. Which made the desire even sharper.

"Sweet Lexie," he whispered, easing his grip on her nape. He wouldn't make the same mistake twice in one night. Let her come to him. "Kiss me."

She hovered, just out of his reach for a moment, then finished closing the gap between them, brushing her lips against his ever so faintly, as though she feared he'd vanish in a puff of smoke if she touched him too hard.

"Like you mean it, Lex," he murmured against her mouth. "Don't be afraid."

Her tentative caress grew bolder, firmer. Short, nibbling kisses changed to a long, smoldering exchange. When she stroked his lower lip with her tongue, heat rushed over him. Unable to contain himself, he took the lead, following her retreating tongue.

A delicious ache of need stoked through his entire body.

When he reached the point where he absolutely had to release her or drag her down onto the bed and do something about relieving that ache, he backed off, letting his head slump into the down pillow. He inhaled deeply, catching another whiff of cinnamon. He held his breath, struggling to control his runaway pulse.

Lexie appeared frozen.

He understood completely. Once again, he hadn't been thinking. At least, not with the head he should have been.

This was *Lexie*.

And he was sporting a hard-on for her. Which was insane. The concept didn't compute, didn't make sense at all. He wrestled to find a logical explanation for it.

It had been a long time since Angela. There'd been no one since. And Lexie was kind and compassionate. She'd saved his daughter's life. He'd always liked her.

She was cute and spunky and smart and…sexy…

Oh, hell. "Lex?"

Her eyes fluttered open. "Hmm?"

Again, smug satisfaction thrummed at her dazed expression. "You okay?"

She nodded slowly. "Did you learn what you wanted to?"

"Oh, yeah. You're a far better jolt than coffee, and twice as addictive."

A sliver of panic chased through her eyes. She shook her head. "Oh, no. Not addictive. That was…"

"Please don't say stupid—"

"Stupid. And it won't be happening again." She rose from the bed and rushed toward the door.

At least one of them had some common sense. But he couldn't resist teasing her about it. "Not even to make your neighbors believe that we really are Sarah's parents? And made her in the regular way?"

His blood pressure shot up again at the concept of making love to Lexie. How different would their lives have been if he'd seen her as more than his best friend's kid sister all those years ago?

But then Sarah wouldn't exist. And no matter what, he couldn't regret the path his life had taken.

She paused in the doorway. She raised her shoulders, then let them drop.

He wanted her to turn back around. To smile at him before she left. "Marc and Kenny would kick my ass, you know that, right?"

She still didn't move.

"It would be worth it, Lex."

She risked a quick glance over her shoulder.

He shot her a wide grin in return.

She blew out an exasperated sigh. "Good night, David." She pulled the door shut on her way out.

David laced his fingers together and cradled his head. Closing his eyes, he willed the throbbing hard-on she'd left behind to subside.

In the back of his mind, the tiny seed of an idea prodded him.

Could that be the solution to all their problems?

Maybe. And just maybe it explained the way he couldn't keep his mind off her curves, her mouth...

The concept definitely bore further exploration.

CHAPTER EIGHT

"No, NO, not pink shoes with a red dress." Sarah snatched the Barbie from David's hand while Lexie fought not to chuckle. She turned to gather dinner plates from the cabinet. The tantalizing smell of roast beef filled the kitchen and a pot of potatoes burbled away on the stove.

"Why not?"

"Momma says so."

"Oh, of course," he muttered. "What was I thinking?"

Almost a full week had passed since their shared kiss in the darkness of David's room. And while he hadn't kissed her again, Lexie wondered if he thought about it.

God knew she had.

The draw between them was something she hadn't expected. At least, not on his part.

But he'd been making slow and steady progress with Sarah, which scared the heck out of her. Her "discard date" loomed closer and closer.

Lexie set the stack of plates on the table. "Sorry, guys, but you're going to have to take the dolls and stuff upstairs now. I need to get the table ready for dinner."

"Oh, darn," David said. "Already? Gee, and just when I was getting the hang of this."

Sarah cocked her head and offered him a pitying glance. "No, you're not. You made Barbie crash the car."

"Women drivers." He shrugged. "I forgot, this is fantasy. Sorry."

Lexie pressed her lips together and glared at him. "What?"

"Try harder," she mouthed over Sarah's head.

David shoved the doll into the pink duffel bag that housed Sarah's "play-with" collection of Barbies and accessories. The bridal doll David had brought her wasn't included—that was still in its box on a shelf in her bedroom. "I'll do better next time, Sarah. Promise. No more car crashes."

As they cleaned up all the little pieces—the shoes, the minuscule purses, the outfits—Lexie rummaged in the silverware drawer.

A quick rap sounded on the back door, then it opened, admitting a cool gust of air—and Kegan.

He waved a manila envelope. "Sorry to interrupt. I know it's almost dinnertime. But I just got these and I didn't think you'd want to wait until tomorrow. Besides, tomorrow's Saturday, and I have the day off. Hopefully."

Lexie's heart crawled into her throat. He'd told David *at least* two weeks. It wasn't two weeks until Monday. She was supposed to have more time. She struggled to speak. "Uh... Sarah. Take those things upstairs and put them away, please."

"But, Momma—"

"*Now,* Sarah."

The child stomped her foot and folded her arms across her chest, giving first Lexie, then David, a sullen look. "I need to stay."

"You need to obey your momma, squirt," Pappy said, entering the room. "Do like she says."

Sullen gave way to sad. Sarah's bottom lip jutted out and she ran to Lexie, throwing her arms around Lexie's right leg. "But—but, I need to stay."

Lexie lifted her off the ground and enfolded her in a bear hug. Knowing the little girl already sensed the tension in the room, she did her best to hold back the turmoil of emotions inside her. "This is important grown-up stuff, baby. I need you to go upstairs. Please."

Sarah wiggled in Lexie's embrace, freeing her arms. She cupped Lexie's face in her hands. "Momma?"

"Yes, baby?"

"I changed my mind. I don't want a daddy for my birfday."

David shifted in his seat. Despite her own overwhelming pain, she felt sorry for him, for how that remark had to cut. Was he as nervous as she was? "Go, baby. We'll talk all about daddies later, okay?"

"Come on, shortcake. You take that stuff upstairs, then meet me in the library and we'll read a book together, okay? You can pick." Pappy gestured toward the kitchen staircase.

"'kay." Sarah kissed Lexie's nose. "Love you, Momma."

Lexie closed her eyes and placed two quick kisses on both of the little cheeks. Barely able to find her voice, she said, "Love you, too. Now scoot."

She waited until she heard the door close behind Sarah to open her eyes, then quickly ran her hand over them, hoping no one else would notice. Pappy's footsteps retreated down the hallway. The chair scraped the linoleum floor as she dragged it away from the table. She dropped into it, gesturing to the one across from her. "Sit, Kegan. Sorry for the lack of hospitality, but could we just get this over with?"

"Sure." After settling down, he unclasped the metal clips on the envelope and pulled out a small stack of papers. "Just to refresh your memory, the way this works is—"

"Get on with it, Doc," David said.

Lexie nodded. "Just tell us."

"Okay." His deep blue eyes softened as he looked at her. He cleared his throat. "Lexie, you were excluded for genetic relation to Sarah. You're not her mother."

Not her mother.

She thought she'd been prepared to hear that, since there really was no way she could have been. But to hear it spoken so plainly...

Not her mother.

Reality sucked. What she wouldn't give for a good fantasy right now.

Lexie forced a trembling smile. "No surprise there, right?" Silently she begged Kegan, God, anyone who was listening, to have *some* surprise here. But she knew from his apologetic expression as he shifted to look at David that the truth was as she'd always known.

"David, you were statistically included above ninety-nine percent. She's your daughter."

He blew out a long breath and a relieved grin filled his face.

Lexie turned away, staring at the steam rising from the pot of potatoes on the stove.

"No real surprise there, either." David reached for the papers. "Are these the test results? Because I need to fax them to my lawyer for the birth certificate."

Lexie clenched her hand into a ball, the nails digging into her palms. Kegan pushed the pile across the table.

"Oh, and while I'm thinking of it, I'll also need a copy of Sarah's medical and vaccination records. Seems the day-care center won't let her be enrolled without them. I'll need them right away, so if I could pick them up Monday morning, that would be great."

"Day-care center?" She hadn't meant to speak the words aloud.

"Well, yeah, Lexie. I have to do something with her while I'm at work, right? I can't exactly leave her home alone, can I?"

Blinking back tears, she shook her head and pushed her chair away, moving toward the stove. Vaguely she heard Kegan assure David he'd take care of the paperwork as she stuck the potatoes with a fork, checking their doneness.

Her baby—despite what Kegan had said, Sarah was

still her baby, always would be in her heart—staying in a day-care center. Being cared for by strangers.

"I'll call her plastic surgeon and get those records, too," Kegan said. "I'm sure her new one in Erie will want them."

The overpowering scent of the roast beef as she pulled it out of the oven made her stomach protest. Lexie slammed the door, threw the mitts onto the counter and turned the knob off. "I need some air."

She plucked a fleece jacket from a peg. "The roast is done," she told David. "Mash the potatoes and feed—" the words stuck in her throat "—feed your daughter, okay?" She bolted for the door.

"Lexie, wait, we have to talk—"

She held up a hand, shaking her head. "Not now. I can't. I just…can't."

The porch door squeaked behind her. David watched her dash from the house. Dr. Riley stood. "I'll catch up with her, make sure she's all right."

David offered his hand. "Thanks for everything, Doc."

"This isn't how I hoped it would work out."

"I understand. She's part of this community now, and so's Sarah. I'm an outsider." David marveled at the quiet strength in the healer's handshake.

"If you need anything while you're here, call. If she—" he jerked his head in the direction Lexie had fled "—needs anything, call. I hope you figure out how to work this out so no one gets hurt any more than they already have." Kegan paused on the porch. "'Night."

Part of David wanted to dance with joy. The papers verifying his paternity, proving Sarah was his, lay on the kitchen table. His daughter. And now he had what he needed to get her birth certificate changed. To replace "Father Unknown" with David Edward Mitchell.

So why did the other part of him feel like hell?

Lexie.

The urge to run into the nippy Montana twilight after her was overwhelming. He, not Kegan Riley, should be the one comforting her.

But she'd given him a direct assignment that involved Sarah. Granted, most of the work was already done, accomplished by Lexie. He wasn't going to let her or Sarah down.

He'd search Lexie out later. And they'd talk. He'd used the threat of the day-care center to get to her, and judging from her reaction, it had worked. Now maybe she'd be more receptive to his plan when he spoke to her about it.

In the meantime... He glanced at all the drawers in the white cabinets. Where did she keep the potato masher?

"LEXIE?" David rapped lightly on her bedroom door. "It's almost time for Sarah to go to bed, and she wants you. I didn't even attempt a bath or anything."

He stood in the hallway for several long minutes, getting no response. He returned to Sarah's room, where the child studied the bookcase. She looked up expectantly as he entered the room, then her face fell as she realized Lexie hadn't come with him.

"Did you pick a book, sport?"

She shook her head. "Where's Momma?"

"I don't think she feels well."

"She said we'd talk about daddies." Sarah folded her arms across her chest.

"Maybe we should wait for her to talk about it."

"Okay." She marched over to the door that connected her bedroom with Lexie's. Fist tight, she hammered on the wood. "Momma! Come here. We need to talk about daddies!"

The little girl waited about three seconds—apparently the limit of her patience—and banged again. "Momma!"

Note to self: Daddy Lesson #2: Being sick—or broken-hearted—is no excuse for not answering.

"Sport, really, I think she's sick. A headache or something. Let her be. Let's get you into bed."

She turned back into the room, her eyes growing large. "I don't want you to," she whispered, pressing against the door. "Only Momma. Momma says no running around naked in front of visitors."

Lesson number one came back in full force. The bruise on his cheek throbbed with the memory. And he hated being assigned "visitor" status by his daughter. He spread his hands out. "No problem. You can either change yourself, or sleep in your clothes, whichever you want. Well, you have to take off your shoes and socks."

"In my clothes?" She offered him a skeptical look. "Really?"

"Sure, why not. Won't hurt anything for one night."

"Okay." She sat on the floor in front of Lexie's door and pulled off a sneaker. "I still wanna see Momma." Yanking off the second shoe, she tossed it at the door. "Momma! Come tuckle me in. And sing me asleep."

A key rasped in the lock and the door opened. Now in the process of taking off her socks, Sarah looked up and smiled. "Hey, Momma. You feel better now?"

The room behind her was dark. Lexie knelt beside Sarah, her eyes puffy and red in a way that made David ache with knowing he'd caused her pain, her tears. "Not really, baby."

Sarah pointed at him. "*He* said I could sleep in my clothes."

"He did, huh?" Lexie's shoulders rose, then fell. "I suppose it's fine."

Sarah jumped to her feet, then framed Lexie's face with her hands. "You promised to talk about daddies later and it's later."

"Yes, it is. But I'm not feeling up to it—"

"You said!"

"Sport, you need to give her a break." David pulled back the pink-and-white gingham covers. "Climb in here."

"It's okay," Lexie said. "Just turn on the Emerald City and turn out the room light…please?"

"Sure." The night-light cast a green glow in the

room that made everything softer, and he understood why Lexie hadn't wanted to talk with the overhead light on.

Sarah scrambled onto the bed. "I get to sleep in my clothes!"

Lexie tucked the edges of the blankets under Sarah, occasionally tickling, sending the little girl into fits of giggles—hence the phrase "tuckling her in." He'd observed the ritual several times but never done it himself. Maybe one day...

Lexie sat on one side of the child and patted the opposite side, indicating he should also take his place.

He settled in...and was struck by the innate rightness of the scene. Him, Sarah, Lexie...a dad, a child and a mom. He'd already realized that raising Sarah by himself wasn't going to be the easy task he'd first imagined.

"Sarah, I want you to listen to me carefully," Lexie said gently.

"Dr. Riley told us the results of those tests. Remember, when he put the Q-tip in your mouth? And mine and David's?"

Sarah nodded.

David found himself holding his breath, unsure how the child would take the news. *No biting this time, I hope.*

"Well, the tests proved what David and I already knew, what he's already told you. He's your daddy, baby. You can tell Fallyn next time she asks that science proved it."

Sarah's bottom lip stuck out slightly. He couldn't

help but feel as if he'd been measured and found lacking. Maybe if he had black hair...and a crown.

"Is he staying with us forever? Or will he go away again like Connor's daddy?"

Lexie's eyes burned. She clenched her teeth together, ignoring the throbbing in her left temple and at the base of her neck. All she wanted to do was crawl back into her bed and cry some more.

"I'm not leaving you, sport."

"No, baby." Lexie cleared her throat, steeling herself to tell the child the whole truth. Laboring to bring Sarah into the world hadn't hurt at all. Not compared to this. "What's going to happen is—"

"That's enough for tonight, don't you think, Lexie? I mean, give her a chance to accept the fact that I really am her daddy, even though I'm not a king."

Once again she wasn't sure if she should kiss him or kick him for the unexpected and merciful reprieve he'd given her. At least one more day before she had to tell the child who was her world that she'd be going back to Erie with her daddy, while her "momma" stayed behind. About day care and God only knew what else David had in store for her.

She couldn't swallow past the enormous tome lodged in her throat.

Sarah snuggled down into her pillow. "Sing me, Momma."

Lexie shook her head. "I'm not feeling good, remember? If I tried to sing tonight, it would sound like someone stepping on a frog." She could barely handle talking.

"Okay." Sarah turned toward David. "You sing me."

He burst out laughing, jiggling the bed. "I always sound like someone stepping on a frog. A big one. And I don't know any good go-to-sleep songs."

"Sing Scarecrow's song. If I only had a brain," the child prompted.

Despite the pain in her heart, Lexie couldn't stifle a small chuckle at that. "Yeah, if only."

But maybe what she needed to be hoping for was that David, unlike the Tinman, had a heart of his own...one that would be generous with the woman who'd carried his baby and raised her, when she asked him again for visitation rights with that child.

"Hey, I have a brain," David protested. "There's no straw in here." He thumped the heel of his palm against his skull to demonstrate.

Sarah rewarded him with a wide smile, one that looked so much like his own, Lexie wondered how she could have doubted the test results for even a split second.

Desperation did funny things to people.

"'kay, if you won't sing, then kiss Momma again."

"What?" Lexie shook her head. She'd stayed far beyond lip distance from David since she'd been tempted into kissing him the other night. "I don't feel well, honey. I might be getting sick, and I'd hate to spread my germs."

"I'm willing to risk it."

Lexie glared at him, then glanced down at Sarah.

"Children do not tell grown-ups when to kiss, or anything else for that matter."

"But, Momma, maybe he really is a king, but you gots to kiss him to make him change," Sarah whispered.

"Then he'd have to be a frog right now, and while I know he said he sings like one, he doesn't look like one to me."

"Ribbit," David said.

Sarah giggled. "Sounds like a frog to me."

God, she was just eating him up tonight. And while Lexie should have been comforted by father and daughter connecting, it just made the looming reality of him leaving and taking Sarah with him an even easier-to-visualize concept.

And she'd be alone.

Lexie pressed her fingers to her temple. "I have to go to bed, too, baby." She leaned down, completed the kiss ritual. "I love you."

"Love you, too, Momma." Sarah crooked her finger. "Come back here."

Lexie leaned over again, and the small lips pressed against her forehead.

"Now you feel better."

"Thanks, baby." Unfortunately, the true pain came from the center of her chest. And she didn't think she'd be feeling better anytime in the near future…anytime in the future, period.

"Can I kiss you good night?" David asked softly.

Sarah nodded, then turned her head, offering him her right cheek. "Here." She fingered the birthmark.

Lexie sucked in her breath and waited, blinking hard. Did David have any idea the child was unconsciously testing him? Despite wanting to keep Sarah a bit longer, she didn't want him to fail.

To his credit, he never hesitated. He leaned over and pressed a gentle kiss where she'd indicated. "'Night, sport," he whispered, voice trembling.

And in that moment, Lexie realized "The Truth." It was as if a magnifying glass had been placed over the fine print and she could read clearly.

David Mitchell was one hell of a man.

And she loved him.

Probably always had. Hiding behind the words *crush* and *puppy love* had been easier than admitting the truth and the pain that went with it. Because he'd never seen her that way. Still didn't, despite the sexual charge between them of late.

Love, pretty though it was, didn't change a darn thing. In fact, it wasn't pretty at all, but damn unpleasant. A side effect she didn't need.

Not if he didn't—couldn't—love her back. The one dream she still had was to have a love like her parents had known for years.

She swallowed a bitter sigh.

"Sweet dreams, baby." Lexie stroked Sarah's hair. How many more nights would she be able to do that?

She rose and checked the door to the hallway, making sure it was locked, since a pair of guests without reservations had wandered in off the scenic highway. David turned on the monitor then followed into her bedroom.

After confirming Sarah's door was closed securely, she motioned him to follow her deeper into her room. "I need to ask you—"

"We need to talk," he said at the same time. Awkwardly, he gestured in her direction. "Sorry. Ladies first. Go ahead."

She paced the width of the room, stopping in front of the window. The streetlight flickered, the only sign of change outside. No cars traveled the street; no one walked the sidewalk at this hour. The calm quiet of the town she called home belied the turmoil inside her. Taking a deep breath and gathering every ounce of courage she possessed, she turned to face him. "David, I want—no, no, I *need* visitation with Sarah. Even if it's just two weeks in the summer." She lifted her chin and met his eyes straight on. "I think you owe me at least that much."

His eyebrows arched. "Oh, really? You do, huh?"

The silence couldn't have lasted more than ten seconds, but to Lexie her entire life could have been compressed into that time.

He shook his head. "I don't think that would be the best thing for Sarah."

"What?" She'd been prepared for a number of answers, but that wasn't one of them. "Did you just say…no? As in, no visitation with her?"

"Pretty much, yeah. I said I didn't think it would be the best thing for her. Or for me."

Lexie leaned against the footboard of her bed. Pain so intense it made giving birth feel like a hangnail flooded her entire body, from the soles of her feet to the tips of her hair. Her *hair* hurt. Beyond comprehension.

David's mouth moved, but she couldn't make out what he said.

No visitation were the only words her brain could process.

Her stomach rolled, and she pressed a hand over her lips. David stepped toward her, eyes wide and full of concern.

A little late for that, buddy. How could she have misjudged him that badly? She backed away, shaking her head. "Go away, David."

"But, Lexie, I need to ask you—"

"I have nothing more to say to you. Go." Another wave of nausea swept over her. She bolted for her bathroom, slamming the door in his face.

CHAPTER NINE

HOURS LATER, David rubbed his eyes, then tried to refocus on the monitor. The line of code blurred. It didn't matter; he'd read the thing four or five times and still didn't know what he'd done.

Because he couldn't stop thinking about Lexie.

He'd spent what had seemed ages outside her bathroom door, listening to her run water in the tub to mask the muffled sounds of her crying. And he'd begged her to open the door and listen to him. But she'd refused. Told him to get lost.

Certain she'd be in better shape to listen to his idea in the morning, he'd opted to work.

Or try, anyway.

He popped his knuckles, then saved the file and closed the notebook. His shirt ended up draped over the back of his chair; he dropped his jeans to the floor. The key in the old-fashioned lamp clicked as he shut it off, then he slid between the cool cotton sheets of the massive bed.

Rolling onto his back, he draped his arm across his face. At least the bruise on his cheek didn't hurt as much anymore.

Sarah's monitor relayed her quiet slumber.

He waited for sleep to claim him.

Thought about the code for the program.

Lexie.

Cramming the feather pillow into the crack between the mattress and the headboard, he flopped onto his stomach.

Somewhere in the house, a board shifted and creaked. Outside his just-cracked-open window a breeze stirred the leaves on a tree in the front yard. As they came loose, their shadows drifted across the top of the bed.

Lexie will think it's a great idea. Now get some sleep.

He yanked the pillow from the crack, punched it several times and curled up on his side.

Eventually his mind shut down. But even in sleep he couldn't escape her. In his dreams he saw the younger version of Lexie as she plied him with ice cream and brownies and listened to his tale of woe, playing down her own losses. Offering to make his dream reality.

Her tearful pleas for him to at least consider Angela as a potential threat to the baby Lexie carried for them.

Her face in the library, a couple of weeks earlier, when recognition had kicked in. The blatant terror when she'd asked where his wife was.

Then the other night, confessing she'd stopped dreaming herself.

"Don't cry, Lex," he mumbled.

"I'm not. You awake now?"

Turning onto his back, he pried his eyes open. And

found a silhouetted form on the edge of his bed. "Lexie?"

"I *need* visitation, David. Photos. Phone calls. I carried her for nine months and gave birth to her. You can't just cut me out of her life completely."

"What was that like?"

"What?"

"Giving birth to her. The labor and delivery." He tried to imagine what she'd looked like at nine months. She'd run at five, and her tummy had just been rounding into an obviously pregnant shape. He'd missed watching her grow large with Sarah...

And so much more.

"Oh." Her outline grew taller as she straightened. "Hard. Painful. Scary."

His eyes adjusted to the light and he could make out her form more clearly. "Scary? Why was it scary?"

"I was...alone. I missed home and my family. And...you—you were supposed to be there."

He reached out, found her hand. Her fingers were cold, and he wrapped them tightly in his own. "I'll always regret not being there, Lex."

"Then the nurse was putting her in my arms. She was so tiny. She needed me. I couldn't be afraid anymore. And I wasn't alone." Her voice cracked. "Please don't take her away from me!" Evidence of her pain tracked down her cheeks.

He sat up, reaching for her face, wiping the moisture away. "Don't cry. You know I can't stand it when you do."

Her lower lip quivered, just like Sarah's. "I'm not crying."

His fingers couldn't catch the tears as quickly as she shed them. "No, not much you're not." The bed shook. It took him a moment to realize her trembling caused the quakes.

"Oh, Lexie." Wrapping his arms around her, he pulled her tight against his chest. "I'm sorry this has hurt you—me—all of us. It wasn't supposed to be like this."

She nodded her agreement. Her dark hair, soft against his bare skin, smelled sweet, fresh, like—well, it sounded corny, but like spring wildflowers or something.

He held her for a long time.

The air in the room grew heavy.

One of her tears trickled down his chest, alongside his belly button, then got caught in the waistband of his briefs. He stifled a groan, and mentally kicked himself for being such an insensitive lunkhead, but it was the most erotic thing he'd ever experienced.

Because it was the most intimate way she'd ever touched him.

And he wanted more.

"Lexie?"

She looked up, no more signs of tears. Her red-rimmed eyes held a spark of the same thing he was feeling.

"I have to kiss you again," he whispered. "Okay?"

She shivered, inclining her head, then raising her face to him.

Leaning forward, he claimed her mouth, nothing hesitant or slow this time, firm and possessive from the onset. With a start, he realized the impulse to kiss her, to claim her, went back a long time—all the way to the night of her prom. He hadn't dared then. But now... Years had slipped by, and he didn't want to wait any longer. He ran his hands through her hair, then let one roam over the planes of her back.

She shivered again, pressing tighter into him.

The tips of her breasts hardened against his chest...and caused his own body to respond in kind.

Sweet insanity burned away the remnants of logical thought as her mouth and deep kisses stoked the fire.

Holding her tight, he rolled, pulling her onto the bed, then stared down at her swollen mouth in the light from the window. "Lexie," he murmured, brushing the hair from her face. "Is this a dream or reality?"

"A dream," she whispered, fingers tracing over his lips, his jaw. "A hot, sexy dream. So don't wake me."

Hot and sexy? She *did* feel the same way he did. "If this is a dream, then you should be naked." He tugged at the bottom of her nightshirt, drawing it up above her waist.

Lexie wrestled with a moment of panic. Naked? With David? She did a quick mental panty check. *Please, don't let me be wearing the holey ones.*

"Last chance to reclaim reality, Lex. Because I really want to make love to you. If you don't want this—"

She silenced him by pressing the tip of her finger against his mouth. "I do."

David wanted to *make love* to her!

The cynic in her ranted and raved about figures of speech and pretty words from soft-hearted computer geeks who hated to see women cry.

The remnants of her dreamer breathed a small sigh of hope.

The realist in her urged her to do it now, before he changed his mind, and have at least one night in his bed and his arms.

He grinned that irresistible grin. "Good. Lift up your arms."

Light streamed in behind him. She hesitated. "Is naked really necessary? Can't we just—"

This time he quieted her with another hard kiss. His mouth left her lips, trailing down her chin. Tipping her head, she offered and he took, teeth nipping gently at her collarbone as he pushed the neck of her nightshirt aside.

Before she'd realized it, he had the fabric bunched just below her breasts. His thumb skimmed the curve and she sucked in her breath, a shiver of desire crawling up her spine. Watching her carefully, he raised the shirt higher. She lifted her arms, letting him peel the garment from her.

He tossed her clothing to the floor and leaned back. His face cloaked in shadows, he simply looked at her. She squirmed beneath his scrutiny.

"Mmm," he hummed. "Beautiful." David lowered his head and used his tongue to tease her nipples to attention. When he closed his mouth on her, she sighed, threading her fingers through his hair. She'd had no lovers since Andrew, and the fact that this was David, object of all her adolescent and not-so-adolescent sexual fantasies, made the sensations even more intense.

Using his nimble fingers and lips, he explored her body, causing the most delicious tension to wind tighter and tighter within her.

He paused over her belly, just below her navel, his fingertip tracing a slight indentation in her skin.

"It's a stretch mark," she said, her face warming.

His eyes widened as he caressed the spot again. "From Sarah?"

She nodded, her own hand snaking down her belly to cover it.

He shoved her fingers aside, then placed his mouth on the mark, kissing it. He raised his head to lock eyes with her. "I love it."

"You do?"

"Yes. It's a reminder of everything you did to make my dreams come true. Lexie Jacobs, have I told you lately how amazing you are?"

The warmth pumping through her sweetened, shifted from lust to love with his proclamation. She shook her head.

"You are." He kissed his way back up her body. The ridge of his arousal pressed into the apex of her thighs when he settled himself against her. Only two thin pieces of cotton, his briefs and her panties, separated them. She needed him with an intensity that almost scared her. She shifted beneath him, seeking more.

"You're beautiful, caring..."

God, she loved this man. Was it possible that he could...?

No, no, the cynic inside her shouted at the dreamer, scaring it back into hiding. *Don't even think like that. You know how the story ends in real life. Shut up and take what he's offering for now.*

"Make love to me, David. Now." She forced her hips up, grinding against him.

He moaned, shutting his eyes. "Lex."

She wiggled again. "We have too many clothes on. I thought you said naked." Hooking her thumbs in the elastic waistband of her underwear, she pushed them down.

With a groan, David rolled off her. "I—I don't have anything with me, Lexie." He cursed under his breath.

"Anything?" Her mind scrambled to make sense of what he meant.

"Protection? A condom?" The bedsprings creaked as he shifted farther away, his breathing ragged.

"Oh." The impact of his words sunk in. "Oh." She wanted to curse, too, but then she started to giggle.

"What's so funny? I'm going to die here, and you're laughing?"

She nodded. "I can take care of this. Don't go away." She jumped from the bed, the wooden flooring cold on her bare feet. Dashing into his bathroom, she grabbed the heavy terry-cloth bathrobe from the hook on the back of the door. She tied the sash around her waist as she left. "I mean it, don't move. I'll be right back."

He laced his fingers behind his head, giving her a lazy, seductive grin, complete with dimples. "I'll be timing you."

She darted into the hallway, avoiding the squeaky board near the top of the stairs. *Don't think, don't think.* In her room, she raised on tiptoe, pulling a box from the top shelf in her closet. Grabbing two packets without looking, she crammed them into the robe's pocket, replaced the box and headed back to his room before she could give herself a chance to change her mind.

He hadn't moved at all, just grinned again as she scurried into the room. She tossed the square packages onto the bed by his side. "There."

"Why, Lexie Jacobs, you *have* grown up. What would your mother think about her girl keeping condoms on hand, just in case?"

Lexie's face scorched. "That she's smart? Look, those were a gag gift from a friend. I really don't go around jumping into bed with guys…"

"I know you don't." He reached over, tucked the condoms under his pillow, then grabbed her by the knot in the belt of her robe. "I'm just teasing you. And I'm glad. Now get back in here."

She tumbled into his embrace as his mouth found hers. He parted the robe, staring down at her. With the end of the belt, he caressed her skin, starting at the hollow of her throat. Down through the valley between her breasts. Then he circled each one, making her push her shoulders into the mattress, a silent plea for more.

The terry cloth brushed lightly over each nipple, causing them to tighten.

Lexie moaned as David cupped one breast, drawing the other into his mouth. The aching need within her spiraled higher with each stroke of his nimble fingers, each hot caress from his tongue. "David, please!"

"That's exactly what I'm going to do, Lex. Please you."

"So get on with it alr—" She gasped when he grazed his finger across the juncture of her thighs.

"Patience."

Patience was the last thing on her mind. But he wouldn't be rushed. The slow smolder became a raging wildfire beneath the ministrations of his talented hands and mouth. The ability to think rationally fled by the time he finally reached beneath the pillow and retrieved the condom.

"Look at me, Lex," he ordered, poised just over her.

She glanced at him, hips straining to join them.

He smiled and slowly sank into her.

"Oh, David. Yes."

He teased her, varying his rhythm, sometimes fast, then slowing to a maddening pace. Sometimes he plunged deep, sometimes he didn't, at one point withdrawing fully while she cried out, writhing in frustration until he rejoined them. She gripped his shoulders, locked her ankles in the small of his back.

"Greedy," he murmured, gently biting her earlobe. "I like that in a woman."

"Stop teasing," she demanded, then gasped as he slid even deeper.

"Whatever you say, princess." This time he set up a steadily increasing pace. Sweat slicked their bodies.

Lexie arched up to meet him, panting, begging.

"Just let go, Lex." He reached between her thighs, stimulating her to the point of insanity.

Her orgasm wracked her body, made her shake and tremble in a way she'd never thought possible. And then he was calling her name, finding his own release.

Their heavy breathing gradually slowed. David rolled them onto their sides, reaching out to caress her face. "Still think it was a dream?"

The heat of a blush crept across her cheeks as she nodded. "An amazing dream. Fantastic."

He grinned. "Don't go anywhere, okay? I'll be right back." He slipped from the bed, heading toward the bathroom.

Lexie pulled her nightshirt on, then searched for her misplaced panties.

She could pretend it had all been a dream, but only if she left now, before he could ruin it with reality.

CHAPTER TEN

SOMEWHERE BEHIND the heavy cloud cover, the sun had been up for several hours. John sat at the kitchen table holding a mug of coffee he'd had to make himself.

Not like Missy to sleep in this late. Even without bright sunshine to wake her.

He had a pretty good idea what Doc Riley had brought in his brown envelope that had shaken up the gal.

He'd never seen her take to her bed like this, not even when she had the flu or something. Poor thing. Another bite of his toast did nothing to settle his own unhappy stomach.

A clumping noise clattered down the back stairs, every other step a heavier thud. The door opened and Sarah entered the kitchen, holding one black boot, the other on her foot. She wore a long-sleeved, green plaid sweater and a pair of purple shorts.

Tarnation. Even he knew that wasn't a good combination.

"'Morning, Pappy." She held the boot out in his direction. "I can't work this. I dressed myself," she said, clearly proud of herself.

"I can see that. How come?"

"Momma's still asleep," the child whispered, as though her mother could hear her all the way from upstairs. "She didn't feel good last night, so I let her sleep."

"You're a good kid, sprout."

"Can we make her breakfast on a tray? Like she does when my tummy is sick?"

"Well, maybe we could make her some toast on a plate, okay? My ole bones ache after running up those stairs the other night. I don't think I could carry a tray up there."

"I can carry toast." Her curls bobbed as she shook her head. "Let's do that."

"Let's get that other boot on first, okay?"

"Okay." She picked the shoe back up and then plopped on the floor in front of him, sticking her foot in his lap. "Don't I look nice, Pappy?"

"Sure are colorful today. Which is good since there's no sunshine." He smiled.

"I wanted to surprise Momma."

"Oh, I'm sure she's gonna be surprised." He chuckled. Somehow the gal would gently suggest a different combination and the young'un wouldn't feel at all like she'd gotten it wrong. Lexie was one of the best mothers he'd ever seen in action, 'cept his own Doris.

And somehow, he had to make sure she kept her child.

Losing a child, even if there wasn't a blood bond, was the worst feeling possible. He'd thought losing

Doris had been the worst, but it had paled in comparison to losing their adopted son, daughter-in-law and grandson to a fire.

Thank God his Doris had been spared that pain.

He wasn't about to let Lexie feel it. Not when she'd been the one to save him from just wasting away the rest of his life.

"There ya go, squirt. Now let's get some toast cooking for your mom, and something for you."

"'kay."

He helped the child pull a chair to the counter and put two slices of Missy's homemade bread into the toaster oven. Sarah pressed the lever down, then propped her elbows on the counter, chin on her palms, to watch it cook. "Pappy?"

"Yeah?"

"Momma said that man is my daddy. Dr. Riley made tests, and they said so."

"Yeah?" He steadied the chair as she wiggled on it.

"Does that mean I gotta call him Daddy now?"

"Do you want to call him Daddy?"

She shook her head.

"Well, then call him what you want to for now."

The little girl giggled.

"What?"

"I think Momma would get mad."

He fought back a smile. "Why?"

Sarah looked around the kitchen, then stood up on the chair and crooked her finger at him. "I call him Mr. Stuffy Pants."

John coughed to hide his laughter. Pasting a stern expression on his face, he said, "I'm sure your momma wouldn't like that, sprout. Maybe you could just call him David for now. And he's trying. Gotta give him credit for that." And he had to. Even though he didn't want to. The man was trying to get to know his daughter. And that was fine. As long as he left his daughter—and her momma—right here in Mill Creek.

"Connor's daddy was here, then he left. My daddy was gone, and now he's here."

He waited awhile for her to say something more. "And? Does that mean something?"

"Is it only mommas who stay with kids all the time, Pappy?"

John rubbed a hand across his stomach. If David Mitchell had his way, the child wouldn't have a momma anymore. "Not always, sprout."

The lever on the toaster popped up and the bell dinged. "Lookie there, it's done." Thank God. 'Cause this wasn't a conversation he should be having with the little one. "No, now git your fingers away from there. You know it's hot."

He helped Sarah butter the toast. She jumped down off the chair and carefully took the paper plate from him. "Okay, you take that up to your momma."

She stared at the food, making very exact steps. Her boots clomped on every stair this time, not just half.

He went back to the table, chugged down the now-cold dregs of his coffee. He glanced out the window as he placed the mug in the sink.

A silver minivan crawled down the driveway and

pulled in to a parking space alongside David's rented SUV. A middle-aged couple emerged from the front seats and a tall young fellow unfolded himself from the back, stretching his arms over his head.

The men moved to the back of the van and hauled out several suitcases.

As far as John knew, they weren't expecting any guests.

Tarnation. Maybe they were from that magazine Missy kept harping about. The "mystery guests" she'd been expecting.

He hollered up the back stairs. "Missy! Looks like new guests." Getting no response, he shuffled down the hallway, heading for the foyer.

He made it to the front door at the same time they did. Opening it, he gestured inside. "'Morning, folks. Welcome to the Mill Creek Bed-and-Breakfast. I'm John Nonnemacher, your host."

The woman, with short dark hair and lively brown eyes, smiled at him. "Oh, you're Pappy! Lexie's mentioned so much about you on the phone." She rushed forward and wrapped her arms around his neck. "I can't thank you enough for taking care of my baby and grandbaby."

John's face got hot, and he tried to gracefully untangle himself from the woman's embrace.

"Honey, you're choking the man. That's not a nice way to thank him," the older man said.

"Oh, sorry, right." She released him and stepped back.

"You think you all could move in just a bit farther,

so I can get in with all this luggage?'' the younger man said.

"Sorry, Marc," the woman said. "I'm just so excited, I'm not thinking straight. Where's my baby?" She glanced around the foyer.

"Maybe we should introduce ourselves properly," the older man said, extending his hand, which John accepted. "I'm Timothy Jacobs, that's my son, Marc, and—"

"Pappy!" came Sarah's shout from the kitchen. "Where are you?"

"In the foyer, sprout."

The black boots clattered down the hallway. "Pappy! Momma said thanks for the toast, she feels better. She's in the shower now..." The young'un skidded to a stop, wrapped her arms around his leg and pressed her face into his blue jeans when she realized there were strangers in the house.

The woman's eyes widened and she stared at the small form attached to him like a burr on a blanket. "And I'm Sarah Jacobs," she completed the introductions.

The little one risked a quick peek at the lady, then hid again. But she tugged on his pants. He bent over. "Pappy," she whispered. "*I'm* Sarah Jacobs."

"Yep, you are, sprout. Tell you what, why don't you head on back upstairs and tell your momma that there's another Sarah here to see her."

Sarah turned quickly and scampered up the stairs.

"Oh, I wanted to surprise Lexie," Mrs. Jacobs said, heading to follow the little girl.

"Now, the young'un said her momma was in the shower, so you probably want to give her a chance to get dressed, right? Besides, I'm sure she's gonna be surprised enough."

"I've waited a long time to see my daughter, Mr. Nonnemacher. I really don't want to wait, not even five more minutes. I've seen her in a towel before." The woman grasped the wooden banister and slowly started up.

"Turn right at the top of the stairs. First bedroom on the right," he said.

Missy's dad chuckled. "Sorry. That woman has had me in a complete frazzle to get her out here. We'd have been here sooner but our son, Kenny, and his wife just had their first baby."

"Don't apologize. Now I know where Lexie gets her determination from." John looked at the luggage, then gestured toward the stairs. "Might as well get yourselves settled, too. You got yourself the pick of the rooms up there, 'cause we ain't got any other guests at the moment. Well, 'cept for the young'un's father, and he's not exactly a guest, I suppose."

Marc's mouth twisted into a scowl. "He's staying here?"

"Marc, you promised you'd behave yourself."

"Tell it to David." He hefted the suitcases and headed for the stairs.

Timothy Jacobs offered John a wry smile and a shrug as he also moved toward the steps. "Melodrama."

Hellfire and brimstone. Between them and David, it

was the most excitement he'd had in his life since Lexie had arrived.

He wanted boredom back.

LEXIE FASTENED a towel around her head, then dried off and wrapped a large yellow one around her body, tucking the end to secure it. The mirror showed only slight bags under her eyes. Sleep, a rare commodity of late, hadn't come till dawn. Too much time spent thinking about what had happened between her and David last night. She splashed some cold water on her face to tighten the skin. Leaving the exhaust fan running in the bathroom, she went out into her bedroom.

A quick rap sounded on the door. "Lex? It's me."

David.

Another gentle knock.

"What?"

"I need something," David muttered into the crack of the doorjamb. "Open up."

She partially opened the door. "I'm not dressed yet," she hissed.

He grinned. "Works for me."

"You needed something?"

"Yes. For starters, this." He shoved the door wider, then cupped her face with both hands and kissed her soundly, spreading gooey warmth through her entire body. Memories of their loving last night increased that languid feeling. Would it be enough to change things between them? Make him more receptive to granting her visitation?

Or had she made a huge mistake indulging herself like that?

"Mmm." She indulged a little more in some exploration of his eager mouth, then pushed against his chest. "We can't do this now."

"Why not?"

Voices echoed from the foyer. Sarah's boots stormed up the stairs.

"That's why not." Lexie backed away from him, tightening her grip on her towel.

"Momma, Momma, guess what?" Sarah rounded the railing at the top of the stairs, took in David's presence and slowed her approach.

"What, baby?"

The child edged closer. "Momma, I'm Sarah Jacobs, but there's another one. A real old lady."

"I heard that." Another pair of footsteps came up the staircase.

Sarah squeezed between the doorway and Lexie, hiding her face in the soft terry cloth.

"Mom?" Lexie's heart jumped as the woman reached the top of the stairs. "Oh, Mom!" She spread her arms open, then had to grab for the top of her towel as it threatened to unfold because of Sarah's yanking on the bottom.

David moved aside in the narrow space, leaning against the door to Sarah's bedroom. Her mother patted his cheek as she passed. "David. Thank you for finding my baby."

His face reddened, and he shuffled his feet.

Suddenly Lexie found herself in her mother's embrace. She hunched over and turned her face into her mom's neck. The scent of Pear's soap filled her nose; she struggled briefly to hold back the tears. Then she let them go. "Mom, oh Mom!"

"I'm here now, sweetheart." Soft, familiar fingers rubbed Lexie's shoulder.

Home. She was home in her mother's arms.

"I've missed you so much!" She sniffled.

"Me, too."

"If this isn't typical of women, blubbering all over each other," said a deep, masculine voice from the top of the stairs.

Lexie straightened up, grabbing for the towel again. "Ohmigosh. Marc! Where's Daddy? He's here, too, right? What about Kenny?"

"Dad's downstairs, honey," her mom said. "Kenny's busy with his new son, but he sends you his love."

"It's getting a little crowded here, Lex," David murmured. "Think I'll head down to the kitchen and get some coffee."

"Good idea. Take a hike." Marc glared at him.

David squared his shoulders and returned the favor.

"Marcus Anthony Jacobs, you promised to behave." Their mother wagged a finger.

"No sweat, Mrs. J." David turned and headed down the back stairs.

"Now, I think we need to get you in some clothes before you lose that towel," her mom said.

"Do you always parade around in a towel in front

of your guests, sis?" Marc dropped the suitcases and headed toward her.

"Momma," Sarah whispered. "Momma!" Her voice cracked and she trembled.

Lexie stroked Sarah's curls. "It's okay, baby." She held up her hand to deflect her brother's advance. "Let me get dressed and..." She jutted her chin in Sarah's direction. "This is a little overwhelming, if you know what I mean."

"Sure."

Her mom's smile wavered. "But..."

Marc took her elbow. "Pick what room you want, Mom, and I'll haul your suitcases there. Let Lex get squared away."

"Put Mom and Dad in the room at the end of the hall," Lexie said, offering her brother a look of gratitude. "It's the honeymoon suite, the best in the house."

"Oh, don't be foolish, dear. We don't need the best room in the house—"

"Mom, please."

"Okay, honey." She followed Marc down the hall.

Lexie eased Sarah into her bedroom and closed the door. Then she sank to her knees and gathered the child into her arms. "You okay, baby? That was a lot of commotion at once, huh?"

Sarah nodded against her neck. "Who is that, Momma?"

"That's *my* momma. And my brother. And my daddy is here somewhere."

"You have a momma?" Sarah drew back and stared at her. "How come we never saw her before? I thought mommas stayed with their kids."

The words cut right through her. "Sometimes, honey, when kids grow up, they leave home and go places far away from their families."

"I'm not leaving, Momma. I'm staying with you forever."

Lexie pressed her lips together and closed her eyes. It hurt to breathe. It hurt to contemplate what the future held.

Maybe after last night…?

"Momma? You okay?"

She opened her eyes, blinking hard a few times. "I think I got some dust in my eyes." She brushed a quick kiss on Sarah's head, then rose to her feet. "Now, I have to get dressed. I need to see my dad!" Pulling a pair of jeans from her dresser, she tried to put on an enthusiastic face for Sarah's sake.

Despite how much she wanted to see her parents and brothers, and how much she'd missed them over the years, she'd give just about anything to turn back the clock a few weeks to when Sarah and Pappy and the bed-and-breakfast were her entire world.

"Is that my grandma? Like Connor's momma's momma?"

Lexie sighed. "Baby, you need to ask your daddy about that."

He was the one turning their lives upside down in so many ways. Let him handle the hard questions.

DAVID RUBBED his forehead. Was there a sign plastered there that said, *I slept with your daughter/sister last night?*

Because it sure felt like it.

Mr. J. sat at the table, poring over the *Mill Creek Gazette,* but stealing furtive looks at him over the newspaper's edge. Marc tipped his chair back on two legs, arms folded across his chest, staring coldly at David.

Mrs. J., oblivious to the men, bustled around the country kitchen, gathering the makings for omelettes, chattering all the time. "Lexie looks like she's lost weight. She needs some good home cooking."

Pappy scowled. "That gal's a whiz in the kitchen. When she first came to town, she lived here, but did some cooking for Jo over at the diner. Sold her all kinds of baked goods. Jo still moans over losing Lexie to this bed-and-breakfast."

David readjusted his stance, leaning against the counter near the coffee machine. Things could get interesting with her family here. Damn it, he didn't need Marc interfering with his plan. He set his mug on the counter. "I'm going upstairs to see if Lexie needs any help with Sarah."

Mrs. J. sighed, cracking eggs into a bowl. "Yes, I saw the way that child was dressed. She needs some coordination, doesn't she? And it's much too cold for shorts. My goodness—"

"I'm sure the gal's helping the young'un change. That child was bustin' her buttons this morning for dressing herself and letting her momma sleep."

David blessed the old man's defense as he climbed the back stairs. Lexie was a good mother.

He rapped on Sarah's door, then popped his head in. "Hey, there. Can I come in?"

"Wait!" Sarah yelped. "I'm not dressed!"

"Okay, my eyes are closed."

"Just a second." Lexie helped the child pull up a pair of jeans and snap them. "Okay, come on in."

"Momma says I can get a pumpkin today. So I hafta wear long pants."

"That sounds like a good idea." David picked up the discarded shorts from the floor and tossed them on the twin bed. "Can I come get a pumpkin, too?"

Sarah tapped her chin with one finger. "Well...will you buy a huge-mongous pumpkin?"

"Humongous?"

"That means big." She spread her arms wide to demonstrate. "I want a huge-mongous pumpkin, but Momma says they're too 'spensive."

A deep pink color stole across Lexie's cheeks.

"I'll buy you whatever pumpkin you want," he said.

"Then you can come." Sarah flashed a smile at Lexie. "Right, Momma?"

"I suppose." Lexie rose to her feet. "Now, I'm going to see my family."

Sarah looked at David. "Is that my grandma? Momma says I gots to ask you."

"She did, huh?" He lifted an eyebrow at Lexie. "Well, actually, she and I need to talk about that.

Think you could run downstairs and get some breakfast while we chat?"

Sarah's mouth drooped, and she wrapped her arms around herself, shaking her head. "Uh-uh."

"All right, then we'll just go next door and talk, okay? And you can stay here..." David glanced around her room for inspiration. A pad of paper and a box of crayons sat on a small desk in the corner. "You can draw a picture of the humongous pumpkin while you wait for us, okay?"

"Okay."

He took Lexie's hand and pulled her toward her bedroom.

"David, what's this about? I haven't seen my family in four and a half years, and—"

"And they can wait just a few more minutes. This is really important. This is about your future role in Sarah's life."

She followed quietly, without resisting his tugs anymore. He shut the door behind them. For a moment, he debated how to go about this. It wasn't exactly real, but would she feel cheated if he didn't go all the way?

Nah. She'd become much more practical.

"Well?" she prodded.

"Okay." He took a deep breath. "Lexie, we— I— Let's get married."

She blinked. Repeatedly. "W-what did you say?"

"Marry me."

Her eyes glazed over, and she blinked a few more times. "Marry you?"

"Yes, don't you see? It's the perfect idea, the perfect solution. Debugs all the glitches. We get married, you can still be Sarah's mom, I'm her full-time dad. I don't have to worry about how I'm going to take care of her, she doesn't have to go to day care... Your mom can be her grandma. Everybody's happy."

Except Lexie didn't look happy. No smile. Blank expression. Her mouth kind of hung open. She looked as if he'd punched her in the stomach without warning rather than proposed to her.

"You want to marry me?"

He nodded. "Lexie, I've realized that motherhood—or fatherhood, for that matter—is more than a strand of DNA. You are her mother, no matter what those tests say. And you're a good one. I don't want to hurt Sarah by yanking her away from you."

"*You* want to marry *me?*"

"Why is that so hard to understand?"

She tipped her head up, locking eyes with him. A glimmer of—hope?—sparkled in the green depths. "I haven't heard the magic word."

He raised his eyebrows. "Please?"

She sighed. "No, that's not it."

"Then what?"

"Do you love me, David?" she whispered. "Is that what last night was all about?"

Love? Oh, hell. "Uh...um... I care about you, Lex. A lot. I always have. I care about your family, and I want to make things right."

"Oh." Her shoulders slumped forward. "Oh." She nodded. "Now I get it. This is about making sure Marc doesn't beat you up if he finds out about last night. Well, you don't have to worry, I wasn't planning on telling anyone!" She spun toward the door.

He grabbed her wrist. "That's not it, Lexie, and you know it. Last night was special. There's incredible chemistry between us. I think it's been there, simmering, for years. And I *do* care about you. I think it could be really good between us, Lex.

"You said yourself that you'd stopped dreaming and believing in fairy tales. I think a marriage based on mutual caring, enhanced with the attraction between us, with neither one of us having false, pie-in-the-sky expectations, would be built to last. Don't you?"

"Built to last. You make it sound like a truck." Lexie tugged on her wrist. "Let go. Don't make me kick you again."

"I'm not letting you go yet." He pulled her into his arms, then kissed her. A soft, coaxing, slow-burn kind of kiss. He nibbled on her lips until she parted them, allowing him deeper access. His mouth glided over the line of her jaw, then planted teasing kisses down her throat. She moaned softly.

He nuzzled the hollow of her neck. "Don't answer me now, Lexie. Take today." He trailed his tongue along her collarbone. "Think about it. Think about this." His hands wandered down her back to cup her butt, pull her flush against the ridge of his arousal. "And this. And how good last night was."

He let her go, then gently stroked the back of his fingers over her cheek. Her eyes fluttered open.

"Think about Sarah. Isn't her love enough? I'm offering you the chance to be her mother forever."

Sarah barged into the room. "No more talking. I'm hungry. And I wanna get a huge-mongous pumpkin."

"Think about it, Lex." Without another word, he turned from her and headed for his daughter, who needed breakfast and a humongous pumpkin.

And a mother.

Hopefully Lexie wouldn't let either of them down.

LEXIE FORCED another bite of ham-and-cheese omelette down her throat. It landed like a boulder in her stomach, along with the other bits she'd managed to swallow to please her mother.

How quickly she'd reverted to the child role herself, doing what pleased her mom. The joy she felt being with her family again was tempered by the awkward realities of the reunion.

David lurked on the edges of the gathering, skulking near the counters, trading barbed looks with Marc, who sat opposite her at the table. Sarah squirmed on Lexie's lap, still hesitant, uncertain with this group of quasi-family.

"Honey, it's hard for your momma to eat with you wiggling on her like that. Why don't you come sit with me?" Lexie's mom held her arms out.

Sarah pressed her face harder against Lexie's shoulder, shaking her head. The fork slipped from Lexie's fingers. "It's okay, Mom. I'm really not that hungry anyway. But thanks for making breakfast. This is my second breakfast today. Wow, I must really rate. Everybody's trying to take care of me today."

Just like old times, her family had ridden in, and they were looking after "Little Lexie." Despite the fact that she'd missed them horribly and was thrilled to see them, it felt…wrong. She was a big girl now, and perfectly capable of taking care of herself. As well as Sarah.

And Pappy. Don't forget Pappy. He looked almost as lost and left out in the confusion as David.

"Isn't it time to head off for the pumpkin patch?" David asked.

"Yeah." Sarah sat up, taking Lexie's face in her hands. "Right, Momma? It's time? Let's go get the pumpkins." Sarah forced Lexie's head into an up-and-down motion. "See? She said yes." Sarah scrambled off her lap and raced to the back door, plucking her jacket from the low hooks Pappy had installed especially for her.

Chuckling, Lexie pushed back from the table. "Not so fast. I have to clean up first. You know the rules."

Sarah folded her arms across her chest and sighed. "Momma says clear your dishes."

"That's okay, honey," her mother said. "I can get—"

"I can get it, too, Mom. Thanks."

"Sweetheart…" Her dad rose from his chair and laid his hands on his wife's shoulders, gently massaging. "This is Lexie's kitchen." He laughed, leaning over and kissing her mother on the cheek. "Pretend you're actually on vacation unless she asks you to do something, okay?"

Her mom's eyes sparkled as she caressed his face. "Anything you say, love."

Marc groaned. "Did you have to give them the honeymoon suite, Lex? Like they don't act enough like lovesick teenagers without your encouragement?"

"Actually, I think it's pretty fantastic that they still feel like that after all this time."

"Watch it, there. All this time? You make it sound like we're old fogies or something," her dad said.

"I'm the old fogy," Pappy said. "You two still got plenty of time ahead of ya. Don't listen to the young folks." He ran his fingers through his white hair. "Just cause there's snow on the roof don't mean there ain't still fire in the furnace, huh?"

"Pappy!" Lexie said. "Okay, now we're going places I don't want to go. Stop it. All of you."

Her dad gave her mother a long, lingering kiss.

Lexie's heart clenched. They loved each other so much, even after thirty-six years of marriage. That's what she wanted. Not some marriage of convenience. David's convenience.

She might not believe in dreams anymore, but she still wanted love.

"Yep, they're your parents. Just like Fallyn said. Mommas and daddies kiss. Just like you and David did," Sarah pronounced.

The entire kitchen went still.

Three pairs of eyes drilled into Lexie.

She forced a dry chuckle and tried to keep the plate

from slipping out of her trembling hands. She carefully set it in the sink.

Marc shoved his chair backward, his gaze now locked on David.

"Spare us the macho-brother demo, Marc, okay?" Lexie ambled for the back door, her leisurely motion belying her emotions. She grabbed her navy fleece jacket. "I kissed him. So what? I've wanted to kiss him for years, and I did." She squinted at him, sending a pointed message—*Butt out, big brother.* "That's what mothers and fathers do." She jerked her head toward Sarah. "Get over it."

She knelt down and zipped the child's coat.

"Did I say somethin' wrong, Momma?"

"No, baby. You told the truth, and that's never wrong." She gathered the little girl into a hug, then stood, taking her by the hand. "We're going to get some pumpkins. Who's coming with us?"

"I am." David slipped on his coat.

"Anybody else?" Lexie asked the still-stunned kitchen occupants. Pappy offered her a wink and a covert thumbs-up. She smiled, pulling back her shoulders.

"I think we'll just get settled in here," her dad said. "Maybe unpack. You kids go on."

"Take the truck, Missy. Don't forget the hay bales and the cornstalks."

"You got it, Pappy."

"I'm getting a huge-mongous pumpkin," Sarah reminded everyone.

And Lexie was getting a huge-mongous…headache.

CHAPTER ELEVEN

"STOP HERE for just a minute." Lexie pointed out the windshield, directing David to stop the truck on Main Street in front of Al's Market, the small grocery store.

Sarah yanked on her seat belt. "Can I come too?"

Lexie kissed her on the forehead. "I'll be right back, baby. Stay here."

David watched the sway of her butt in her faded jeans as she dashed into the store. He loved the way she'd stood up to her brother.

Her kisses, her touch...she made him crazy, in a way he'd never thought possible. Last night had been incredible. The idea of losing her when he'd just realized how perfect they could be...it didn't sit well. He'd have to convince her that his idea was best for all of them.

"David?"

He turned to face the child in the seat beside him. "I'd like it if you'd call me Daddy."

"David?"

He broke into a broad grin. Had to give it to his kid. She knew what she wanted, and what she didn't. "Yes?"

"What are you gonna be for Halloween?"

"I hadn't thought about it. Am I supposed to have a costume?"

She nodded. "Everybody gots to have a costume. First we do trunk or treat, then we have a party."

"You mean trick or treat."

"No." She shook her head. "I mean trunk or treat. So, what will you be?"

"What are you going to be?"

"I wanna be Dorothy." She frowned. "But I want a real Toto, and Momma says no dogs 'cause guests might be 'lergic. Maybe you could be a dog? But you're too big to be Toto."

"Well, I don't know. I'm not crazy about costumes."

Sarah murmured something low under her breath. He wasn't sure, but it sounded like...stuffing pants?

The door to the truck creaked open and Lexie jumped back in, a bottle of water in her hand. She propped her purse on her knees and dug in it, pulling out a small green bottle. "Here we go." She downed two capsules, then recapped the water. "Much better. Let's go get some pumpkins now."

David put the truck in gear and pulled away from the curb. "We were discussing Halloween costumes and trunk or treat. You want to explain that one to me?"

Lexie laughed, sending warmth cascading through him. "People are so spread out that trick or treating is kind of tough. So we do trunk or treat. Everyone decorates the trunk of their car or the bed of a pickup, and we all gather in the parking lot of the firehall. The kids go from vehicle to vehicle to get their treats. Then there's a potluck supper and a dance inside the hall to benefit the new fire truck fund."

"That's different."

She nodded. "It is. But it's a lot of fun. Being part of a community like this is wonderful." She sighed. "I love it here."

"Does that mean you don't want to come back to Erie?"

"Where's Ernie?" Sarah asked.

"Erie. It's where I live," David said. "Where your momma lived before you were born."

Lexie stared at him over Sarah's head, eyes wide. He knew it was the first time he'd referred to her as his daughter's momma.

"Is it nice? Does Ernie have mountains?" Sarah pointed at the snowcapped peaks in the distance.

"No. There's some not too far away in New York State. Actually, the highest point near Erie is the garbage dump."

"Eeewww," Sarah said. "Garbage is not pretty like mountains."

David laughed. "Actually, when you cover it with snow, you'd never know it's garbage. They cover it with dirt all the time anyway."

"What else?"

"There's the lake," Lexie said. "Talk about humongous. Lake Erie is really big. And there are beautiful sunsets."

"And there's an amusement park and stores and

theater and a zoo." David felt like a travelogue for Erie. "You'll like it a lot."

"I'm going there?"

"Look, there's Mr. Harvey's farm! We're here." Lexie pointed out the window and David guided the truck to a parking place, feeling like she'd conjured the place just when she'd needed it. At some point they had to explain to Sarah exactly what was going to happen.

But maybe Lexie's instincts were right. Not yet. Not when Sarah was just warming to him, and when Lexie hadn't agreed to marry him.

IT TURNED OUT that humongous, like beauty, was in the eye of the beholder. Or in this case, the arms of the holder. Sarah had hers stretched as far as they would go around her pumpkin and she staggered toward the porch with it. Hands out, Lexie stayed nearby, ready to avert disaster should the pumpkin slip.

The day had cleared and the afternoon sun beat down onto the leaf-littered yard, illuminating the red highlights in Sarah's hair—and the chestnut ones in Lexie's. A sense of peace filled David. His daughter. And, if she'd go along with it, his wife. The idea of marrying again, as long as it was Lexie, didn't scare him at all. No way there'd be any ugly surprises with Lexie like there had been with Angela. He'd known Lexie darn near her whole life.

"Bring the cornstalks to the front porch," she yelled to him. "And the other pumpkins, too, okay?"

"You got it!"

They spent the afternoon tying bunches of cornstalks to the porch supports, and painting faces on some of the pumpkins. Even Mr. J. painted one, a tiny pumpkin he decorated with a goofy purple grin and green hair that earned him a giggle from Sarah.

She held up a dripping red paintbrush. "There. He's done."

"Does he have chicken pox?" Marc asked from his perch against the porch railing.

Sarah shook her head.

"Bet I know what they are," David said. "They're angel kisses, right?"

The smile she beamed at him once more had him melting into a puddle of absolute mush. A lethal weapon, that's what that smile was. She could convince him to do just about anything with it.

Daddy Lesson #3: Do not, repeat not, *let the child know how powerful her smile is.*

"What's an angel kiss?" Mr. J. asked from the wicker swing, his arm draped around his wife's shoulders.

"This." Sarah fingered her cheek. "David says the angels kissed me before I was born."

David says...for once, it wasn't Momma says. Nope, it was David says. He didn't even mind he hadn't progressed to Daddy yet.

"Aww," said Mrs. J. "That's sweet."

Lexie grunted as she came out the front door, a trayful of mugs in her hands. "No, this is sweet. Who wants some special hot chocolate?"

"Me, me!" Sarah rushed over as Lexie set the tray on a white wicker table and passed out mugs.

"Why is it special?" David accepted a cup with a heart-shaped handle and a teddy bear on it.

"Best hot chocolate you've ever had," she said confidently. "Whipped cream, shaved chocolate garnish. Go on, try it."

He sipped the drink, enjoying the burn of the rich liquid, the sweetness of the cream and chocolate. "Not bad. Probably won't replace coffee with me, but not bad."

Her gaze fastened on his mouth. Warmth spread through him that had nothing to do with the hot chocolate and everything to do with her. "What?"

"You've got a whipped-cream mustache." She smiled, raising her index finger and stroking it over his upper lip. Then she popped the fingertip into her mouth. "Mmm...sweet."

"Lexie," he said softly. The urge to pull her into his arms and taste *her* sweetness nearly short-circuited his reasoning capacity. But her family was here. He closed his eyes but it didn't make the temptation go away.

"What about me?" Marc called. "Don't I get any?"

"Sure you do. I've got one with a worm in the bottom of the mug just for you."

"Momma!" Sarah sounded scandalized. "Really?"

Lexie laughed and David opened his eyes to watch the joy fill her face. "No, baby, not really, but it would serve him right for some of the stunts he pulled on me when I was a little girl."

"Hey, yeah." Sarah set her mug on the table, then propped her fists on her hips. "You took Momma's doll. You were mean to her."

"That's what brothers do, kiddo."

"Then I'm glad I don't got a brother."

"They're not all bad, honey. They have their good uses, too." Lexie passed Marc a cup, then patted him on the cheek. "They protect you from bullies, teach you humility and your place in the grand scheme of things and bring home cute friends."

David didn't catch what Marc mumbled under his breath, but he could guess it had something to do with wishing he'd never brought David home with him.

"Stop it," Lexie said quietly. "He's her father. Mind your mouth."

For a long moment the siblings stared at one another. The only sounds were the light rustle of the leaves in the breeze and the creak of the swing's chain as it gently swayed to and fro. Lexie's parents watched their kids with amused expressions.

David wouldn't have missed their youngest putting the oldest in his place for anything.

Marc finally inclined his head. "Sorry, sis."

David raised his mug to her in gratitude and acknowledgment of her victory. What exactly did her defending him mean? Was she considering his proposal?

He couldn't wait to get her alone to find out.

Lexie slipped from Sarah's room into the hallway, enjoying the quiet of the house. With the little girl asleep, maybe Lexie could take some time to sort out the events of the crazy day. Light shone underneath David's door, his keyboard clicking away as he worked on some program, no doubt.

She clenched her teeth at the memory of his proposal. Logical, methodical, all planned out, it galled her to know that marriage to her was something he viewed as a "way to debug the glitches" in his life.

The sounds of the piano floated up the stairs, making her jaw relax into a smile. She eased down the steps, stopping at the entrance to the living room. Hiding in the shadows of the archway, she watched her father's fingers caress the keys. Her mother sat beside him, her face raptly concentrating on her husband. The haunting melody "Somewhere Out There" filled the room.

Lexie blinked back tears. The song and the movie it came from had been a favorite of hers as a child.

"He's hardly played at all since we lost you. That's one of the few pieces he would," Marc whispered from behind her. He wrapped his arms around her and pulled her against his chest, resting his chin on the top of her head. "He held on to that song like a magic spell that would bring you back home to us."

Would it break her father's heart to know his little girl no longer believed in dreams coming true, or magic?

"We've missed you, Lex."

She gripped his forearms, hugging herself tighter into his embrace. "I missed all of you, too."

Her mother rubbed circles on her father's back. When he stopped playing, he turned to her. "I told you to keep the faith, that we'd see her again."

Her mom's smile quivered. "Yes, you did."

Her dad pulled her into his arms, rocked her, then lowered his head and kissed her.

Lexie's heart ached—for the pain she'd caused her family, with envy of the love her parents shared and for the uncertainty of her future.

She pushed Marc backward. "I feel like I'm intruding. Let's go in the library." Untangling herself from his embrace, she took his hand and led him across the foyer. She clicked on the small red-domed light that sat on the end table. The leather sofa crackled as she sank onto it. "Sit," she told her brother. "Let's talk."

"If I talk, li'l sis, are you going to listen?" He chose the oversize chair across from her.

"I suppose that depends on what you want to talk about, big brother." She infused as much sarcasm into the final words as possible.

"How can you possibly trust him? After he wouldn't listen to you?"

Lexie shrugged. "At this point, I don't have much of a choice, Marc. David is Sarah's father. He's trying really hard with her. He has all the rights. I have none. I suppose I should be grateful he didn't decide to press charges and have me hauled off to jail."

"Jail." Marc scowled. "How do you feel about the whole Angela thing now?"

Her cheeks warmed. "I'm ashamed to admit it, but I'm...relieved that she's dead."

"That's it, just relieved? Doesn't it make you even madder at David that he didn't believe you, and your fears were justified?"

"Justified? What do you mean?"

Marc stared at her for a long moment, then he exhaled deeply, sinking back into the chair. He cursed under his breath. "You don't know the whole story, do you?"

"What story? I know Angela's dead. David said they were already divorced when it happened, but I didn't want to pry. He didn't seem like he wanted to talk about it. I know he loved her." Yes, he'd loved Angela. But he "cared about" her. That realization stung.

"Angela died in jail, Lexie. Another inmate murdered her. They don't like baby killers in prison."

"B-baby killers? Marc, what are you saying?"

He leaned forward in the chair, reaching for her hand. "I'm saying you were right about Angela all along. She probably did kill her first baby. She was awaiting trial for the murder of her new husband's first grandchild when somebody saved the taxpayers some money by doing her in."

Cold crept through her, making the hair on the back of her arms stand up and her hands go numb. She wiggled her fingers but couldn't feel her brother's reassuring grip. "She—she killed another child?"

He nodded. "The evidence seemed to say so."

"Ohmigod." Lexie shot to her feet, freeing her hand. "That means…"

"That means you did the right thing by running away," Marc said. "You saved that little girl's life by keeping her away from Angela."

Lexie darted out of the library and up the stairs before she'd even thought about it. Entering Sarah's room, she crossed to the bed and just stood there. The light caressed the child's sweet, sleep-softened face.

Lexie pressed her lips together, hard, but still a whimper escaped. Tears welled up and spilled over. "Oh, my poor baby," she whispered. She climbed into the bed and gathered Sarah into her arms, rocking her against her chest.

"Momma?" she asked groggily. "You woke me up."

"I'm sorry, baby. Go back to sleep. Momma will hold you and sing, okay?"

The curls bobbed agreement.

The singing didn't happen, because Lexie couldn't get sound past her swelling vocal cords. But it didn't matter because Sarah had already fallen back to sleep. The rocking disintegrated into uncontrollable shaking.

A shudder crawled along Lexie's back. This precious child shared DNA with a monster. How was that possible?

Whose child was she? The child of her genetics? Or the loving environment in which Lexie had raised her? What kind of legacy would she inherit from a woman like Angela?

Outside the room, a pair of masculine voices rumbled. David and Marc. At the moment, she didn't want to see either of them.

Eventually the arguing subsided and the bedroom door creaked open. Lexie lifted her head from Sarah's.

"Lexie? What's wrong? I heard you on the monitor." David pointed to the night table.

If she'd been a superhero from a comic book, red laser beams would have shot out of her eyes and vaporized him on the spot.

But she wasn't a superhero. She was just a mother.

She gently released Sarah, lowering her back down to the pillow, tucking the covers around her. She kissed her forehead, and then both cheeks, lingering on the birthmark as more tears spilled down her own face.

Without a word, she marched from the room. David followed silently. Down the back staircase, through the kitchen, she strode purposefully, certain he was only one step behind. Grabbing a coat from a hook, she shrugged into it on the way out.

"Lexie? Where are we going?"

The dew on the grass wet her shoes as she crossed the lawn to the gazebo in the backyard. She whirled on him as he joined her. She curled her hand into a tight fist, fighting the urge to smack him.

He stopped to stare at her. "Lex? You're freaking me out, here. What's going on?"

"What's going on? I think there are a few things you forgot to tell me. Like your wife was arrested for murdering another baby. Like I was right. That she would have killed Sarah if I hadn't run away. That you were wrong and should have listened to me!"

"I'm sorry. It wasn't something I wanted to talk about. You think I'm proud of the fact that I wouldn't listen to you? That I was so damn inept as a father even before my child was born that I didn't know a threat to her safety lurked right under my own nose?

"I married a woman who was so screwed up in the head...and I didn't even realize it. You know how they say love is blind, Lex?" He slapped his chest. "I'm living proof it's blind *and* stupid. That's what love does to people, Lexie. Encourages them to make bad choices."

Lexie leaned against the gazebo's railing. The crisp night air cooled her anger, as did his words. Her fingers relaxed. "I'm sorry, too. I just wish you'd told me all this when you got here."

"I had other things on my mind. Like getting to know my daughter."

"I guess there's enough pain to go around, huh?"

He nodded. "Yeah. But we can fix that. Have you given any thought to my proposal? We'll create a nice, stable, two-parent family for Sarah. A family like yours. She never has to know you're not her biological mother."

"My parents love each other, David."

He exhaled slowly. "I thought you'd put aside the romance novels and fairy tales, Lex. Didn't you tell me that this whole thing had killed the dreamer in you? Where's your practical side now?"

Clamoring to be heard. But she didn't want to listen. She shook her head. "I won't marry a man who doesn't love me, David. Not even you. Not even for Sarah. I can't."

"So, you're saying no?"

"I'm saying no." Her stomach rolled. She reached behind herself to grab the railing for support.

"Fine." He shoved his hands into his pants pockets. "Then we need to come up with a plan to explain everything to Sarah and get her prepared to go back to Erie with me."

Lexie's lower jaw quivered. "Will you—will you give me until her birthday?" she whispered.

"I want her settled by her birthday."

"So, you're saying no?" she echoed his earlier question.

"I'm saying no."

Since she couldn't have spoken if she'd wanted to, Lexie just nodded.

"I'll give you through Halloween. That gives us a little more time to get comfortable with one another, get her used to me. But, November first, we're on our way back east."

November first.

Two weeks and one day longer.

So little time to cram a lifetime's worth of love into a little girl. Holding her tears carefully in check— she'd be damned if she'd cry in front of him ever again—she nodded once more and strode back toward the house.

The leaves in the yard crunched beneath her feet as David watched her rush away. The porch door squeaked. Silhouetted by the kitchen lights, she poured herself into her brother's waiting arms.

David turned away, chest tight. He had a pretty good idea just how much he'd hurt her. But if he gave in on any grounds, from visitation to staying through Sarah's birthday—then it would be Thanksgiving, and then Christmas—what reason would she have for marrying him? He had to play the cards he had, use what he could to change her mind.

They might not love each other, but she did love Sarah, with everything in her. Eventually, he was certain that love would be enough. He might have to push a bit, let her see just what she was giving up.

The wind rustled the leaves louder and he shivered, turning toward the gazebo's opening. As he stepped down, something solid and hard connected with his stomach.

He doubled over, gasping for breath.

"You son of a bitch. I've waited a hell of a long time to do that."

David gagged, then sucked in a lungful of air. Straightening up wasn't an option, so he braced his hands on his knees and focused on continuing to breathe.

"That's it, Mitchell? You're not even going to take a swing at me? Christ, you've gotten soft."

"What—took—you—so—long?"

"I didn't want to interfere with your search for my sister. I figured you were our best hope for seeing her again. Which only seemed fitting since you were the one who drove her away in the first place."

"Wasn't how it was supposed to go." Clenching his teeth, David stood up. Fire burned along his abs.

"I don't give a shit how it was supposed to go. All I know is my baby sister's been gone for more than four years. She missed Kenny's wedding and the birth of his son. You can't give that back to us. And now you're breaking her heart. You made my sister cry."

"You made her cry regularly when we were growing up."

"That's different. I'm her brother. I'm allowed. You're not. Besides, we're supposed to be grown-up now."

"She's grown-up, all right," David murmured, thinking how she'd stood up to her brother and mother, and all the other changes in her…

It was all those other changes that got him into serious trouble. That had led to last night…

"That better not mean what I think it does," Marc growled. "I've seen you watching her. You keep your hands—and lips—off her. You've done enough damage."

"I'm trying to make things right."

"How? By taking away a child she loves? A child she carried and gave birth to for *you?*"

"I asked her to marry me," David said.

Marc blinked a few times. "Run that past me again?"

"I asked her to marry me. That way she could still be Sarah's mom, and I'd get to raise my daughter, too. Be a real father, not like the lousy excuse for one that

I have. Your parents would be Sarah's grandparents, you and Kenny her uncles...a real family."

Marc studied him for a while.

"What?"

"I'm trying to decide if that's the most brilliant thing you've come up with so far, or if I need to finish beating the crap out of you."

"Go with brilliant."

"I'm not sure I like all the implications of her being married to you."

"Marc, I swear to you, if she changes her mind and marries me, I'll take good care of her. She'll never want for anything." *Except to be loved.*

And he hated to disappoint her. But he just— couldn't. Never again.

Sarah's love would just have to be enough.

For both of them.

Marc reached up to the nape of his neck and flickered his fingers in the back of his hair, a habit he'd had since they were kids.

"If I'd gotten Lexie pregnant the old-fashioned way, you'd have hustled me down the aisle in a hurry."

Marc groaned. "There's an image I didn't need." He pulled at his shirt collar. "I told you then surrogacy wasn't a good idea, I told *her* it wasn't a good idea, but does anybody ever listen to me? Of course not."

"I just want to be a good father, Marc. It's all I've ever wanted. Listen, this situation is not entirely my fault. She caused me pain, too, you know. I lost four years with my daughter. Four years Sarah didn't have me, just like I didn't have a dad growing up. That kills me."

Marc turned away and rubbed his hands over his face. "I know that," he said. "But it's my job to protect my sister. I don't want to see her hurt any more than she already has been. She's devastated that you're taking Sarah away from her."

"I'm offering her the chance to be Sarah's mother forever. I'd prefer never to tell Sarah about Angela."

"I take it Lexie didn't leap at your proposal, or else we wouldn't be having this conversation. Mom would already be planning the reception."

David shook his head. "She wants the one thing I can't give her, Marc."

"What's that?"

"My heart. I care about her a lot, don't get me wrong, but I am never going to be so blind again."

This time the impact into his stomach not only left him desperate for air, but also hurling what was left of his dinner into the little shrubs planted around the gazebo.

"Idiot. This is Lexie we're talking about. She dreamed of princes and being swept off her feet. If you'd told me you loved her, I might have helped you pull off this plan of yours. But now you can rot in hell for all I care. Stay away from my baby sister." Marc stomped off toward the house, leaving David to finish puking in the bushes.

At least his former best friend was talking to him again. That progress was worth a couple of belts and a lost meal.

Somehow he'd get Lexie to see that his idea would work. For all of them. He wasn't certain how, but somehow he'd convince the mother of his child to marry him.

CHAPTER TWELVE

"I THINK YOU should marry him," her mother said, leaning onto the suitcase perched on the luggage stand and latching it.

"What?" Lexie paused in the middle of yanking the sheets off the honeymoon suite's cherry four-poster bed. "Mom, why?"

"Because he's right, it's the perfect answer. You get what you want, which is Sarah; David gets what he wants, which is Sarah, and what he needs—a mother for that delightful child. Because face it, he's trying hard but he doesn't quite get how to take care of a four-year-old little girl yet." Her mom zipped the matching carry-on bag. "And Sarah gets what she needs—two parents who both love her."

"But David doesn't love *me,* Mom."

"Sometimes love grows where you least expect it, honey."

Lexie shook her head as she peeled off a pillowcase. "I don't think so. He'd make any Vulcan proud, Mom. Logical, rational—love doesn't compute for him anymore. Not after what Angela did to him."

"Can you blame him? That witch made him doubt his ability to make good choices. If anyone can change his mind about that, it's you, honey."

"And what if I marry him, and he changes his mind? What happens then? What if he falls in love with someone else later on?" Lexie rolled the dirty linens into a ball and tossed them on the floor at the foot of the bed.

"Ah, there's the truth, right there. You're afraid he'll hurt you." Her mom patted the uncovered mattress. "Sit with me a minute."

The box spring creaked as she sank down at her mother's side.

"Lexie, look me in the eye and tell me that you don't love David, that you haven't loved him since you were a teenager."

She tried. She lifted her chin and stared into her mother's eyes. "I—I had a crush on him, that's all. It's over with now. I've outgrown it."

"Lie to yourself, but don't lie to me." She wagged a finger at Lexie. "Honey, you didn't have Sarah out of the goodness of your heart. You had her because of your love for David." She sighed. "Noreen and I used to laugh when you kids were really little about you and David someday getting married. As you grew, I watched you watching him. Saw him being kind to you, and your puppy love develop. But sometimes puppy love can become something more. And sometimes a marriage that starts off with the love of a child can grow into something absolutely wonderful." She took Lexie's hand and squeezed it. "Take my word for it."

"What does that mean?"

"If you tell your brothers this, I'll deny it until my

last breath. But I think it's time for you know my biggest secret. Woman to woman."

"What, Mom?"

"I just hope you don't think any less of me."

A tingle of anxiety stirred in Lexie's stomach. "I don't think there's anything you could tell me that would make me think less of you, Mom."

She sighed. "Your father and I have lied to you kids all these years. We've actually been married a year less than we've said. I was already pregnant with Marc when we got married."

"No way!" Lexie clapped her hand over her mouth. "Sorry," she mumbled. "That just kind of slipped out." She tried to process her mother's revelation. "Wow. But you guys were madly in love, right? I mean, that's what led to uh…Marc?" Her face heated. Not exactly a discussion she'd ever expected to have with her mother.

"*I* was madly in love. I don't think your father was so certain about it."

"But now…"

"Now neither of us can imagine life without the other." She squeezed Lexie's hand again. "Which is exactly my point."

"But Dad's a poet. A musician." So much more than the actual job he held of English professor at Erie University. "He's got a dreamer's soul, Mom." Which was where she'd gotten hers, at her father's knee as he'd read her stories of knights and princesses and sang ballads to her. "David wouldn't know a dream these days if it walked up and introduced itself to him."

"I think you're underestimating him. He has a good heart. This has hurt him, too. Don't forget that."

"Hey, you're supposed to be on my side," Lexie said, then felt foolish as soon as the words left her mouth.

"There are no sides. I'm for Sarah getting what she needs." Her mother smiled. "It may be just what all of you need."

"You ready, sweetheart?" Her father stuck his head in the doorway. "All the other bags are loaded."

Lexie tried not to stare at him, but the idea that there had ever been a moment when he doubted loving her mom…it boggled the mind.

As did the concept that they'd gotten married because there was a baby on the way.

She and David shared a child. Sort of…

Still, she'd compromised so much of herself already. To give up on the idea of marrying a man who actually loved her… Lexie wasn't sure she was willing to—or even able to—do that.

"I'll get this one." Marc pushed into the room to collect the suitcase from the luggage stand.

Lexie held on to her mother's hand as they all tromped down the stairs. They stopped in the foyer, setting the bags on the floor. "It's nasty out there, so we'll say our goodbyes here," her mom said as her father helped her with her coat. "Where are Sarah and David?"

"I'm in here, Mrs. J." David's voice came from the

library, where he'd been working online. He appeared in the doorway. "I didn't want to intrude."

"Good thinking, but a little too late," Marc said.

Her mom slapped him on the shoulder, then went to enfold David in a hug. Lexie strained to hear what she said to him, but the words were spoken too low. Pappy and four-year-old Sarah came from the living room and the old man shook hands with her father. Lexie leaned over and picked her daughter up. Then she exchanged quick hugs with her mom and dad, each of them planting kisses on Sarah's forehead—the most she'd allow.

Her dad leaned closer and whispered in Lexie's ear, "Have faith. I know you'll do the right thing. You always do." He tweaked her nose, then turned away to shake David's hand. The front door opened, letting in a blast of cold air. Marc lingered a second longer as their parents headed out and Pappy and David disappeared into the other rooms.

"If you need anything, Lex, you know where we are." Marc set the suitcase down once more and wrapped his arms around both her and Sarah. "And you are worth all of it, sis. Don't you dare settle, you hear me?" he said. Sarah fidgeted, whining, in the tight embrace, so he backed off. "Whatever you decide, we'll be here for you."

"I know. Thanks." Lexie smiled past the pain of their leaving. "Better hurry, you know how Dad gets." She kissed him on the cheek. "Give that to Kenny. Oh, wait." She gave him another one. "And that's for the baby."

Marc laughed. "The baby, okay, but if you think I'm kissing Kenny, forget it." He stopped in the doorway. "Take care of yourself, sis."

"I will."

"I'm proud of you." Marc leaned closer to Sarah. "Can I kiss you goodbye?"

She nodded shyly.

He placed a gentle smooch on the birthmark. "There, now I kissed you in the same place the angels did." He lightly pressed on her nose. "You take care of your momma, okay?"

Sarah nodded, then hid her face in the crook of Lexie's neck.

Lexie cuddled Sarah, comforting herself with the little one as the door clanked shut. Moving to the side window, she shifted the curtain, watching as they pulled from the driveway and onto Main Street.

Her mother wanted her to give marriage to David a chance. Her brother said she was worth a man's love and not to compromise. Her father had faith in her.

Hopefully that faith wasn't misplaced. But what was she supposed to do?

David came back out of the library. "You okay?"

She nodded. "No tears for you to worry about."

"Good. Because we need to talk."

God, she hated when he said that. "About what?"

Sarah squirmed. "Down, Momma. I need to finish my puzzle with Pappy."

David waited until Sarah skipped into the living room, then he turned to Lexie. "I'm taking Sarah away for a few days. She and I need to spend some time alone. I want a chance for her to start building a relationship with me, to start to *depend* on me."

She stared at him, mouth gaping, not quite sure she'd understood him. Taking Sarah? Now? "Uh, uh…"

"I'm taking her to Missoula. Figured we could do some shopping, maybe go see Danny Dino again."

Yep, she'd understood, all right. And so it began.

He was taking her baby away from her.

"I WANT MOMMA to come." Sarah hugged Annie closer.

"I know, sport, but this is going to be a special time. Just you and me." David fumbled with the zipper on her coat.

Lexie watched for several seconds, then sighed. "Let me show you." She knelt beside him and grasped the two sides, keeping the flap of flannel away from the teeth. "Like this."

"Oh. Okay."

"Momma, you come, too." Sarah flung her arms around Lexie's neck so hard Lexie rocked back on her heels and would have fallen over, if not for David's steadying hand against her spine.

Lexie rose to her feet with his help, Sarah still clinging to her, her doll wedged between them. "Baby, I'd love to come with you, but you're going to have fun. David—your daddy will take good care of you."

"I want you!"

"Tell you what, I'll walk you to the car, okay?"

Sarah sniffled, but nodded her head.

"All right. I'm going to set you down so I can put on a coat. It's nippy out there." Lexie placed Sarah on the floor and shrugged into her fleece jacket. "Oh, wait." She fished in the front pocket of her jeans and handed David a square of folded-up notebook paper.

"What's this?"

"A list of her sizes and the stuff she needs right now. Since you're going shopping, I'm helping you out. She needs new shoes, snow boots, a winter coat." Lexie pointed at the paper. "It's all on there."

"Can I get a coat with a zipper that works easy?" Sarah asked, looking up at David.

"That sounds like a good plan to me."

David wouldn't have to shop at the secondhand stores the way she did, so it shouldn't be a problem for him.

The hollow ache in her chest grew larger.

"Hold my hand, Momma." Sarah's small fingers slipped into her palm as they went out to the driveway.

If only she could hold this child's hand forever.

David opened the SUV's door. "I've installed her booster seat, but maybe you could check it to make sure I did it right."

"Sure." She tugged on the straps, making certain everything was secure. Sarah's safety depended on it. "It's good. You can climb in, baby."

Sarah shook her head, folding her arms across her chest, Annie inside the grip. "Not without you."

Lexie picked her up, hugged her tight. "Oh, baby." Her voice cracked. "It'll be fun. I promise."

"He don't know how to wash my hair right." The

small voice dropped to a hushed whisper. "He can't see me take a bath. And who will sing me asleep?"

Tears fogged Lexie's vision and she fought to hold them back. "David will croak for you, baby." She forced a smile.

"Come on, sport. Time to go." David reached for Sarah, grabbing her below the arms and prying her from Lexie in a move that was becoming altogether too familiar.

"Noooo! I wanna stay with Momma! Don't make me go! Momma, please!"

Lexie closed her eyes behind David's back as he tried to fasten the struggling child into the restraints. *Please, God, let my voice sound normal.* "Have fun, baby," she managed to get out. "Listen to your daddy. Be a good girl for him."

"Momma!" Sarah sobbed.

The car door slammed, muffling her pleas.

Lexie bit into her bottom lip, the bitter metallic taste of blood a pale imitation of the bitter pain in her heart.

"Doesn't have to be this way," David said. "You can change all this with one little word."

"Please?" She opened her eyes to find compassion in his.

He shook his head. "Yes. Say yes, and we'll add a set of wedding rings to the shopping list."

"You still haven't said the *magic* word, David. So don't count on hearing me say yes anytime soon."

He shrugged. "Okay. Have it your way." He waved the note, then tucked it into his pocket. "We'll be back in a few days. Thanks for the list."

Lexie clenched her hands into fists, nails digging into her palms. She'd like to tell him what to do with that list, but there was a child present.

He was fighting dirty, using Sarah like this.

She pressed her lips together and waved as the car eased down the driveway. Sarah's arms stretched out in her direction, reaching, tears cascading down her face.

When they turned onto the street, a sob broke loose from deep inside her, and she fought the urge to run after the car and beg him to let her go with them. "B-bye, b-baby." She snuffled.

"Here, Missy." Pappy held out a faded blue handkerchief.

Lexie jumped. "Pappy. I didn't know you were out here."

"That's clear." He waved the scrap of fabric again. "Take it. You're dripping."

"Thanks." She wiped her nose, then tucked the hankie into her pocket.

"You okay?"

"No."

"Didn't think so." He draped a thin arm around her shoulders and turned her toward the house. "Let's git you inside." He jerked his head in the direction of the neighbor's house. "You don't want that old biddy Casterlin seeing you out here crying, do ya? She'll be on the phone in minutes, spreadin' the tale all over the county."

She let him guide her steps, since the tears made everything all quivery.

"What do I do now, Pappy?" Back in the kitchen, she hung her coat up on the hook.

"Well, I know you got chores to git done. Do them. Then you can put your feet up and read, or go over to Nola's house and have a gabfest, or I got a tape of the latest Griz game. You could watch that with me, if you want."

"Now there's an offer I don't get every day." A tiny smile tugged at her mouth. What would she do without this angel in her life? Strange, but he felt more right than her parents and brother had. She loved them, but he knew her better now. "But I meant more in terms of the big picture, Pap." She dragged out a chair and sank down, pressing her forehead against the table. "I don't know what to do."

The chair next to hers scraped the floor. "My Doris always said if you followed your heart, you'd never go wrong. What's your heart tellin' you, Missy?"

"My heart hurts so much I don't know what it's telling me."

A gnarled hand patted her back. "Well, you work on listening to it. It will tell you what to do."

"I wish…"

"What, Missy?"

She shrugged, not knowing what to wish.

The hand on her back hesitated a moment, then resumed offering comfort. "It will all work out right in the end."

If only she had his faith. Or her father's. But working out right, and working out well, those were two different things.

She could let David take Sarah away from her, and have her heart shatter into a million pieces.

Or she could marry a man who didn't love her, and probably never would.

Neither option was a happy ending.

Reality sucked.

Give her fiction any day.

"AREN'T YOU GOING to eat?" David nudged the plate a little closer to his daughter, who sat on a green plastic booster seat across the table from him.

She shook her head.

"I cut it up the way you like it." When she wouldn't tell the waitress what she wanted, he'd ordered pepperoni pizza for her.

"My tummy feels funny." She cuddled her worn doll closer.

"Maybe that's because it's hungry. You need to eat." When she still didn't even attempt the pizza, he tried another approach. "How about you just drink some of your orange pop?"

"Momma says pop's just for special 'casions."

"Well, this is a very special occasion. This is our first daddy-daughter trip." David pushed the covered cup of soda forward. "A few sips? That might help your tummy."

She shook her head again. David swallowed an exasperated sigh. Surely she'd eat when she got hungry enough. She wasn't going to starve to death until then. It wasn't worth getting upset about or antagonizing her over.

"Okay, do you want to go back to the motel room and lie down?" The first thing he'd done when they'd arrived in Missoula was get them checked in to a motel. Sarah had inspected the room and pronounced it "not as pretty as the rooms we have at the bed-and-breakfast."

"No."

"What do you want to do then?"

"I wanna go home," she said softly.

He smiled to hide the fact that her words tore at him. She seemed determined to make this as difficult as possible. Or was it just that his kid didn't like strangers, didn't like crowds and simply wanted to be in her own home? He could relate to a lot of that.

But if she wouldn't trust him on a short trip like this, how was he going to get her to go to Erie with him?

"I was thinking more along the lines of doing some shopping, sport." He dug in his pocket and pulled out the paper Lexie had given him. "Your mom's got quite a few things on this list. I think it's going to take a while to get all this stuff, so we should probably get started."

On the way out of the restaurant, he offered Sarah a red-and-white peppermint. "This might help your tummy."

She accepted the candy, giving him back the wrapper. "Why do they call it peppermint? It don't taste like pepper."

David chuckled, opening the door to the SUV. "I don't know, sport. That's a good question."

At the Southgate Mall, he parked outside JCPenney. "Don't you think you should leave your doll in the car? I wouldn't want her to get lost."

Sarah nodded solemnly, then placed the doll in the car seat. "Be good, Annie. We'll be back."

David lifted her down from the SUV. "I need you to hold my hand while we're here." He held his out.

She looked at it, then tilted her head to stare at him for several long seconds. When she placed her fingers into his palm, he smiled and gripped them carefully, afraid to spook her if he tried to hold too tight.

Once inside the department store, she edged even closer to him, practically attaching herself to his leg. "Let's start with a coat, okay?" he said. After finding the little girls' section, he made his way through the closely placed racks. "How about this one?" He held up a beige coat.

She shook her head.

So, he tried again. With a pink one. Same response.

The scenario repeated about eight times. Finally, he asked, "Why don't you tell me what kind of a coat you do want. Besides one where the zipper doesn't get stuck."

"Can I really have whatever I want?"

"Sure."

Her eyes widened. "A purple one," she whispered. "With fuzzy stuff around the hat and bottom."

They searched through the entire stock of coats, but didn't find one that matched her criteria. Sarah's mouth turned down, her whole face looked so dejected he felt miserable.

"Don't worry," he said. "This is just the first place. There are more we can look at."

"Really?"

"Really." David loved the way her hand felt in his as they wandered into the main mall. The fact that she stuck so close to him, obviously using him as her security system, sure felt good, too. Right. The way a daughter should feel about her father.

"That's Momma's favorite store." Sarah pointed out Waldenbooks as they passed. "We should get her a book."

"We can do that." As long as it wasn't a romance book. Or some fantasy novel. Maybe they should get her something nonfiction. Did they have a book entitled *Creating a Happy Marriage with the Father of Your Child?* Maybe *12 Steps to a Successful Platonic Marriage?*

Except he didn't want it to be platonic. One night with her had more than convinced him of that. "On the way back. And there's always tomorrow, too."

"We're gonna shop tomorrow, too?"

"Depends on how much stuff we manage to find today, I suppose."

Farther down the hall, David paused outside a photography studio, then looked down at Sarah. The plastic photo holder in his wallet was empty. No evidence of his child, no pictures to whip out to share with other proud parents. "Let's go in here a minute."

Inside, a poster advertised holiday backgrounds and Christmas cards with adorable children. Several young women jostled strollers, a pair of twin boys sat in chairs along the wall, feet dangling, kicking at the rungs. Most of them gave Sarah a quick once-over. David winced at some of the stares. One child pointed a finger at her; his mother poked him in the side and whispered harshly at him.

Sarah wrapped an arm around his leg and pressed the marked side of her face into his khakis.

He caressed her hair, letting the soft texture soothe his desire to lash out at the people in the store.

"Can I help you?" asked the young woman behind the counter.

"Do I need to make an appointment to have my daughter's picture taken?"

"As you can see, we're kind of clogged up right now. If you'd like to come back in about an hour, we should be able to do it then."

Sarah shook her head against his leg, and tugged on his pants. He bent over.

"I don't want my pitchure took," she whispered. "Let's go get a purple coat."

David unwrapped her arm and knelt on the floor. Using one finger beneath her chin, he lifted her face until she looked at him. "I need a picture of my beautiful little girl." He leaned forward, brushing his lips over her right cheek. "I love you, Sarah."

Ignoring the soft *awww's* and gooey looks he was getting now from the moms in the studio, he took Sarah's hand and rose to his feet. "We'll be back in an hour, then."

"Child's name?" The woman held a pen over a pad.

"Sarah Mitchell."

Another tug on his pants had him bending over again. "I'm Sarah Jacobs," she murmured.

He cleared his throat, straightening. "Sarah Jacobs Mitchell."

She nodded, obviously satisfied with that.

"Let's go find your purple coat."

CHAPTER THIRTEEN

LEXIE THREW herself down on the bed. The guest rooms were once again pristine and ready for new arrivals, the bathrooms all clean and three loads of laundry washed, dried, folded and put away.

Four loaves of bread baked. Just over two dozen chocolate chip cookies—there would have been more, but she'd eaten enough of the raw dough to make herself queasy.

Now what?

The silence in the house, especially from the room attached to hers, echoed inside her.

Lexie bounced back off the mattress and hustled downstairs to the library. Bypassing the shelves full of paperbacks, she ran a finger along the spines of the old leather books she'd collected, some from the attic, many from flea markets and garage sales.

"Pick one and sit, Missy. I'm exhausted jest from watching you today."

She turned. "I don't know that I can, Pappy. When I sit, I think too much."

"So, go next door and gab with Nola. Do something. Take advantage of the free time."

"I don't want free time, Pap. I want Sarah." And

she didn't want to gab about it with Nola, who didn't know the whole truth of the situation. If her friend knew David had proposed, she'd be lobbying full force for a marriage.

"I know you do." He shuffled his feet. "You know I'll help you however I can, right? I mean, if you need a lawyer, we'll git one."

"Oh, Pappy." Lexie moved toward him. "Where would I be without you?" She embraced him, nose twitching, trying not to sneeze at the scent of cherry pipe tobacco that clung to his old gray sweater. He thought he was fooling her, but she knew he hadn't quit. The only thing she didn't know was where he was hiding his stash. "I love you, Pap."

He cleared his throat, patting her awkwardly on the shoulder. "I love you, too, Missy. And I'm the one who'd be lost without you." Backing from her arms, he shook a finger at her. "Now find something to do afore you drive us both crazy tonight."

"I think I'll take a walk."

"That sounds good. So, go on. Git."

The streetlights were coming on as she left the house. Pulling up the collar of her jacket, she turned right and headed down the sidewalk. Wood smoke rose from Mrs. Casterlin's chimney. Leaves crunched beneath Lexie's feet as she passed Nola's house. Farther down, light spilled from the market.

A half block later, she waved to Bob Schrieber as he locked the front door of the old Victorian house he'd converted into a bookstore. They shared the same passion for books. Lexie suspected he ran the store not to make a profit so much as to give himself something to do and to bring books into the lives of other people.

The whole town had the feel of a comfortable flannel shirt. Though she'd been born and raised in Pennsylvania, she'd actually grown up here. These people had embraced and welcomed her and Sarah, made her part of their homes.

The odor of fresh paint drifted to her as she passed the building Frank Colton was converting into a martial arts school. Maybe she'd enroll herself, so the next time the urge to kick or kiss David came over her, she'd be fully trained in the kicking department.

As for the kissing...

Much as it galled, her lips could remember every nuance of the way he kissed.

And they wanted more, too.

Stupid lips.

She rubbed her fingers over her mouth, like it would erase the thought. The sidewalk gave way to dirt beneath her feet, and Lexie crossed Main Street, ending up in front of the firehall. By next year, if everything worked out, there'd be a new engine parked inside.

Lexie walked briskly back toward the other end of town, arms swinging. But even the activity couldn't keep thoughts of Sarah and David from her mind.

Did her baby miss her?

How was David making out, taking care of her by himself for the first time?

SARAH CAME OUT of the bathroom and crawled onto the double bed closest to the wall. The tag on her pajama shirt stuck out in front of her neck—she'd put them on inside out and backward.

David pulled the covers down, and she slid between the white sheets.

The night hadn't been a complete disaster. He'd gotten the employees at the photography studio to keep other people out, and had even coaxed a tiny smile from his daughter. She'd eaten cookies from the mall, and he'd been happy enough with that.

They hadn't found a purple coat with fuzzy stuff yet.

And he hadn't been crazy enough to try to attempt getting her to take a bath, let alone washing her hair.

Sarah's curls sprawled across the pillow as she lay down. "My tummy feels funny again."

"Are you hungry?"

She shook her head.

Probably just homesick. She'd moped all the way back to the motel, pleading to go home. "Here's your doll." He placed the little rag body next to hers, then tucked the covers securely around her sides. "Is that better?"

"No."

He brushed his hand across her forehead the way his mom had done when he was young. She didn't feel warm, but what did he know? "Would you like to call your momma and say good night to her?" Amazing how easy it had become to call Lexie Sarah's momma.

Damn, he hoped Lexie wanted to keep the job. Hoped she was discovering at this very moment how much she didn't like being apart from the little girl she'd made her own.

"Can I?" Sarah rolled onto her side to face him.

"Sure." He punched the number into his cell phone.

"Mill Creek Bed-and-Breakfast. This is Lexie, how may I help you?"

"I've got a little girl here who wants to say good night to her momma," David said. "You wouldn't happen to know where I could find her momma, would you?"

Lexie inhaled sharply. "David! I didn't expect you'd call."

David passed the phone to Sarah, who didn't stir more than needed to take it and prop it against her ear. "Momma? I miss you."

While he listened to the one side of the conversation, he sat on the other double bed and kicked off his brown hiking shoes. Sarah didn't talk about much, offering one or two words here and there in response to whatever Lexie said.

"Sing me asleep." Sarah's eyes slid shut. Her features softened as she listened, and the edges of her lips turned up a bit.

That look of contentment reinforced for David that by cosmic intervention, his child had the perfect mother.

How could he have been so blind as to overlook Lexie, who'd been right under his nose his whole life, and have fallen for someone like Angela?

Though at first, Angela had been fun. Adventurous. Slightly daring. Definitely exciting.

And now, the thing he found most exciting about a woman was the fact that she could love a little girl with a passion and devotion he wished every kid could have.

Hell, a part of him wished he could have it.

How fair is that, to want her to love you so deeply, and you're not willing to love her back?

He hated that voice of reason.

Sarah sighed, eyebrows scrunching up. "My tummy's funny, Momma." After a pause, she opened her eyes and held the phone out toward him. "Momma wants to talk to you."

"Hey."

"Is she okay?" Concern filled Lexie's voice. "Is she running a fever?"

"I don't think so. She doesn't feel warm." He rose from the bed and moved near the door, lowering his voice. "I was thinking maybe it's just all the excitement, you know? Homesickness."

"What did Sarah have for dinner? Maybe something didn't agree with her."

"Uh, well, she wasn't very hungry."

"Does that mean she didn't eat anything for dinner?"

"Of course not. She ate. Just not much." Just three big cookies from the bakery in the mall. But somehow he didn't think that news would make Lexie very happy, nor qualify him for Father of the Year.

"If Sarah's stomach's upset, you could try giving her some flat soda. A clear one, like Sprite."

"How do I get pop to go flat without waiting hours?"

"You take two glasses, and pour it from glass to glass. It'll go flat pretty quick."

Sarah rolled onto her back and moaned. "I want Momma."

"David? Was that Sarah?"

"Yeah. Look, I have to go—"

Sarah sat bolt upright in the bed, sheer panic on her pale face. "I need a bucket!"

"Uh-oh, did she say she needs a bucket?"

David moved toward the bed. "Yes. What does that— Oh God. Never mind. Sarah just showed me what she meant by that." He sighed. "I really liked those shoes." Next time he'd be sure to order the waterproof style.

"I can be there in about an hour and a half—"

"No! I can handle it. Look, I have to go."

"Call me in the morning and let me know how she is!"

"I will." David closed the phone and dropped it on the night table. Trying hard not to gag and follow suit himself, he went to comfort his sick child and clean things up.

Daddy Lesson #4: When a sick kid says, "I need a bucket," get a bucket immediately.

"YOU SURE YOU'RE OKAY?" David asked as he helped Sarah out of the truck. "That breakfast is staying put in your tummy?"

She nodded. "I'm better now."

"Good."

She offered her hand without hesitation this time, and he resisted the crazy urge to dance through the parking lot.

In a part of the mall they hadn't explored yesterday, twinkling pumpkins at a costume store caught Sarah's attention. "Can we go in there?"

"Sure."

"Not by the scary stuff." She tugged him to the left, entering the store as far away from an animated, life-size Frankenstein as they could get.

"Okay. What do you want to look at?"

"Look at this!" She pulled him toward a cut-out display of the main characters from *The Wizard of Oz*. Growing more lively with every step, she actually let go of him. She rushed to a shelf and held up a pair of red shoes. "Ruby slippers! These are magic." Sarah placed them on the floor next to her own feet and frowned. "They're too big."

David pulled out Lexie's list, then scanned the boxes. "Here, sport. Try these."

She plopped onto the floor and pulled off her sneakers without untying them. The red shoes sparkled in the light. She stood up, holding out one foot. "Pretty!" She glanced shyly up at him. "Can I—can I have them? Momma's making me a Dorothy dress, but I don't got ruby slippers."

"Absolutely you can have them." It was the first thing she'd actually asked him for. No way he'd deny her anything, if he could give it to her.

Her smile and little dimple turned the world right for him. "Really? They're not too 'spensive?" She lifted the box toward him.

A jab of guilt prodded him as he pretended to consider it. Things must have been hard for Lexie financially. Memories surfaced of his own mother trying to hide her anxiety over the bills from him. If his father had been more generous in the early years, she'd have shed fewer tears.

Still, it wasn't David's fault Lexie had struggled. Okay, some of it was.

Most of it. Why hadn't he listened to her, instead of ignoring her concerns?

"David?" Uncertainty shifted Sarah's tiny features; the dimple vanished along with the smile.

"Yes, you can have them."

"Yay!" She took off the red shoes and carefully wrapped the tissue paper around them, reverently placing them back in the box. "Thank you."

He tied her sneakers, then propped the box containing the magic slippers beneath his arm. "Shall we see what else they have?"

They explored farther through the shelves and racks. When Sarah gasped, David's head snapped in her direction so fast the muscle in the back of his neck twinged. She pointed. "That's bee-u-tiful. Momma would love that. Wouldn't she look pretty in it?"

David reached for the filmy pink dress. "What's this supposed to be?"

"It's Glinda, the Good Witch." Sarah clapped her

hands. "Let's get it for her. And find something for you. We'll have fun costumes for Halloween."

"Do you think she'd like it?" He lifted the dress from the rack. With Lexie's dark hair and curvy figure, she'd be a knockout in it. His pulse picked up at the image forming in his mind. Lexie in this dress, the dance at the firehall...holding her close.

"Yes! Please, get it for her? And something for you?"

"Okay, we'll buy this for her and look for a costume for me." He draped the dress over his arm. They wandered the aisles in search of something for him. What would appeal to Lexie? "How about a pirate?" He picked up an eye patch, shuffling the other items. "Arrgg, matey, swab the deck and hoist the sails."

Sarah giggled. "That's silly."

"And look, I can have a parrot on my shoulder, too." A stuffed parrot attached to the costume with Velcro.

Her smile was all the answer he needed. He gathered the items and looked around for a checkout. In the center of the store, they both skidded to a stop. Sarah's mouth dropped open. "Wow. That's the most huge-mongous pumpkin ever."

"I'll say." The air-fan inflatable jack-o'-lantern towered over his daughter. "That would look cool in the front yard, don't you think?"

Sarah nodded, and he added it to their now-humongous tower of purchases.

They headed for the register, David staggering under the awkward load balanced in his arms. As he signed the credit card slip he felt Sarah press against his leg. Accepting the huge bag from the salesgirl, he turned, shuffling awkwardly with Sarah glued to him like that, finding a pair of teenage girls staring at Sarah.

One shook her head. "Your poor little girl. What's wrong with her face?"

"Nothing. What's wrong with your manners? Or didn't your parents teach you any?"

The girl's pierced eyebrow rose, taking the silver ball with it. "Whoa, take it easy. I was just curious."

"Curiosity is fine. Hurting a child's feelings is something else. Usually it's called rude." David cupped Sarah's head. "Come on, sport. Let's take these things to the car, and go find your purple coat."

Several yards out of earshot, David stifled a few muttered curses. Sarah giggled.

Amazed, he looked down at her. "Why are you laughing?"

"What's wrong with your manners?" she repeated, looking at him with wide, adoring eyes. "That's funny. Momma says ignore rude people. Would she get mad if I said that?"

"I have absolutely no idea." And he didn't. But he puffed out his chest and added a spring in his step. He'd championed his daughter, and she liked it.

They made their way down the long corridor, stopping in several other stores. They added a pair of white-and-pink sneakers and black snow boots to their collection of purchases. One department store remained to search for her coat, but first they returned to the SUV. David's fingers had ridges pressed into them from all the handles of shopping bags. "That's better," he said, slamming the back window of the vehicle. "Just one thing left to find, and that's your coat. We'll try this last store here, and if we can't find it, I guess we'll have to go someplace else."

"'kay."

Back inside the final department store, Sarah tugged on his arm.

"What?"

Her cheeks pinkened. "I have to go potty."

"Okay." He turned around. "Let's go to the motel. We can come back after lunch to look for your coat."

She danced from foot to foot. "I gotta go now."

Uh-oh. That sounded like a potential Daddy Lesson if ever he heard one. He glanced around. Rest rooms were usually by customer service, right? Taking Sarah's hand, he headed across the store. Past the beauty salon, and the catalog pick-up counter. Just near the exit doors, there was a long corridor with a sign indicating the rest rooms in that direction.

"Hurry, David." Sarah waddled, her legs pressed tightly together.

At the end of the hallway, he halted, staring at the two options: Women. Men.

Where the hell was a single dad with a little girl supposed to go?

Sending her into the women's room by herself wasn't an option. No way he'd risk anything happening to her. Letting her out of his sight and possibly losing her again...no way.

She wiggled, hopping around. "David!"

A middle-aged man came out of the men's room.

"Hey. Anybody else in there?" David asked him.

"Don't think so," the man replied as he sauntered down the corridor.

David pushed the door open, looked around. "Anybody in here?" When no one answered, he pulled on Sarah's hand.

"Hey! I can't go in there! That's the boys' room."

"You can't go in the ladies' room by yourself. Come on."

"I wish Momma were here."

At the moment, so do I. He tugged his daughter inside, checking it out further.

No feet under the stalls, so the coast was clear.

Sarah wrinkled her nose. "This bathroom stinks." She pointed at the urinals. "What's that?"

David turned the dead-bolt lock on the main door. "Never mind. I thought you had to potty?" He urged her toward one of the green metal stalls. "Go on."

"You hafta put a seat cover on. Momma says so."

"Of course." Entering the stall, he reached for the dispenser. "It's empty."

"Momma puts paper on it then." Sarah danced more urgently, like she had a pocketful of fire ants. "Hurry!"

Male anatomy made things so much easier. He draped toilet paper over the seat for her. "There. Okay?"

"Yes. Now go away!"

He left the stall, holding the door closed at the top.

A few minutes later, Sarah pushed against it. He stepped aside and let her out. "Okay now, sport?"

She nodded. "Gotta wash my hands."

Over at the sink, he adjusted the water for her, then picked her up so she could reach the foul-smelling soap.

The outer door rattled. "Just a minute," David yelled over the splashing water. "Be right out."

Sarah took her sweet time drying her hands with the paper towels he pulled from the dispenser for her, meticulously stroking each finger.

"Hurry up, sport. Someone else needs to get in here."

She tossed the wadded-up paper in the trash can as he unlocked the bolt and opened the door. Ushering Sarah into the hallway, he stopped just outside the rest room.

A baby-faced security guard blocked the way. "Put your hands up and step away from the kid!"

"What?" David glanced around. A uniformed woman security officer stood behind the first man as backup.

Another woman, armed with shopping bags and an enormous black purse dangling from one arm, pointed. "See, there he is! I told you he'd taken a little girl in there with him!"

David held his hands out in front of him. "Look, I'm not sure what's going on here, but this is my daughter."

Sarah locked her arms around his leg.

"Sure. I said hands up and move away from the kid. The cops are on their way." The young rent-a-cop lowered his hand toward a nightstick.

Cold sweat beaded across the back of David's neck. Becoming the beating victim of an overzealous wannabe-cop wasn't his idea of a good time. He slowly raised his hands over his head. "Look, if you'll just—"

"Shut up! Turn around and face the wall."

As David started to comply, the woman guard rushed forward and grabbed Sarah, whose scream echoed in the confined space. His leg shook as she tried to pry his child off him. "Hey! What do you think you're doing?"

His hands came down and he spun back toward the guards as a pair of patrolmen raced into the fray, making the narrow hallway feel even tighter. He shoved at the security guard, who went sprawling onto the tile floor, then David reached for Sarah.

"What the hell is going on here?" the uniformed cop yelled. "You!" He pointed at David. "Turn around and get your damn hands on the wall, now! Get that kid outta here!"

Sarah's terrified shrieks tore at David's heart. "Sarah, it's okay. Just go with the police. Everything's going to be fine." He turned and placed his palms against the rough plaster surface.

The cop pressed against the small of David's back, and began frisking him. "Got any weapons? Anything else I should know about?"

"No. Like I said to security, that's my daughter. I didn't know taking a child to the bathroom was a crime."

"Put your hand behind your back. I'm cuffing you for both our safety while we get this figured out."

David lowered his right hand. Metal snapped around it. Before he knew it, he stood, hands cuffed together, pressing his forehead against the cold wall. In the background, he could hear Sarah's sobbing and a woman's animated voice. "The little girl told him she didn't want to go in the men's room and that she wanted her mother, but he just pulled her in there. Last week I saw on TV some creep did that in Florida and molested the child."

"Yes, ma'am," said the other patrolman. "We all saw that. You were right to tell security."

"Turn around and talk to me," the cop said.

David sighed, then launched into the explanation of how a simple trip to the bathroom had gone very awry.

The cop grabbed David's elbow, led him to the end of the corridor. "You got ID?"

David nodded. "Back pocket."

The cop fished out the leather wallet. "You stay right here. Don't move."

A small crowd had gathered, all of them eyeing him as though he was lower than the dirt inside a keyboard. He anxiously looked for Sarah, but she was hidden behind the cluster of security people and police.

Time ticked by one agonizing second after another.

Hell. Would she repeat her initial reaction, that he wasn't her father? That her daddy had black hair and a crown? That would likely earn him a quick trip to jail. Or would she remember all the things he and Lexie had told her about the scientific tests that proved he was her father?

"I want my momma!"

David's chest tightened. Poor thing was going to be totally traumatized by the whole thing. Shoot, so was he.

"Don't touch me!" Sarah shouted.

A woman yelped. "Ow. The kid bit me."

Sarah's face appeared around the side of the woman security guard. Her eyes locked onto his.

"Daddy!" she cried. "I want my daddy!" She darted around the woman and raced to David, once more latching on to his legs, making him rock backward against the wall. The handcuffs bit into his skin, and the circulation got cut off, but he didn't care.

His baby had called him daddy.

That was worth being cuffed and treated like the scum of the earth. But he wished his hands were free so he could stroke her hair, gather her into his arms and hold her.

"It's okay, honey."

She sniffled, then looked up at him. "I told you I can't go in the boys' room! Now look!"

A chuckle burst from deep inside him. "You're right. I should have listened to you. Next time I'll go in the ladies' room."

Sarah stomped her foot. "You can't do that, either."

"No, you can't. Then I would have to arrest you."

The cop reached behind David to unlock the cuffs. "We called the Mill Creek Bed-and-Breakfast, where the child said she lived. The woman there corroborated your story about being the kid's father."

"Dr. Riley did a test," Sarah said. "I told you that. He's my daddy."

David rubbed his wrists, closing his eyes for a split-second, wanting to enjoy the moment. *He's my daddy.* Then he opened them again. Some aspects of this scene, like the cuffs, didn't qualify as the best of his life—not a Kodak moment by any means.

Lexie was probably freaking out after a call from the police. She'd need reassurance as much as Sarah. As soon as they got back out to the car, he'd give her a call.

The cop handed David his wallet. "Next time find a store with a single rest room and avoid all this, okay?"

David tucked the black trifold into his rear pocket. "Yes, Officer. Thank you." He knelt down and wrapped his arms around Sarah. She pressed her face tight into his neck and began to sob again. "It's okay, honey. I'm sorry that scared you so much."

"They taked me away from you! That was wrong."

"Yes, it was. But they were trying to protect you. They thought I was a bad man."

"You're not a bad man. You're my daddy!" Sarah hiccuped against him.

"Yes, I am." He rubbed her back. "And no one is ever going to take you away from me again."

Not the police. Not Lexie. No one.

CHAPTER FOURTEEN

"THANKS FOR PHONING, David. Yes, I'm okay. Bye." Lexie pressed the Off button on the portable phone and dropped it onto the table.

She called me Daddy, Lex.

David's words echoed through her mind.

Sarah had made a breakthrough in accepting him. Granted, neither of them would have chosen the particular experience that had led to it, but now... David had been thrilled.

Lexie wanted to be happy for him. But it hurt too much. Sarah was slipping away from her.

She rubbed at the center of her chest. Short, shallow breaths were all she could manage. Her heart thudded, skipped a beat, then pounded harder. Sweat beaded just below her hairline on her forehead.

"Missy? Who was on the phone?" Pappy strolled into the kitchen, heading for the jacket hooks on the back wall.

"D-David." She gasped, massaging the spot harder.

"You okay? You look kinda pale."

She shook her head. "Hard to breathe. Some—something's wrong."

Pappy grabbed her by the forearm and pulled her out of the chair. "Let's go."

"Where?"

"Across the street, where do you think? I ain't got the strength to carry you, gal, so keep those feet moving."

The cold air that rustled the cornstalks on the porch helped ease the tightness around her chest. She let Pappy guide her across Main and into the clinic. "I—I remember the last time we did this."

"Shh. Concentrate on breathing. You talked too much that time, too. Funny, but I thought next time we did this it would be the other way 'round, with you helping me." He opened the glass doors to the clinic. "Need a hand here," he announced to the place at large. "Missy's having trouble breathing."

The room came to life, the women behind the reception desk springing to action. Martha, the clinic's nurse, came to take her arm, while Sue Ann dashed down the exam-room corridor. "Dr. Riley? We need you right now!"

Before she knew it, Lexie was on an exam bed, staring up at the white drop ceiling in the small emergency bay recently added to the clinic. Martha pressed her fingertips to Lexie's wrist, took her pulse, then checked her blood pressure. Kegan came around the curtain, concern etched along the lines of his face as he removed the stethoscope from around his neck. "What's going on, Lexie?"

"No big deal." She forced a smile.

"Hey, I decide what's a big deal and what's not in this clinic, okay?"

Lexie nodded. "My heart feels funny, like it's missing a beat every once in a while. It's hard to breathe—my chest is tight."

"When did this start?" He looked over the things Martha had jotted on Lexie's chart.

"About ten minutes ago."

"And what were you doing?"

"I'd just gotten off the phone."

"Sit up for me." Kegan helped her up, then warmed the metal end of the stethoscope against his palm. "Was there something about this phone call that upset you?"

She shook her head. "Not really."

Kegan snorted. "That didn't seem convincing to me." He made her breathe slow and deep, listening to her lungs and heart. Gradually she began to relax.

"Lungs sound okay, heart not bad. A little fast. But still, better safe than sorry. Martha, get her into a gown and hook her up." He inclined his head toward some sort of machine at the side of the gurney.

"What's that?"

"EKG." He slipped his stethoscope into the pocket of his lab coat.

Sue Ann poked her head around the privacy curtain. "Doc? Your sister is on the phone. She sounds really upset. It's your nephew again."

Kegan sighed. "If you need me," he said to Martha, though his gaze included Lexie, "I can be back here in about ten seconds."

"If that's meant to reassure me," Lexie said, "you just scared the stuffing out of me."

"I'm sure it's nothing major, Lexie. Try to relax." He followed Sue Ann.

Martha produced a gown and helped her remove her shirt and bra. After "gluing" some patches onto her chest, Martha hooked up the machine. "Okay, Lexie, now just lie back and relax."

Soft footsteps on the tile floor announced Kegan's return. "We're good here now, Martha. Would you please go tell Mr. Santos that I'll be in to check on him as soon as I can?"

"Sure." Martha's sneakers barely made a sound as she left the emergency area.

"Everything looks good right now, Lexie," Kegan told her. "Why don't you tell me more about that phone call you had earlier. Who was on the phone?"

"David."

"He's out of town, isn't he? Took Sarah off for some sort of daddy-daughter bonding adventure?"

Lexie opened her eyes, blinked against the fluorescent lights. "How did you—never mind. I should know better than to think anything's a secret in this town."

"There are more secrets in this town than you think. *Your* biggest secret is still safe, I promise."

Lexie coughed hard as her heart fluttered again.

"Okay, saw that," Kegan said, glancing at the readings. "You're not skipping, you're getting in extra beats. So, did David's call upset you?"

She called me Daddy, Lex. "No. Not really."

Kegan studied the machine for a minute, then looked back at her. "That's not what this says. This says it did. Makes a pretty good lie detector at times. But despite that little stress-induced flutter, your heart seems fine, lungs sound clear. How have you been sleeping?" He disconnected the wire leads running to the sticky patches.

Lexie sat up, swinging her legs over the side of the table. "Not too great."

"For how long?"

"Since David came to town. Most nights I get some sleep, but not enough. Last night I didn't sleep at all."

"Because?"

"Because without Sarah there, the house is so empty," she whispered. "*I'm* so empty." She blinked rapidly, not because of the brightness. This time it was the darkness that hurt. Darkness inside her. The bleak outlook of her future.

Kegan sat on a wheeled stool and patted her knee. "Lex. I'm so sorry. You seem to get along well. Is there any chance the two of you could…I don't know, share custody of her?"

"He asked me to marry him."

"Really? Congratulations, that's wonderful news."

"I said no."

"What?" The chair squeaked as Kegan scooted backward an inch. "Why?"

"He doesn't love me. What kind of marriage would that be?"

"Good grief, Lexie, no wonder you're not sleeping, and you're having anxiety attacks. You've got yourself all twisted into knots, don't you?"

She nodded. "I suppose so."

"And have you been dealing with the lack of sleep by dosing yourself with extra caffeine?"

"Yes. I've had a lot more coffee than I usually do."

"That'll do it. Ectopic beats are usually caused by caffeine, anxiety, fatigue and stress. And right now, I'd say you've got all those things going on.

"I'm going to give you some medication that should let you get a good night's rest. Stay off the caffeine. If the extra sleep doesn't help with the breathing and heart fluttering, come back, we'll try something else to take the edge off."

Kegan picked up her chart, tore a piece of blank paper from the back. He drew a line down the center of it, placing a plus in the right column and a minus in the left. "Now, for the stress and anxiety... As your friend, and the guy who delivered Sarah and who's watched you be a wonderful mother to her, let me see if I can't help you think this through a little more. What are the pluses to marrying Sarah's father?"

"Sarah. She's the big one."

"What else? Has to be something else."

"He's a good man," Lexie whispered. "He's been sweet to me all my life."

"Okay." Kegan jotted that down, then handed her the chart. "I'm going to get some medication samples for you. Just toss those patches into the garbage can over there once you get them all off. Get dressed. Then work on the T-chart. I've used the same thing to help me make decisions in the past. Maybe it will clarify things for you."

Early that afternoon, Lexie stared down at the paper

on her nightstand. She'd added more items to the plus column:

He's handsome
Sarah would have two parents
Good chemistry between us/great in bed
Strong character
Smart
Sarah wouldn't have to go to day care
Financial benefits
I love him
I love Sarah and feel lost without her

In the minus column, there were only two items:

He doesn't love me
Pappy needs me

So, did the list mean she should marry him? Because the pluses far outweighed the minuses? Maybe she just needed to think a little harder. He had faults. Heck, he was a man, right? Maybe she should add that to the minus side. Although...there were times when being a man was a very good thing. Her body warmed with the memory of their night spent together in his bed. She already had that one listed in the pluses. Could something be both?

More minuses: stubborn, pigheaded... that probably only counted as one since they were synonyms.

She ran her index finger down the paper.

What was she thinking? This was how David would

make an important decision, with his head, not his heart. She crumpled up the paper, tossing it toward the small waste can in the corner. It hit the edge and bounced to the floor.

She'd followed her heart when it had told her to run to protect Sarah. If she'd made a logical chart like this, listing all the minuses of running away, she'd have stayed.

Lexie sighed. Obviously there was still more dreamer in her than she wanted to admit. She'd trust her heart when it came to Sarah and David. Now she just needed to know what it had to say.

The whine of an engine signaled a vehicle easing into the driveway. Lexie rose from the bed to peer out the side window. Two men climbed from a rust-spotted, green Volkswagen van. Each collected a small suitcase from the sliding side door. Great. Guests. Just what she was in the mood for right now.

SARAH GIGGLED. David grabbed her foot tighter. "Stop squirming. I'm almost done." He dabbed the brush on her little toe. "There. What do you think?" A few telltale smudges surrounded some of the nails. He scraped at them with his finger.

Propped up on pillows against the headboard, she glanced down at her toes. "Good. It really glows in the dark?"

"I don't know. Should we find out?" He rose from the end of the motel bed, then flicked off the light switch by the door.

Twenty faint dots of green danced on the far bed. "Cool!" Sarah waved her hands. "Lookit!"

David chuckled. "I can see it." He flipped the lights back on, causing Sarah to whine in protest. "No, now you've got to get ready for bed so we can watch our movie. Go brush your teeth." She'd changed into her pajamas before their "nail session" or whatever you called it. And she'd even let him help her straighten out the top.

Would wonders never cease?

A few minutes later they both lay propped on Sarah's bed, an animated movie on the television. She rolled onto her side, using his chest as a pillow. Afraid to startle her, he took shallow breaths. Tentatively, he stroked her soft curls.

"Daddy?"

He closed his eyes and smiled. If he lived to be the oldest man on the planet, he'd never get tired of hearing her say that. "Yeah, sport?"

"I had fun today. Not with the police," she quickly clarified. "But shopping with you."

"Me, too. We've still got to find your coat. The waitress at dinner told me about some other stores. We'll try those tomorrow, okay?"

Just the low hum of the cartoon came from the TV. Sarah's back rose and fell evenly beneath his hand. David picked up the remote and turned off the TV. The light faded slowly from the set, the only illumination coming from the bathroom—Sarah insisted it stay on all night long.

Loath to leave the warmth of his child snuggled

against his side, David lay there for a long time. This was perfect.

And yet, a small bit of…loneliness?…prodded him. Lexie.

Perfect would be Lexie snuggled up against his left side.

A whole family. A real family.

The child shifted, sighing in her sleep. "Momma," she murmured.

David rubbed light circles on Sarah's back. "Shh. We'll see her tomorrow."

The thought was like a blast of sunshine in mid-February. *Well, I'll be damned.* He actually missed Lexie, too.

GRIPPING THE PORTABLE phone in her hand, Lexie paced the width of her bedroom, the wooden floorboards cool beneath her bare feet. She eased onto the rug beside the bed. The numbers on the clock blinked to 10:36. She'd been staring at the thing for well over two hours. Her fingers tightened around the hard plastic in her hand. Obviously they weren't going to call her tonight. By this time Sarah was generally sound asleep.

She sighed. It was the first time in Sarah's life she hadn't wished the little one good-night.

Lexie rubbed her knuckles over her eyes. She set the phone down and picked up the little pill Kegan had given her. In the bathroom, she chugged some water. The little white pill went down easily. Back in her room, the emptiness from next door—and inside her—wasn't as easy to deal with. She pulled on a long-sleeved satin nightshirt lined with flannel—perfect for fall Montana nights. She fingered the bottom of a sleeve, picturing Sarah's tiny fingers doing the same.

Sarah loved the smooth fabric. As a baby, she'd clung to a yellow blanket that was trimmed with satin. She'd stroke it whenever she was falling asleep. Though Sarah had given up on "blankie" a few months ago, it was folded and tucked away in the bottom of Lexie's dresser

Lexie crept into Sarah's room and clicked on the night-light. She settled on the edge of the bed, brushing her fingers over the gingham bedspread. On the seam, she found the stitches she'd painstakingly put in to repair the damage that had been in the pretty spread when Sarah found it at a yard sale.

Lexie eased herself down, inhaling Sarah's scent from the pillowcase.

Sugar and spice and everything nice...

That's what little girls were supposedly made of.

Everything nice—hugs and kisses and laughter—sometimes tears—and rainbows and sunshine and love...

Sarah was all that.

Lexie's eyes slid shut, closing out the green glow from the Emerald City light. Life without Sarah meant losing all those wonderful things. Until David had taken Sarah away on this shopping trip, Lexie hadn't realized how big the empty space would be without the little girl in her life.

Marry David. Keep Sarah.

As sleep crawled in like fog around the edges of her brain, those were her last conscious thoughts.

The warmth of keeping Sarah stayed with her, giving her an overwhelming sense of peace.

Her heart had spoken.

COTTON FILLED Lexie's mouth, and her head felt like the Scarecrow's—full of straw. She forced open her eyes, groaning when the bright sunlight hit. She blinked, then glanced around the room, slightly off balance.

The Yellow Brick Road. Gingham bedspread. She'd fallen asleep in Sarah's room.

Bright sunlight? Kegan's wonder pill had done a number on her. She stumbled from the room and headed for a quick, cold shower. Maybe the new guests were late risers.

When she cautiously made her way down the back stairs, she found Pappy on his way out the door. "Took care of breakfast for them young fellers, don't worry about it."

"You did? What did you feed them?"

"Hotcakes and sausage. They loved it." He thumped his chest. "I'm not useless yet, you know. I was baching it here for a few years before you showed up."

Lexie skated across the kitchen floor in her socks, then wrapped her arms around him, catching the faint whiff of his tobacco on his worn coat. "Of course you're not useless. Thank you." She gave him a quick peck on the cheek.

He scoffed, shaking his head, as though he didn't enjoy it when she fussed over him. "You look like hell, Missy. Didn't you take that stuff Doc gave you?"

"Gee, thanks. Yes, I did."

But even after a whole night's sleep, she was dragging. She glanced longingly at the coffee machine and its half-filled glass pot.

"Don't even think about it." Pappy wagged a finger at her. "Doc said no caffeine."

"I'll stay clean if you will."

His blue eyes sparkled with mischief. "I have no idea what you're talking about, gal. But git yourself something good to eat. Mitchell called. He and Sarah are coming back today."

Marry David. Keep Sarah.

Had she really thought that last night? Yes, she had. She couldn't live without her child. "Have fun at the diner, Pap. Tell the guys I said hello."

"I'll do that."

After he left, she fixed some herbal tea, trying to convince herself it would perk her up.

What would marriage to David be like? Would he come to love her later? She sighed. Giving up on love was hard. But Sarah was worth it.

FOOTSTEPS ON the front porch mixed with the low murmur of a man's deep voice. Lexie grabbed her book from the end table and threw herself down on the leather sofa in the library. No point in looking overeager for Sarah's return. She needed to feel David out on a few things, and didn't want him having the upper hand. Or at least, didn't want him *knowing* he had the upper hand.

The front door opened and Lexie rose, sauntering to the archway. "Oh."

The two guests each with a black photography bag in hand, paused on their way to the stairs. "Hi there," said the taller of the pair. "We missed you at breakfast."

The shorter one— Ted? Yes, that was it—frowned. "Yes. At a bed-and-breakfast it usually is customary for the hostess to be present at breakfast."

"Don't mind him," Ryan said. "He's just miffed because everyone in town says you make the greatest baked goods in a hundred-mile radius, and he wanted some."

"I'm very sorry. I'll make it up to you tomorrow morning with fresh cinnamon rolls. My doctor gave me some new medication and it knocked me for a loop."

"Understandable. Even bed-and-breakfast hostesses are only human." Ryan grinned. He jerked his head back toward the front door. "Love the decorations."

"Thanks."

Ted scowled. "Are you just going to stand here and make time with her, or are we taking this stuff upstairs?"

"I suppose we'll have to take this stuff upstairs." Ryan spoke to Ted, but his eyes never left Lexie. "But once we get it stashed, I'd like you to tell us more about the house, how you transformed it into the B&B, the family history, all that good info."

Lexie nodded. "Sure. I'll be down here in the library."

Old books and newspaper clippings spread across the coffee table several hours later. Lexie educated the two men about the town and house. The back door slammed, and Sarah's voice filled the air. "Momma!"

Lexie jumped from the sofa. "Excuse me, gentlemen, but that's my little girl." Lexie flew down the hallway, pulling up short at the dining room, trying to compose herself. She forced herself to walk slowly into the kitchen.

"Momma! Look at my new coat!" Sarah rushed across the room.

Bending her knees to squat lower, Lexie opened her arms and enfolded the child. "I missed you, baby."

"I missed you, too, Momma." Sarah wiggled from her embrace and smoothed a hand down the front of a purple coat. "Look. And see?" She stroked white fake fur that surrounded the hood, which she had pulled up over her head.

"It's beautiful, baby. But is it really that cold out?"

The back door had opened again, and David, arms overloaded with shopping bags, trudged in. He dumped his burdens next to another set of boxes and bags already on the table. "No, it's not that cold yet. But she wanted to wear it like that. That coat was hell to find, let me tell you."

"Daddy," Sarah admonished. "Don't swear."

Lexie rocked back on her heels. Although David had mentioned Sarah calling him Daddy during the police incident, she hadn't realized that meant the child had taken to doing it all the time. And hearing it for herself... "Geez, did you guys leave anything for the other shoppers?"

Sarah giggled. "Of course, Momma. We got stuff for you, too. And—" she turned to glance at David and lowered her voice "—Daddy got a special surprise."

"He did, huh?" Lexie rose and went to the table, looking over some of the labels on the shopping bags. Sure enough, not one of them looked as if it came from a thrift store.

"You didn't have to get me anything," she said to him.

He grinned, and her stomach got all squishy. Those dimples should have been registered with the FBI. "Yeah, we did."

"So, where's the special surprise?"

"You have to close your eyes," David told her.

"And promise to say yes, Momma. Please?" Sarah clutched her hands together, begging.

"Uh-oh. I'm not sure I like the sound of that."

"Stop worrying, Lex. It's something every kid should have. Something I always said my kid would have." David waved his hands at her. "Now, close your eyes and I'll be right back."

She sighed. "All right." She closed her eyes as the back door heralded his departure. *Something every kid should have and he'd always said his kid would?*

Two parents? Had he gotten her a ring in the hopes of persuading her to marry him?

"Remember, say yes, Momma," Sarah whispered.

A fresh blast of cool air, along with another house-rocking slam of the door announced his return. "Okay, Lex, put your hands together and hold them out in front of you. Don't drop it."

Excitement thrummed through her. Okay, so maybe he didn't love her, but maybe there *was* a little romance in him, surprising her with a ring. And if he asked her again, before she told him she'd decided to go ahead and marry him, then that put her in the top position, and maybe he'd be willing...

"Here you go."

Something warm and fuzzy filled her cupped hands. David's large palm supported hers. Lexie opened her eyes to find a puppy blinking up at her. Its wiry gray hair tickled her fingers and its tiny black-button nose twitched. Suddenly its mouth opened in a huge yawn, revealing a pink tongue and needle-sharp puppy teeth.

"Can I keep him, Momma? Please? I named him Toto."

Lexie sighed. Sarah's eager face would be too hard to resist, so she swung her glance to David, who stood so close she could smell the crisp fall air clinging to his jacket, mixing with his spicy aftershave. "Sarah knows the rules of the bed-and-breakfast, David. No pets allowed. Guests could have allergies."

He shrugged. "I know, she told me, but I figured it wouldn't be for long, so, what the heck?"

Wouldn't be for long? The words struck hard. Lexie straightened. *We'll see about that, buster.*

"Can I keep him, Momma?" Sarah shrugged out

of her purple coat, dropping it on the floor and reaching for the pup.

"That's not how you treat the beautiful new coat your father bought you. Hang it on your peg."

The tiny dog whimpered. Lexie lifted him higher. "Toto, huh? He does sort of look like a Toto."

"Except he's a she," David whispered as Sarah picked her coat from the floor and went to hang it up. "I tried explaining, but Sarah didn't want to hear it. This is Toto, and that's that."

"How could you do this to me?" Lexie whispered back. "Why not just wait until you got to Erie to get her a dog?"

He lifted his shoulders again and another huge grin filled his face. "She smiled at me, Lex. Do you know what that does to me?"

Oh, yes. She knew exactly what it did to him. Sarah took after her daddy in many ways. "It's the dimples."

He nodded. "Yep."

"Can I have him, Momma?" Sarah held her hands out. "I wanna show Pappy. He's gonna love Toto, just like me."

"I still haven't decided if she can stay or not."

"Oh, Momma! Please?" Sarah's lower lip quivered. "I *need* him! He's so cute."

"Who is taking care of this dog?"

"I am," Sarah said.

"Yeah, right." She stared at David. "Well?"

"I will be one hundred percent responsible for the dog."

"If it piddles on the floor?"

"I'll clean it up."

"If it chews up my furniture?"

"I'll fix it or replace it."

"If my guests are allergic?"

"I'll pay for the canceled reservations." David scooped the puppy from her hands and held her up near his face. "Satisfied?" The tiny pink tongue darted out and licked David's nose, making him chuckle and Sarah giggle.

She'd lost the battle even before Toto had entered the house. Winning the war was more important. "Okay, she can stay."

"Yiiippiee!" Sarah danced in place, waving her arms around.

The puppy trembled in David's hands. "Easy there, sport. You're scaring Toto. Remember, she's just a baby."

"Oh. Sorry." Sarah stilled, then slowly reached out. "Can I have him now? I wanna show Pappy."

"Her," David reminded, placing the dog carefully into the child's hands.

"Right. Her." Sarah hugged the pup, giggling when Toto licked her face. She carefully strolled from the kitchen, leaving Lexie and David alone.

David unbuttoned his coat, draped it over the back of a chair, surveying the piles on the table. "I had no idea we'd bought so much until I saw it all together."

"You'll spoil her," Lexie murmured.

"Isn't that what dads do?"

"No, usually I think that's the grandparents' job."

"We got a few things for you, too. Does that mean I'm spoiling you, too?" His mouth twitched.

"No." But...a part of her wanted him to. "You don't have to buy her love, David." *Or mine, either.*

"Is that what you think I'm doing? Hey, I missed out on buying anything for her for four years. I don't think this—" he swept his arms in the direction of the table "—even begins to make up for that. I didn't get her first pair of shoes, but I bought her three this trip. I bought her a new coat and a puppy." He folded his arms over his chest. "When you think about it, I'm still way in the hole."

Uh-oh. She tried to look mollified. "I'm sorry, David. I guess I'm just...a little jealous, that's all."

"You're jealous of me? You were here for her first steps and her first word. I missed all of that. I'm jealous of you, Lexie. We made a lot of progress, but right now she's still more your child than mine. And..." His lips tightened against each other, as though he didn't want to let the words out.

"And what?"

The radiator running along the wall clinked and hissed, filling the silence of his hesitation. Finally, he confessed. "And that hurts."

"Oh, David." Lexie went to him, wrapping her arms around his waist, hugging him. Beneath all his bluster, he was a sensitive soul. And she had to remember how much this—how much *she*—had hurt him, that the pain went both ways here. After a moment, he responded, drawing her closer.

David held her tight, her warmth soothing, inviting.

Her compassion unnerved him. No matter what he did or said, Lexie proved time and time again what an incredible person she was.

Woman. With her soft body pressed against him like that, *person* wasn't the right word. Incredible *woman*.

Loosening his grip, he leaned back, waited for her to look up at him. When she did, he bent forward, brushing his lips over her cheek before moving to her mouth.

He took his time, nibbling, caressing, coaxing, in no rush to take the kiss deeper. His fingers stroked her spine, traced the curve of her waist.

She cupped his head, urged him on, her mouth open, begging for more. Her tongue slipped past his lower lip, stirring fire that flashed through his body. Determined to give her what she sought, he changed the tone, hungry, needy, wanting. "Lex…"

She froze, stiff in his arms, mouth no longer pliable beneath his. She placed her palms on his chest and pushed him away.

"What? What's wrong?"

"Shh."

The sound of raised male voices came from the front of the house, followed by the yip of a terrified puppy. Something crashed. One male voice cursed.

"Who the hell—"

Lexie was already rushing down the hallway, David one step behind her. Pappy stood in the library archway, Sarah clinging to his legs, face pressed against the old man's jeans, sobbing. A tall, lean guy stood in the center of the room, Toto in his hands, petting the dog and crooning calming words as he glared at a short blond man who was standing on the sofa, one hand extended as if to ward off the vicious beast. Books and papers were scattered across the floor.

"What's going on?" David demanded.

"Momma!"

Lexie scooped Sarah into her arms. "I'd like to know that myself."

"Keep it away from me!" sofa-guy said. "Oh, I can feel it already." He lifted his hands to his face. "I'm puffing up." He jumped from his perch and dashed toward the door. "Ryan, pack our stuff, we are out of here."

He skidded to a quick stop in the archway. "This is supposed to be a pet-free hostelry. Look at me."

The guy's red-rimmed eyes watered. David had never seen such a quick allergic reaction to an animal. "You're not going to stop breathing or anything, are you?" he asked. "The medical clinic is just across the street. Maybe we should take you there."

"No, thanks." The man stopped at the front door. "But don't think you're getting a good report out of me. I'll be in the van. Hurry up, Ryan. Change your shirt and wash your hands before you come out, too." The house quivered as the door slammed.

"Oh, nuts," Lexie murmured.

"He don't like Toto." Sarah sniffled.

"Why 'oh nuts'?" David asked.

The other guy crossed the library, extended Toto to

David. "Cute dog. Sorry about Ted. He tends toward histrionics where his allergies are concerned."

"You guys are my mystery guests, aren't you?"

"Afraid so." He looked at Lexie with a combination of apology and something else that made David want to slug him.

"Shhhh—oot."

David knew she'd changed the end of the word out of deference to the child in her arms. "What's a mystery guest?" David took the dog, and the man headed up the stairs two at a time.

"Now do you see what I meant? Why I had this rule? Damn it, David, you can't fix this by paying their night's fee. It's much bigger than that."

"Don't swear, Momma," Sarah said, lifting her tear-stained face from Lexie's neck. "I'm sorry. Toto's sorry, too. Right, Toto?" She turned to look at the dog.

"It's not your fault, baby."

"You still haven't told me what a mystery guest is."

"Somebody from a bed-and-breakfast magazine Missy's tryin' to impress," Pappy said. "And I don't think we did too great, huh?"

Lexie shook her head. "No. I don't think we did." The cold fury in her eyes as she glared at David over Sarah's head clearly said she wished to heaven he'd never found them.

CHAPTER FIFTEEN

LATER THAT NIGHT, after Sarah was tucked safely in bed and sound asleep, David followed the whir of the sewing machine into the dining room. He balanced a bowl carefully on top of a napkin in the palm of either hand. Lexie sat at the far end of the table, head bent over the fabric, feeding it through the machine. "I didn't know you could sew."

She glanced up, the machine's chug-chug noise slowing to a halt. "Some of the ladies in town taught me. Makes the funds go a bit further. I made all the curtains in the house."

"That's great." He hefted the bowls. "I brought a peace offering."

With a wary look in her eyes, she carefully laid the fabric that had been draped into her lap alongside the sewing machine, then came to join him. She glanced down at the contents of the bowl. "Drown-your-sorrows sundaes?"

"Yeah. I know you'd probably rather drown me right now, but I just thought..." Actually, he had no idea what he'd thought. "I'm really sorry for the mystery-guest disaster, Lex."

Picking up her spoon, she swirled it through the

sticky syrup. "You forgot the whipped cream and shaved chocolate."

"I had to improvise. There's no brownie on the bottom, either. I used chocolate chip cookies."

"Hmm. Sounds interesting." She scooped out an overflowing spoonful and put it into her mouth.

"Well?"

She nodded. "Not bad. Not as good as my version, but not bad." Another scoop, another nod.

David started on his sundae, not that he really felt like eating it. But he wanted something to reconnect them. Ever since the Toto fiasco this afternoon, she'd felt far away from him. Not what he wanted.

"I-I've been thinking about your proposal," she said quietly.

He dropped his spoon, spattering vanilla ice cream all over the table. "You have?" He scrubbed at the white blobs with his napkin.

"Yes."

Cautious optimism flowed through him. "And?"

"Not that I'm saying I will, understand, but *if* I marry you, then..."

"Then what, Lexie?"

"We have to live here in this house." Her words tumbled out, running into one another.

He'd already figured that. The new Lexie thrived in this community, and it had been Sarah's only home. He could relocate part of his business here without a problem. After all, he'd already been working here for almost three weeks. Technology made the world a lot smaller, and that was what his business was all about. "Done."

"Pappy needs me. It's not fair to leave him after all he's done for Sarah and me, and—" She stopped, mouth gaping for a moment before she closed it and swallowed hard. "Did you say 'done'? As in okay?"

"That's what I said. If you want to live here, that's fine with me. I like this town. My business can move—that's not a problem."

Her eyes widened and she eased back from the table. For a long while she just stared at him.

"What's making you reconsider, Lex?" he asked.

She rose from her chair, moving to the far end of the table. She fingered the blue-and-white gingham material. "You know." She turned to look at him again. "I love her, David. She's my whole life, and if you take her away from me, I don't think I'll survive."

The light from the chandelier reflected off the moisture welling in her eyes.

"Don't say that." He shot from his seat, at her side in a few strides. Cupping her face in his hands, he thumbed away the first tears. "And don't do this. Just tell me that you'll marry me so we can give Sarah a real family."

She blinked hard. "I will," she whispered. "I love her. And...I love you."

Her words buzzed through his head. "You do?"

She nodded. "My mom was right. I've loved you forever, I think. That's why I gave you Sarah."

She loves me.

His brain went off-line. The old house creaked.

From the next room, David could hear the low roar of the television as the old man watched some program.

Fresh tears spilled down her face, onto his hands. "I'm sorry. I shouldn't have said that—"

He did the only thing he could think of. He leaned forward and kissed her gently, shutting off her apology.

Lexie Jacobs, mother of his child, fabulous woman and all he could ever want in a mate, loved him.

And he loved her.

A wave of panic raised goose bumps along his arms. Could it be? And would he be as blind this time, or could he keep his eyes wide open? This was Lexie. The girl next door. He knew all there was to know about her. No crazy surprises, as there had been with Angela. Lexie was a compassionate, warm woman, who cared so much about his daughter she was willing to sacrifice her final dream.

Warmth spread through his chest, that funny constricting feeling taking his breath. He cleared his throat. "I love you, too, Lex." As soon as he said it, he knew it was true.

For the second time that day, she stiffened in his arms, muscles going completely rigid. She pushed away from him, shaking her head. "Don't, David. Don't be condescending. I don't need to hear empty words. I know what I'm getting myself into."

"They're not empty words, Lex. I wouldn't do that to you."

Her eyes grew large, and she stepped back. "Stop

it. This is hard enough on me. Please, don't do this to me.''

"Do what? Love you?"

"Don't pretend. We both know you're a head person. You said you'd never love anyone ever again. That it makes you too blind. I can accept that."

"But you can't accept that I might actually love you?" He shook his head. "I will never understand women."

"L-let's talk about what you expect from our marriage."

"Expect?"

"Like, do you want a prenuptial? Will we have more children?" Her face flushed and she glanced down.

"Do you want more children?" The idea of sharing her bed, making more babies with her, this time the usual way, sent heat coursing through his body. He stepped toward her.

She nodded as she stepped back. "I do."

"One that's really yours this time?" He moved in her direction again.

Her eyebrows tightened in the center of her forehead and her eyes sparked. "Sarah *is* really mine, David. I can't believe you don't get that after all this! Her genetics don't matter to me."

"Just checking." He edged her closer to the wall. He smiled as she backed against the door frame. An amazing woman. His woman. "What does this tell you?" Pinning her between the wall and his body, he pressed against her, claiming her mouth in a way to leave no doubt in her mind. He drew his lips down her throat, nipping at her collarbone, tracing his tongue along the hollow, dipping just below the neckline of her shirt.

She moaned and tipped her head, exposing the soft skin farther. "David." His name came out as a breathy little sigh that kicked his own pulse a notch higher.

He lifted his head. "God, Lex. I'd give up coffee in exchange for some of you every day."

One corner of her mouth twitched. She lowered her head and opened her eyes. "Now, *that* I can almost believe."

He leaned close to her ear. "Believe all of it." He nibbled on her lobe, delighting in the shudder she gave. Still wedged against her, her reaction sent the most fantastic sensations through him. He leaned away again so he could see her face. "You know what I want, Lex. Your family has been my ideal ever since I was a kid. That's what I want." He grinned at her. "Hey, we've even got the dog already. And the white picket fence."

She rolled her eyes.

He let the smile fade. "I want it all, Lexie. Sarah, you, other kids...and I only want one prenuptial agreement."

She inhaled deeply—he was willing to bet she didn't know how that felt on his part as her breasts rose and pressed harder against his chest—as if steeling herself. "Okay, what is it?"

"You believe that I love you."

"And until I do?"

He stepped away from her. A cold chill ran through the skin that had pressed against her without her body heat to keep it warm. "I won't marry you."

"What?" she shrieked. "Okay, so I believe you. I love you, you love me." The irony of the words struck her, and she launched into the rest of the song from the children's television show.

"Don't. I'm not willing to settle, Lex. And I'm not willing to let you, either. Not now that I know how we both feel. You said you wanted a guy who loves you. You got it. It's everything or nothing."

"And until I believe you're not just being condescending?"

"I'm going to do everything I can to convince you I'm telling the truth. I love you, Lexie Jacobs. I'm going to marry you. But not until you believe me."

He smiled. "And now, I have some work to do. Good night." He turned abruptly, leaving her standing against the door frame, kiss-swollen mouth partially open.

DAVID SHOVED his hands deeper into the pockets of his sheepskin-lined coat and paced the length of the storefront again. He checked his watch. Nine minutes after ten. The sign hanging in the Sapphire Mine's front door posted hours from ten till five.

They were late.

And he was running out of time.

A week since his revelation, Lexie still wasn't buying his attempts so far. The pop-up declarations of his love on her computer had been ignored. The never-ending loop of "I Love You, Lexie Jacobs" on her monitor had only made her demand he fix her computer *immediately* so she could use it, and admonitions to keep his hands off it in the future.

David pulled out his cell phone and flipped it open. Sure enough, the green light indicated he had a signal. He'd have to remember that. Certain spots in town worked, others didn't. He chose a number from the directory. The voice that answered sounded groggy. "Kenny, you sound like hell, man."

"No kidding. How I'm supposed to get any work done is beyond me. The baby doesn't sleep for more than two hours at a time. Both Jess and I are slowly losing our minds. Thank God for Mom. She comes over in the afternoon so Jess can have a nap."

"Enjoy it. The years go by very fast." Hard to believe in just over a week Sarah would turn four.

Kenny grunted. "You didn't call to find out about my baby. How's my sister doing? Marc is still way pissed at you."

"Big surprise there. Kenny, I've, uh, run into a complication."

"Don't like the sounds of that. David, I swear, if you hurt her, Marc and I will both be on the next plane out there, and this time we'll take turns punching you out."

"I'm not going to hurt her, Kenny. I love her."

"What? Marc said he hammered you because you didn't love her. What gives?"

David sighed. "Suffice it to say I've seen the light. The only problem is, she doesn't believe me."

Kenny laughed. "Sounds like our Lexie all right. But why are you calling me?"

"I'm out of ideas for how to convince her. I'll take any suggestions you've got."

"And you're asking me?" A loud snort echoed through the line. "Oh, Jess will love that. Besides, Marc says Lex's changed a lot in the time she's been gone. Said he barely recognized her. I don't think I can help you except to say remember she loved all those books with knights and stuff. Halloween's just two days away. Why don't you dress up as a knight and sweep her off her feet?"

"No way. Talk about cheesy and cheap. And cliché. She'd definitely find that condescending. Besides, I already have a pirate costume. Got something else?"

A woman flipped over the sign in the jewelry store and waved her hand at David. He smiled and held up one finger.

"Nope, sorry. But whatever you do, make it good. I'd like to see you, her and Sarah together as a family. It just feels right."

"I know what you mean. Thanks, Ken."

"Give my sister a hug for me."

"I will." David turned the cell phone off and stashed it in his pocket, heading into the store. Hopefully at some point soon, Lexie would give him reason to need a ring.

"PARK THERE, right next to Pappy." Lexie directed David to a space in the firehall parking lot, which was brightly lit up by floodlights.

"Okay." Shutting off the SUV, he flipped down his eye patch. "Arrgg. Are ya ready to do some looting and get some treasure, mateys?"

"Daddy, you look so cute." Sarah giggled in the back seat of the Blazer.

"Thanks, sport." He lowered his voice. "I feel like an idiot. Think I can get away with not taking off my coat?"

"Nope." Lexie sighed. "And neither can I."

David shut off the SUV and pocketed the keys, then glanced over at her. "I can't wait to see you in that dress, you know."

"She looks bee-u-tiful, just like I knowed she would," Sarah piped up.

"I don't think it's fair that you got to see her and I didn't." David leaned over the seat and grabbed Sarah's knee, sending the child into a fit of giggles. "Come on, let's go trunk-or-treat."

Lexie waited while David got out and went to the back seat, unbuckling Sarah. He'd become a natural at operating the booster safety seat. Just like he'd become a natural with Sarah. Even with the Barbies.

A great dad. Just as she'd known he would be.

"You coming? Or are you just going to sit there all night with that dreamy expression on your face?" David asked her as he helped Sarah from the high vehicle.

She scowled at him. "I do not have a dreamy expression on my face."

"Oh, that's right. I forgot, you're practical now. A

woman with her feet on the ground and no crazy dreams in her head. No romance in your soul."

Lexie heard the tightly controlled pain in his voice as he tossed her own words back at her. The ones she'd spoken when he'd offered flowers and chocolates, her favorite chocolates, as a matter of fact, and she'd called the move too predictable and not what the new Lexie would want. And when he'd asked what she did want, she'd shrugged. "Sarah," she'd said.

"You'll get her," he'd replied. "As soon as I convince you I mean it when I say I love you."

"I believe you already. Let's get married."

But he'd known the truth—she didn't believe him.

"Momma, come on! All the other people are ready."

"All right, baby." Lexie slid from the Blazer, smoothing her long gray coat over her legs. The filmy dress, more appropriate for a fairy than Glinda, certainly wasn't cut out for Halloween weather in Montana. Most costumes weren't, unless you went dressed up as a skier or a snowmobiler. But that was one of the reasons the party at the firehall was such an important bash. They could show off costumes without freezing.

Pappy unfolded a webbed lawn chair, setting it alongside the lowered tailgate of his ancient truck. He eased himself into it, a large plastic bowl of chocolate bars at his feet. "You run along and take the young'un round to get her treats. I'll stay here and hand out ours."

"Hey! The truck looks great. You've outdone yourself this year, Lexie." Ray Henderson, owner and one-man operator of the *Gazette,* the town's weekly newspaper, lifted his camera. "Can I get a shot for the paper? That scarecrow is fantastic."

"Sure." Lexie climbed into the truck. David hoisted Sarah up, then clambered up himself. Once they all stood on the tailgate, they removed their coats, tossing them to Pappy. In the middle of the truck, fastened to a pole, hung the scarecrow they'd created. He wore one of Pappy's old flannel shirts and a torn pair of jeans. Straw stuck out of the sleeves and pant legs, and a pair of old battered work boots made the scarecrow's feet. His head was crafted from a burlap sack.

Lexie straightened the crown on her head, adjusting the bobby-pin anchors. David put the parrot on his shoulder.

"Okay, pirate, you go over there," Ray directed. "Straighten your bird. Fairy, let's have you on the other side."

"She's Glinda, the Good Witch, not a fairy," Sarah informed him.

"Sorry. I'll make sure I get it right in the article, okay?" He smiled at Sarah. "Dorothy, I want you right in the middle. That's it. Hold up your wicker basket. Turn a little bit that way. Good."

Lexie gave Ray a grateful glance. Trust the compassionate man to make sure he shot Sarah's left side.

A breath-stealing breeze flapped the gauzy end of her dress around her ankles, and Lexie shuddered. Goose bumps sprouted along her arms and the hair on them stood straight up. That should look attractive. "Hurry up, Ray."

"Yeah," Sarah shouted. "I need treats!"

"Everybody smile." His camera flashed. "One more."

With the pictures done, Sarah leaped from the end of the truck into Pappy's waiting arms. David jumped down next. Lexie carefully navigated across the strewn hay. The pumps she'd borrowed from Nola were already killing her, and she wasn't about to have Ray capture a picture of the Good-Witch-turned-klutz falling out of the back of the pickup.

David stretched out his arms to her. She laid her hands on his shoulders and moved forward. He grabbed her by the waist, slowly sliding her down his chest. Suddenly the chill in the air vanished, replaced with heat from his body—and hers. She glanced up at him. "David, I—"

"That dress is a knockout on you, Lex. Just like I predicted. My daughter has great taste."

She arched an eyebrow at him. "*Your* daughter?"

"Okay, our daughter." He leaned forward and kissed her, sending her heart into that skip-extra-beat pattern.

Obviously I'm still not getting enough sleep.

"Oooooo, look at Miss Lexie," came a sharp little voice. "K-i-s-s-i-n-g."

Lexie put her hands on David's chest and pushed, but he struggled to hold her close. "Don't, Lex," he whispered. "Don't get too far away. Not yet."

The mixed panic and fading lust in his voice made

her suddenly aware of just how tight his black biker pants were. She eased back in his embrace and turned her head. "Hello, Fallyn. Have you gotten a lot of treats?"

A silver-garland halo bobbed as the child nodded her head, holding up a pillowcase for Lexie's inspection. "Mom says I can go around twice if I want."

Pappy leaned forward in his chair and dropped a chocolate bar into the fabric sack. "There ya go."

"That's not fair," Sarah said, zipping her coat. "You should only take one." She looked up at Lexie. "Right, Momma?"

"I think one is enough, yes. But I'm not Fallyn's momma and I don't make the rules for her."

And she wouldn't make the rules for Sarah, either, if she couldn't get David to marry her. Why didn't men have a built-in love barometer that was as clear as their lust barometer?

"That's the only halo that child will ever wear," David murmured into her ear. "A monster of some sort really would have been a more appropriate costume."

Lexie coughed to cover up her laughter.

He cleared his throat and let go of her. "My black beard makeup smudged onto you. Sorry." Using his fingertips, David brushed at her face. "There. I think it's time we took Sarah around, how about you?" He picked up his jacket from the tailgate and slung it on, then held out Lexie's, helping her into it.

"Yeaaah! Let's go!" Sarah grabbed for David's

hand and started dragging him off while Lexie still fumbled with the buttons on her long woolen coat.

"Catch up with us," he called back over his shoulder as they merged into the crowd of people milling around the parking lot.

"There goes my baby, Pap," Lexie said. "And here I am, left behind. Alone."

"Aw, Missy. You ain't ever gonna be alone. I'm here."

Lexie shot him a quivering smile. "I'm very grateful for that, Pappy."

"I'm the one who ought to worry about you going off with that young man, leaving me alone."

Lexie knelt down in front of him. "I won't leave you, Pappy. I promise. I already told David if he marries me, we have to live here. In Montana. In the Bed-and-breakfast."

"You'd do that for me?"

"Of course." She caressed his whiskery cheek. "I love you, Pappy. You've been there for me, and I'll do the same for you. We're family. Family's not about blood, it's about love, right?"

"You know it, gal." He lifted her hand and placed a quick kiss in her palm. "Now run along. I'll see you inside later."

She smiled at him with a tenderness that warmed his aching bones and headed off in the direction the young'un had gone with her father.

John chatted with his neighbors, accepting their praise of the truck's decorations on Missy's behalf. The pile of chocolate bars got smaller and smaller as he doled them out to the kids. But all the while, he kept thinking about Missy. And Sarah. And David.

It seemed it was long past time for him and junior to have a chat.

IN THE FRONT of the hall, the band began playing "Monster Mash." On one side, near what David assumed to be the kitchen, a long table offered all kinds of treats and several punch bowls. Women carried steaming casserole dishes to the tables against the far wall.

"I have to go make sure they put out my graveyard," Lexie said to him. "I worked for hours on that and want to make sure they didn't leave it in the fridge." The special dessert consisted of chocolate pudding, whipped topping and Oreo cookies he and Sarah had crushed into crumbs. Then she'd used oval cookies to create tombstones in the "dirt."

Connor, wrapped in white bandages up to his neck, ran over and grabbed Sarah's hand. "Can Sarah come with me and play pin the nose on the pumpkin?"

Lexie looked to David. "It's okay with me."

"Please, Daddy?"

"Well—" he glanced around the room "—I guess. Meet me by the dinner table when you're done, okay?"

Sarah nodded, and hand in hand with Connor, skipped away, her dress bouncing merrily.

"How come she's not standing here with her face pressed into one of our legs?" David asked Lexie.

"Do you see anyone staring at her? These aren't

strangers, David. Many of these people have known her since the day she was born. No one's going to gawk at her. Well, except maybe Fallyn, and Sarah's learning how to cope with her." She waved toward the kitchen. "I'm going to check the situation out. I'll meet you over there, okay?"

"Sure." He watched her move away, the light pink dress swishing. The nipped waist accentuated her form. She'd curled her dark hair into tight ringlets, and he was tempted to pull on them and watch them spring back.

To gather them all in his hands and press his face in them, enjoy the softness, her softness. Inhale the sweet floral scent of her...

Damn it, thinking like that was going to get him into a lot of trouble in his already-too-tight pants.

Female laughter made him turn around. Nola, dressed as a living replica of Sarah's rag doll, broke into a big smile. "Don't you look yummy. Care to plunder me?"

David shuffled his feet. "A lovely offer, but I'm a one-woman pirate."

"Good thing. I'd have to poke out your other eye if you took me up on the offer. Where's Lexie?"

David pointed toward the kitchen. "She went that way."

"Thanks." Nola headed off, glancing over her shoulder at him once and giggling again.

A hand grabbed his elbow. Pappy stood at his side. "Been lookin' for you."

"Why? Is something wrong?"

The old man let go of his arm. "You tell me. What are your intentions toward my girl?"

David arched an eyebrow—a mistake because the hairs got caught in the elastic of his patch—but he didn't comment on the "my girl" bit. "Look, you don't have to worry about losing Lexie. I've already promised her we can live here."

"So, why ain't we planning a wedding already? We can announce it tonight."

Damn. Well, if anyone knew how to reach her, it would be Pappy. He knew her better than anyone else did. "I can't convince her that I really love her. I want her to know that I'm marrying her because I do, not just because of Sarah."

"Ah." He fingered the whiskers on his chin. "What have you tried?"

"The usual stuff. Love notes on her computer. Flowers. Her favorite candy."

Pappy shook his head. "Boy, that's courtship stuff. That's to woo a woman, not convince her you love her."

"I'm open to all suggestions at this point."

The old man's expression softened. "Years ago, I had these autographed baseballs my cousin from New Jersey got me. A Babe Ruth and a Lou Gehrig. Well, it was Doris and my anniversary, and I wanted to git her somethin' special, you know? But the ranch—this was back when we lived out on the ranch—weren't doin' too well that year. So, I sold them balls to buy her a pair of pearl earrings to match a necklace that had belonged to her momma. And you know what?"

David shook his head.

"She'd sold the necklace to buy me a special custom-made display case for my baseballs. It was made from mahogany and had a velvet lining." The old man's smile trembled. "We had us a laugh over that. Doris said it was just like that story 'Gift of the Magi.' She wore them earrings every Sunday till the day she died. Called them her love earrings 'cause they proved how much I loved her." A whisper of a sigh escaped him. "I buried her wearin' them, too. I still got the display case."

David tried to unravel the threads of the story. "So, exactly how does that apply to me and Lexie?"

Pappy shrugged. "Figger it out."

CHAPTER SIXTEEN

"Momma." Sarah tugged on Lexie's dress. Dinner had long since been completed, and the second rounds of games for the children begun. Soon the band—Rico and the Mudsharks, a group of local guys, a few of whom taught at the high school—would start the dance music.

"What, baby?" Lexie leaned down.

"Give these to Daddy." In the center of Sarah's palm she held a little packet of M&M's. "I winned them."

"Those are you favorites."

"I know. He likes them, too. I want to share."

"That's very sweet, baby. I think that will make your daddy very happy. But I think he'll be happier if you give them to him." Sarah caught David's eye as he looked up from what appeared to be an intent discussion with Nola, Pappy and Kegan. David grinned at her, the potent effects magnified by the eye patch and stubble beard. He certainly made a great rogue. She'd walk the plank for him anytime.

"Will you come, too?" Sarah slipped her hand into Lexie's.

"Of course I will. Are you having fun?" Lexie led

the child around small clusters of people, nodding to them. Didi Ericson, the owner of the local jewelry store, waved to her, and Lexie returned the greeting.

"Yep. But it would be funner if Toto came."

Lexie laughed. "Sorry, no dogs allowed."

David watched as they came across the hall. He said, "Here are my two best girls."

Sarah let go of Lexie's fingers and went to stand in front of David. Waving her hand, she motioned for him to scoot down.

He bent over. "What can I do for you, sport?"

She extended the offering. "I winned these and I want you to have them."

"That's nice, honey. But I thought you told me those are your favorite chocolates?"

"But you like them, too. I want you to have them."

"Why?"

"Because…" In a sudden fit of shyness, Sarah bent her head to study her feet. "'Cause you're my daddy and I love you."

David's mouth opened, then shut again. He quickly looked from Sarah to Lexie, and she cursed the patch that made his face harder to read. But the shimmer of tears in his exposed eye was clear.

"Oh, sweetheart." He scooped Sarah up into a bear hug. "I love you, too," he whispered, locking gazes with Lexie. "More than anything. Thank you."

Lexie smiled, hoping the quivering of her lips wasn't obvious. The moment was the culmination of his dream. David Mitchell's little girl loved him.

That was how it should be.

Lexie's stomach lurched, and she was pretty sure it wasn't because of Mrs. Casterlin's potato salad. Why did she feel so miserable? Like she'd lost something? Sarah still loved her as well.

"Lexie? Are you okay?" David held Sarah in his arms, the little one's head slumped against his shoulder, knocking the parrot sideways. Her eyelids drooped. Too much excitement had worn her out.

"Actually, I'm not feeling that well. And it looks like Sarah's ready for bed. Would you mind if we went home?"

Kegan sidled next to her and clamped his fingers along her wrist, glancing at his watch.

She yanked her hand back. "Not like that, Kegan. I'm just a little under the weather, that's all. Probably something I ate."

"You didn't eat the potato salad, did ya, Missy?"

"Maybe you should let him check you out, Lex. I heard about what happened while Sarah and I were on our shopping trip." David readjusted his grip on the child.

Lexie glared at Kegan, who held up his hands in mock surrender.

"Don't look at me. I respect doctor-patient confidentiality. Talk to him." Kegan jerked his head in Pappy's direction.

The old man had the good grace to look sheepish. "Now, Missy, don't get your knickers in a knot. I was jest worried about you. Plum forgot he didn't know."

David studied Lexie carefully. Her color had faded

some, but she didn't appear ill. Had Sarah's declaration of love for him upset her?

He tightened his arm around his daughter, her warmth perfect against his chest. "I'm game to go home and get out of this costume."

"Great. Let's go."

As Lexie came closer, he snagged her around the waist with his free hand. "Just one thing. I was really hoping for a slow dance with you tonight, so you have to promise me one at home," he whispered. "After I get this makeup off my face so I don't get it all over you when I kiss you."

She didn't answer him as he ushered his family toward the pile of coats on the table near the doorway.

His family.

God, that felt so right. If only she'd come around…

Sarah's gift had given him the clue that decoded the old man's story. Love was about sacrifice. Putting the other person first, no matter what you had to give up, just as Lexie had sacrificed so much for Sarah. But David didn't know if he could bring himself to follow her example.

Especially now.

MUCH MORE COMFORTABLE in a pair of jeans, long-sleeved denim shirt, bare feet and a washed face, David rapped on Lexie's bedroom door. When she acknowledged him, he stuck his head in. "Did Sarah fall asleep already?"

"Just about. If you hurry you might be able to catch her." Crown already removed, Lexie fumbled with the back of the fairy dress. Despite Sarah's insistence, David couldn't think of Lexie as a witch, good or not. She'd looked more like a fairy princess to him.

"I might need some help with this hook and eye."

"You owe me a dance," he reminded her, entering the room. "And I kind of wanted it to be with you in that dress. Leave it on."

When she stared at him, he added, "Please?"

"Okay. But then you have to wear the eye patch."

"Like that, do you?"

"It does lend a certain…mood."

He flashed a grin at her, then went through the connecting door into Sarah's room. She lay on her left side, one hand tucked beneath her cheek, the other curled under her chin. He knelt on the braided rug alongside the bed. The glow of the green night-light glinted off her hair.

David stroked her curls, his chest tight.

Her eyelids flicked open, and a small smile lifted her mouth. "Daddy."

"I came to say good night." He leaned over and kissed her forehead. "Tonight was really special to me, honey. *You* are really special to me. I love you so much."

"More than chocolate?"

"More than chocolate."

"More than Christmas?"

"More than Christmas. More than anything."

Drowsy smile fading, her eyes fluttered closed again.

"Sarah?" He stroked her hair again. "I have to go

back home to Erie. I've got things I need to do there, and your momma needs some space to think about things."

One eye cracked open. "You said you'd never leave me."

The pain in his chest stabbed hotter. "I know. But if you keep me here—" he touched her forehead "—and here—" he tapped her just below the hollow of her throat "—I'll never be gone. And I promise, I'll think about you all the time, and I'll call you every day."

"Will you come back? I don't want you to go, Daddy!" She flung her arms around his neck.

"Shh." He didn't want Lexie overhearing this conversation. Not to mention that if Sarah asked him that again, he'd never be able to go through with it. "I'll see you again, honey. I'm not leaving you forever. Just for a little while."

"What about my birfday? Will you come to my party?"

"I hope so, honey. I hope so."

She released him, sinking back into the pillow. "Sing me asleep, Daddy." She closed her eyes again, sighing deeply.

"Okay, but no making fun of my croaking."

A tiny smile—and her dimple—made a fleeting appearance. He pressed his fingertip to the indentation in her cheek. Very, very softly, he began to sing the song he'd heard Lexie sing many nights. "'You are my sunshine...'"

His voice quivered, and the room blurred. How was he supposed to live without his sunshine?

Sacrifice was the pits.

If there were another way to prove his love to Lexie, he'd do it in a heartbeat. But Sarah's gift of her favorite chocolates and Pappy's story had made it clear—playing the mean ogre who could take away her child wasn't going to prove his love. Maybe—oh, God, he hoped so—by leaving, and giving Sarah to her, freely, she'd understand just how much he loved them both.

His plan *would* work. It had to.

Sarah rolled over onto her back, flinging one arm wide. Her breathing evened out into slumber. He rose to tuck the bedspread around her sides, then dropped kisses on her forehead and both cheeks, ending with the birthmark. "I love you, sweetheart," he whispered again.

Four weeks ago, if anyone had told him he'd be leaving Montana without his daughter, he'd have sent them to see a shrink. No way David Mitchell would ever turn his back on his child.

And if they'd even implied that he could be this love-blinded optimist again, he'd have slugged them.

He'd never known love could hurt so much. He softly pulled the door shut behind him as he crept into Lexie's room.

Perched cross-legged on the edge of her bed, rubbing one foot, Lexie looked at him curiously. "Everything okay?"

"Yeah. No problem." He moved to her dresser,

where a small boom box sat. He hit the power button and a soft melody filled the room. The bed creaked when he sat beside Lexie, pulling her feet into his lap. "Can't dance on sore toes," he told her. He pressed his thumb into the ball of her foot, rotating it gently.

"Ah, damn, that feels good."

"Don't swear," he admonished with a sad smile.

"Why do you look so glum? I'd have thought you'd be walking on air tonight. Sarah told you she loved you." Lexie couldn't stand to see him looking so...pensive and down. David wasn't a down kind of guy. Pensive sometimes, yes. A head man. But he looked like she felt.

"Absolute music to my ears, and my heart." His face grew more animated, his smile more real, happier. "She's fantastic, Lex. You've done a hell of job raising her so far." He stopped rubbing her feet, and she groaned as he stood up, holding his hand out to her. "But I don't want to talk about Sarah. I want to dance with the prettiest woman in town."

She let him take her fingers and pull her from the bed, wrapping his arms around her waist and holding her flush against him. She reached up, caressed the hair on the nape of his neck. Getting a little long, it had a slight curl in it at the end, just like Sarah's.

They rocked slowly in time to the tune from the radio, bare feet occasionally brushing against each other's. One song faded, and another started—Eric Clapton's "Wonderful Tonight."

Lexie lifted her head and looked at him. He smiled down at her. "Yeah. I remember."

It had been her prom theme.

"You wore a yellow dress that set off your eyes and dark hair. You looked wonderful then, but you look even better tonight, princess." He bent his head and kissed her, tenderly, as though she were a fragile thing he might break.

And it was true. He'd always had the power to break her heart if she'd let him close. Now more than ever.

Not just because of Sarah. Because of her own feelings.

The backs of her legs brushed against the bed, and David lowered her to the mattress, followed her down, mouth still connected to hers. Draped along her side, he splayed one leg over hers. He placed teasing kisses on her cheeks, eyelids, the end of her nose. The tip of his tongue traced the curve of her ear. "Sweet Lexie," he whispered. "I want to make love to you again tonight."

He nipped on the fleshy part of her lobe, then dragged his mouth down the slope of her throat.

"Mmmm." Desire surged through her, and she arched her neck. "Yes, David. Love me."

He went very still, then lifted his head. Opening her eyes, she found him staring down, his gaze intent. "I do love you, Lex. And I'm going to prove it."

"Sounds good to me," she whispered, letting her fingers skim his cheek. "Prove it."

He rose from the bed.

"Hey!"

He glanced over his shoulder as he retrieved something from the top of her dresser. "Just making sure we're not interrupted by a certain munchkin."

The key scraped in the lock. His wicked grin in the flickering candlelight made her heart race as he stalked slowly back toward the bed. His expression turned more feral, and a wild glint sparked in his eyes as he unbuttoned his shirt. "Shall I go get the patch? Or should I ravish you without it?"

The temperature in the room climbed. Or maybe it was just her. "Ravish me?"

"Isn't that what pirates do to princesses?" He slid his shirt down his arms and dropped it to the floor.

He held out his hand. She reached out to take it, and he pulled her from the bed. Her fingers closed around his bare shoulders, then wandered down his chest, toying with the soft golden-brown hair. When she fumbled with the snap at the top of his jeans, he sucked in his breath, grabbing her wrists. "Hold it."

"I want to." She chuckled. "But you won't let me."

His soft laughter washed over her. "I had no idea you were so bad, Lexie Jacobs. But I like it." He turned her around, tugging on the back of her dress. The zipper rasped, cool air stroked her spine, then the material puddle around her feet.

She shivered.

"Cold?" he whispered, then pressed his mouth to the back of her nape.

"No. Definitely not cold."

"Good." His kisses blazed a path down her back until he knelt behind her. "Nice." He stroked her new peach lace panties. "Very nice. But this—" he slid them down her legs to join the dress "—this is even better."

Lexie fidgeted as he caressed her skin, alternately using his strong hands and warm mouth. "David…"

"Hmm?" He spun her around again.

She made the mistake of looking down. When he glanced up, an ember flared in his eyes. He grinned, then ran his tongue over his lips.

Her knee shook. "You're not going to—"

The heat of his mouth descended, hovered for a moment just out of reach, teasing, tormenting. Then he touched her.

Oh yeah, he was going to.

And it felt wonderful. Lexie closed her eyes, head back, then lost herself to the sensation, threading her fingers into his hair.

Instead of shouting his name as she wanted when his actions gave her release, she moaned, then sighed with delight. "Mmmm."

He rose. "Don't go anywhere. I've only just begun to ravish you." His lips brushed across her forehead before he moved away.

Lexie pried open her eyes to catch him yanking back the bed covers. "Aye-aye, Captain." She gave him a languid smile that slowly faded as he pulled a condom from his pocket and tossed it to the night table, then reached for his zipper. "Wait!"

He hesitated. "What?"

"Let me."

He smiled, holding his hands out to his side. "By all means."

By the time she worked the zipper to the bottom, he was no longer smiling, but panting, a thin sheen of sweat glistening over his lip. "You're killing me, Lex."

"Turnabout is fair play." She knelt and tugged at his jeans, wiggling them down until his erection popped free. "Oh. Why, David, I'd never have thought it of you. Going commando." She tsked, shaking her head, then ran her tongue over her lips, blatantly imitating his earlier behavior.

He groaned. "Lexie." He infused a note of warning into her name. "I never said anything about playing fair."

"What's wrong, my strong pirate can dish it out, but can't take it?" She closed her hand around him.

"I can take anything you can dish out, princess." He gasped as she flickered her tongue over the top of him.

She set herself to discovering just how true that was, delighted in the power she held over him, enjoying this more playful lovemaking. Every twitch, every stifled groan from him gave her pleasure.

David didn't know how long he could withstand her loving torment, but finally he reached down and grabbed her arms, yanking her to her feet, then pushing her gently onto the bed.

"Do you surrender?" She giggled.

"No surrender." After peeling off his jeans, he turned away from her a moment, opening the condom and rolling it on. Then he crawled onto the bed over her. "I'm just changing the terms of the battle."

Soon David had her writhing beneath him, begging him to join her. When he did, every part of him cried out with the rightness of it. She met him stroke for stroke, her ragged breathing and soft cries urging him on. She gave her passion so freely, he could only hope her heart would follow, that come tomorrow she'd believe in him, in them.

She had to.

Or he'd lose everything.

SOMETHING WET and cold nuzzled her cheek. David? Kissing her? Lexie struggled upward from the cozy cocoon of sleep. "You have to go," she mumbled.

The moist thing lapped at her face again.

She forced her eyes open to discover Toto, standing on the bed beside her, tiny tongue licking her nose. Sarah's anxious face hovered just inches beyond the dog.

Lexie groaned, pushing the puppy gently away from her. "What's going on? I thought I said no dogs on the beds?"

"Toto has to go potty, Momma."

"That's your father's problem, not mine."

Sarah's bottom lip trembled. "Daddy's gone."

"Gone? Where did he go now?" She scooped Toto against her chest with one hand and tossed back the blankets with the other. Figures. Leave it to a man to promise to take care of something, and then take off to the diner, or shopping, or...had he headed off to his lawyer again?

"Back to Ernie."

Lexie's feet hit the floor, and she froze in the middle of rising from the bed. "Ernie? You mean Erie? Honey, you must be mistaken."

Sarah's curls bounced as she shook her head. "Last night he said he had to go home."

He left? Surely not. Toto shivered in her arms. "Baby, take Toto downstairs and put her leash on. I'll be right there." She placed the puppy in the child's arms and rushed into the hallway.

The wooden floor creaked beneath her bare feet. She skirted the stairwell and raced into his room. The bedspread lay unwrinkled since she'd made the bed herself yesterday morning. He hadn't slept in it. The usual things she'd become accustomed to—his balled-up socks lying next to his discarded shoes on the rug by the bed, a pair of his jeans slung over the back of the chair, his notebook computer and printer on the desk—all gone.

The room felt so empty.

Something just wasn't right. David might walk out on her, but not on Sarah. Although after last night, she hadn't expected him to walk out on her, either. Her stomach churned. She scanned the room once more.

A brown envelope lay on the night table, her name written in precise print. She opened it, unfolded a sheet of paper filled with typing. Inside the envelope was a check made out to her. A check for more money than she'd seen in forever. Absentmindedly she tucked it into the breast-pocket of her nightshirt and began to read the letter:

Lexie,

I'm not good with words, so forgive me. I'm going back to Erie. I'm giving you what you want the most—Sarah. And your life back pretty much the way it was before I found you. I'll be calling Sarah every day, and I will provide for her. This check should be enough for now, and I'll send you more next month. If you need more sooner, just let me know.

Why am I doing this? Because I love you, Lexie. I have nothing more to offer you to convince you than this. I'm leaving my daughter with you, and becoming a check-writing daddy.

The words smeared together there, the ink from the printer had run as if the page had gotten wet. *Tears?* David had always vowed he'd never be like his own father, who sent a check once a month and that was all. Lexie glanced back at the paper:

It's killing me to leave either one of you. But I want you to feel like you have choices, Lex. You can choose to marry me and make us a family. Or you can choose to just go on the way you did before.

Make no mistake. I want you, Lexie. I want you in my life, in my arms, in my bed, because you're in my heart, and I don't think you'll ever leave there.

Your decision. And as further proof of my sincerity, I'm leaving you a copy of Sarah's new birth certificate.

You know where to find me when you make up your mind.

It was signed with a sprawling script: *Love Always, David.*

And there was a PS:

I'd really like to be with my daughter on her birthday.

Lexie sank to the edge of the bed. She pulled out the final sheet of paper in the envelope. An official-looking document with a raised seal stamped on the bottom. Sarah's birth certificate. Lexie skimmed her fingers over the seal, then over the names listed. It registered the birth on November 8, of a female child, Sarah Jacobs Mitchell, to the parents, David Edward Mitchell and Lexie Ann Jacobs.

Lexie's hands shook as she set the papers down on the quilt. David had made her Sarah's mother. Legally. And logistically, by leaving his daughter in her care.

He really did love her.

Tears flowed freely down her face.

CHAPTER SEVENTEEN

"Damn it, old man." David slammed one hand into the top of his desk, scattering papers. The other hand tightened around the portable phone until his knuckles turned white and the plastic housing creaked. "Where are they?"

"Told you, I don't know exactly."

"I'll take approximately."

"Can't say."

David shoved the chair away from the desk and rose to pace his home office. He paused in front of the long window. Outside, a gray Erie morning heralded the coming winter. A kid rode a bike on the quiet neighborhood street. Wet leaves littered the yards. "Please. It's Sarah's birthday."

The old man cleared his throat. "I know that."

"Last year I didn't even know today was her birthday. This was supposed to be the first one I spent with her. Instead, I'm back to wondering where my daughter and the woman who has betrayed me *again*, are."

"I know. I'm sorry."

David inhaled deeply. "If you hear from her, please tell her I want to at least talk to my kid on her birthday." He jabbed the Off button, then moved away from the window. Setting the phone on top of his metal file cabinet, he yanked open the second drawer and pulled out a large manila envelope. Inside, a business card with plain black printing held two phone numbers. He dialed the cell number, then resumed pacing, wearing a visible track in the nap of the cream-colored carpet. "Hello, Betty? I'm sorry to disturb you on a Saturday. This is David Mitchell."

"David! It's good to hear from you." The private investigator hesitated. "It *is* good, isn't it?"

"Uh, no, not exactly."

In the background, David heard the shriek of children playing. "Boys, quiet down. Grandma's going into her room to take this call." The laughter and noise got softer, and a door closed. "Okay, sorry. What's going on?"

"Guess I spooked her."

"Oh, David." Compassion filled her voice. "I'm sorry. What happened?"

"I wish I knew. Everything was great. Sarah…" His chest tightened and he struggled to speak. "She was fantastic. Took us a while, but we bonded. I thought Lexie and I had worked things out, too. I proposed to her."

"But?"

"I came home to prove to her I wasn't going to yank Sarah away from her, to prove how much I love her, offer her choices and now they're gone again."

The rustle of paper came through the phone line. "Tell me exactly when you lost contact with them. The quicker we start looking, the more likely they won't get far."

"The first few days after I left were fine. I called,

spoke to Sarah on the phone every day. Lexie seemed fine. Not that we talked much. She said she was thinking things over. Didn't want to rush. Monday of this week was the last time I spoke to either of them. Tuesday I bought into the old man's excuses. Wednesday I started to get suspicious, but by Thursday, I just knew she wasn't there anymore."

"You've called her family?"

"Yeah. If they know something, they're not telling me." Not even Kenny would say if he'd talked to his sister or not.

"Okay, David. Give me a few hours, let me make some phone calls, see what I can dig up."

"Today's her birthday," he said. "My baby's four today."

"I remember. Don't worry. We found them once, we'll find them again. I'll call you soon."

"If you can't reach me at home, try my cell. I'll have it with me."

"Will do."

The phone returned to the base on his desk, David trotted down the stairs. In the living room, he paused just long enough to admire the picture of Sarah he'd placed prominently on the wall. The photograph from their shopping adventure. "Damn you, Lexie. I can't believe you did this to me again. You had no reason this time."

Served him right for being a love-blind fool. An optimist. Following his heart instead of his head.

He'd expected her to call the next day and tell him she believed him, and they'd be waiting for his return. *Fool, fool, fool.*

Unable to stay in the house any longer, he marched into the kitchen, and from there, into the garage. He stabbed the overhead-door button. His leather coat hung on a coat tree. In his mind, though, he saw the pegs near the back door of the bed-and-breakfast, with Sarah's new purple coat on one of the lower hooks.

Cursing under his breath, he slid into his SUV, cranked it to life.

Cruising town did little to soothe him. He drove out on the Peninsula, intending to traverse all fourteen miles of roadway. In the far background, the landfill rose up, bringing to mind Sarah's wrinkled nose at learning that was what substituted for mountains in the immediate Erie area.

He found himself turning up State Street, the road that divided Erie into east and west. He shifted one block west onto Peach. Signs for the Erie Zoo had him imagining taking Sarah there. Had she ever been to a zoo? Mill Creek, Montana, didn't have one. She'd probably love the train and the carousel.

The Saturday prelunch traffic—the "Peach Jam" in local vernacular—crawled near the mall. Sarah could have a field day shopping with him there. With his luck, it probably had a purple jacket with fuzzy stuff on the hood in every department store.

Connie's Ice Cream, the movie theaters, all things he'd intended to share with his daughter.

He gripped the steering wheel tighter, and eventually found himself parked in front of Chuck E. Cheese. A minivan pulled next to him. A man and woman got out of the front seats, and three kids spilled from the sliding door. The woman reached back inside, retrieving a gaily wrapped present with long, multicolored ribbons that swirled in the breeze.

David watched them enter the place he'd intended to take Sarah for her birthday celebration.

A deep, hollow sensation crawled up from the pit of his stomach. In all the time he'd spent looking for them the first time, he'd never known pain and despair quite like this.

Because then he could only imagine what he was missing.

Now, he knew.

THE TWO-LAYER CAKE pitched to the right. Little clumps of the yellow cake showed in the chocolate frosting. David licked the spatula and nodded. He hadn't made a cake since food science class in high school. It wasn't perfect, certainly nowhere near what "Momma" would have made for Sarah, and Mrs. Wachter, his former teacher, probably would have given him a C on it, but by damn, he'd made it himself. Water splashed as he dropped the utensil into the sudsy bowl in the sink.

When the phone jingled, he slung a dish towel over his shoulder and peered down at the caller ID display. He snatched the handset up. "Betty! That was fast. Have you found out anything?"

"I've got a rental car in John Nonnemacher's name, on his credit card, rented from the airport in Butte. But John's at the bed-and-breakfast. So, I'd say that makes it pretty clear what she's driving, anyway."

"Any idea where she's headed?" He kneaded the tight muscles in the back of his neck.

"Haven't found anything else yet, but I'll keep on it. We can find out where the car gets returned to Avis. You sure you don't want to notify the police? I've got the make, model and plate. They could put out an APB, or maybe even issue an Amber Alert."

"No! Cops swarming them would terrify Sarah. She's been through enough lately. Like you said, we found them once, we'll find them again. I have faith in you, Betty."

"Okay, it's your call. I'll let you know ASAP if I find out anything new."

"Thanks." After replacing the phone, he dropped the towel on the counter. He stuck pink candles into the cake, then carried it to the kitchen table. Outside the sliding door to the deck, twilight gathered. Orangey clouds streaked the sky.

Sinking down into one of the chairs, David propped his chin in his palm. Next to the cake, the gold velvet box from the Sapphire Mine displayed the ring he'd bought for Lexie, another prop to flog himself with.

God, how he missed both of them.

How stupid could one allegedly intelligent man get?

He glanced back to the cake. Matches. He needed matches. Fumbling through the junk drawer, he shoved aside string, tape, keys, and eventually found a battered book of matches.

The doorbell rang.

A small, irrational spark of hope flickered to life. Cutting through the living room, he forced himself to stroll to the front door. He flung it open. "Mom." Disappointment filled him, and he hoped it hadn't come through in his voice. "What are you doing here?"

She pointed over her shoulder at the Lincoln parked near his mailbox. "Actually, it was your father's idea. He said it was your little girl's birthday, and he thought maybe you'd need some company. And you wouldn't answer my phone calls."

Despite the nippy November air, his face grew warm. "Sorry, Mom." He looked out to the street. The Judge had suggested the visit?

David opened the door wider. "Why don't you come in?" He cleared his throat. "Both of you."

His mother arched her well-groomed eyebrows in shock. "Both of us?"

"Yeah. Come on, it's cold out there."

She waved at the car, motioning for his father to join them. Clad in a long woolen overcoat, the Judge strode briskly to the front step. He inclined his head in greeting. "David."

A confusing swirl of emotions rolled through David. This man had let him down, missed out on his entire childhood. He'd been a check-writing father when it suited him.

And yet, now David found himself in a similar position. Never in a million years had he expected to feel some connection with the Judge. "Come on in." Taking his mother's coat and hanging it in the foyer closet, he turned to accept the gray overcoat, and couldn't stop his jaw from dropping open in surprise. "You're wearing jeans?"

Phillip Wysocki ran a hand over his hair, chuckling.

"Yes, and I put them on one pant leg at a time like everyone else, too."

"Guess I've only ever seen you in a suit," David muttered, embarrassed by his reaction. But it wasn't his fault he didn't know much about his old man.

Or was it? After all, he'd been the one who'd refused to have anything to do with him once his mother had told him the truth, after the Judge's wife had died. Thirteen was a hellish time for a kid, and dropping the bombshell of his father's identity on him then hadn't helped.

At least his mother hadn't forced it on him. And she'd waited to continue her own relationship with the man.

It had taken him months to even phone his mother after she'd married the Judge, the pair eloping to Hawaii while David had been away at college. He'd never gone back home after that, spending summers at his apartment near school.

Maybe it was time to put aside all the hurt he'd carried over the years and find out what his father's story really was. "You guys want some cake?"

"That would be lovely, dear." His mother headed for the kitchen, but stopped short at the photograph on the wall. "Is that your Sarah? Oh, David, she's adorable."

"Thanks. I think so, too, but then I'm probably biased."

"It's not easy to have only photographs of your child."

David turned to face the man who was his father.

"So, why'd you settle for that while I was growing up?"

"I think I'll make some coffee to go with the cake," his mom said, slipping into the kitchen.

"I told you, son, that sometimes a man makes mistakes. My mistake wasn't in creating you, but in not having the courage to acknowledge you sooner and let the chips fall where they may."

"Why didn't you?"

"Because all my life I'd wanted to be someone important. A judge. Maybe a politician. My wife was in a car accident three years before I met your mother. The crash left her severely impaired. I had to put her in a nursing home." Creases appeared in the Judge's forehead as he frowned. "It was hard. Really hard. Some days she knew me. Most days..." He shrugged.

"But then I met your mom." He smiled.

David fought the impulse to step backward as a dimple appeared in the Judge's right cheek.

"She made me feel alive again, hopeful. I shouldn't have let things go as far as they did. But I don't regret it. I don't know if I would have survived those days without your mother."

"But the affair and an illegitimate kid?"

"Would have ruined my chances for a bench if they'd become public knowledge. Which is why your birth certificate read 'Father Unknown.' Because your father was a coward who put his career before the people he cared about." He held out a large envelope. "Your phone call got me thinking. Hope you believe in better late than never, son."

David took it, lifting a sheet of paper from inside.

The raised seal of the state of Pennsylvania bumped beneath his curious fingers. "A new birth certificate? For me?" Phillip Edward Wysocki was listed under "Father's Name."

"I hope you don't mind. After all, it is pretty late."

"I—I don't know what to say." Besides, the huge lump in David's throat made it tough to talk. He swallowed hard.

"Don't say anything. Except that you'll give your old man a chance to get to know his son after all these years."

"And if it wrecks your career now?"

His father grinned. "Scandal has become much more commonplace these days. With the right spin…" He shrugged, and the grin slowly faded. "I think you'd be worth it."

"Sure as hell took you long enough."

"Yes, it did. And I'm more sorry about that than you'll ever know." His father held out his hand. "What do you say?"

David took the offered grip, letting his fingers close around his father's hand for the first time. Though he'd met with the Judge on rare occasions, they'd never shaken hands, never touched. The Judge was now willing to put his career on the line—to sacrifice—for him. "I say, nice to meet you. Dad."

Moisture glistened in the man's brown eyes as David pumped his hand. The Judge cleared his throat. "Good." Releasing David's hand, he cuffed him on the shoulder. "What do you say we go see how your mom's making out with that coffee?"

"Sure."

In the kitchen, they found David's mom staring at the coffee machine as the dark liquid dripped into the pot. "Mom?"

She turned to face them, tears coursing down her cheeks.

"Aw, Mom. Don't. Don't cry." David rushed forward, taking his mother into his arms. "Why are you sad?"

"I'm not." She sniffled against his chest. "I'm happy. I never thought I'd live to see this day."

Over his mother's head, David glanced at his father, who lifted one shoulder and rolled his eyes. *Women,* the look said. Who could understand them?

Not David. He was done trying.

The doorbell rang again, twice in rapid succession. "Now who?" David asked, releasing his mother. "Be right back."

This time when he opened the door, he discovered a huge bunch of Mylar balloons. His heart thudded against his chest wall as he glanced down. The balloons wore a purple coat with fuzzy stuff along the bottom, and farther down, a pair of ruby slippers.

Stunned, he stood there for a moment. The balloons rustled impatiently. "What in the world?" he finally managed to say.

The shiny silver balloons rose on a set of entwined ribbons, and Sarah's beaming face came into view. "Surprise!" she yelled. "Happy birfday, Daddy!"

"Sarah." He rushed out onto the step, the storm door slamming behind him. The child giggled as he scooped her up into his arms. "You're here! In Erie!"

"Easy, Daddy, the balloons will fly away!"

He kissed her soundly on both cheeks. "I can't believe you're here."

"We surprised you?"

"Oh, yeah, I'm surprised all right." He glanced around. "But where's your momma?"

Sarah's nose wrinkled. "Toto gets carsick. He barfed on the front seat right when we got here."

David stifled a chuckle. "Oops. Bet your mom isn't too happy about that."

"No, she's not."

Lexie slogged up the driveway, Toto under one arm, and a blue plastic bag dangling from her other hand. Her mouth was set in a thin, tight line, and her hair blew in her face. She looked tired and cranky.

And he'd never seen a more beautiful woman in his life.

She hadn't betrayed him. She'd come to him.

She marched up the steps and thrust the puppy at him, forcing him to shift Sarah into one arm and take Toto in the other. "You forgot your dog," she said. "If you think you're getting off that easily, I've got news for you, buster."

"Okay, so what is it?"

"What's what?"

"What's the news for me?"

The features of her face softened, and she offered him a tentative smile that wiped the weariness from her eyes. "I believe you."

"You do? What do you believe?" He couldn't stop the grin that appeared on his face.

"Do we have to do this on the porch, or are you going to invite us in?"

He didn't want Sarah getting a chill, or else he wouldn't have budged until everything was resolved. "Welcome," he said, opening the storm door. After Lexie went into the foyer and dropped the bag, he followed. Their coats got draped over the stair banister. He set Sarah and Toto on the floor, then pulled Lexie into his arms and kissed her soundly. Then, he whispered, "What do you believe, Lexie?"

She smiled at him, reaching up to cup his face. Happiness twinkled in her eyes. "That you love me. Will you marry me, David Mitchell?"

"Lexie Jacobs, it would be my pleasure to marry you."

"Yeaaayy!" Sarah yelled, jumping up and down and clapping her hands. Toto yipped, running in circles on the wooden parquet floor. "We're getting married!"

"What's all the commotion?" David's mom and dad appeared in the living room. "Who's getting married?"

Sarah ran to David, pressing her face against his leg.

David lifted her into one arm, and wrapped the other around Lexie's shoulders. "We're getting married," he announced. "But first, we're having a birthday party. Mom, Dad, this is Sarah, our daughter. She's shy," he explained as the child hid in his neck. "Maybe, before we light the candles on the cake, we should call the rest of the family and get them over here." He looked at Lexie. "Kenny and Jess and the baby, Marc, and your parents should be here, don't you think?"

She nodded, moisture gathering in her eyes.

"Don't," he warned. "Don't you dare cry, or I'm not giving you the present I got you."

Sarah's head snapped up. "Hey, it's *my* birfday. I get the presents, not Momma."

"Oh, I have stuff for you, sport. But your momma worked hard on your birthday, and I wasn't there for her. She gave me you, the best present in the whole world. I think she deserves something, too." He leaned forward to whisper in the little girl's ear. She nodded, and when he set her on the floor, she ran into the living room, giving her newly found grandparents a wary look and a wide berth.

"You got me a present?" Lexie asked.

"Yep. Come on in the kitchen." Arm still slung around her shoulder, he guided her to the table. Sarah stood beside it, arms behind her, rocking back and forth on her feet.

"Did you make the cake?" Lexie asked.

"Yes, I did. All by myself."

"It looks delicious."

"It looks ridiculous, but thank you." He nodded to Sarah. The little girl came forward and held out the box.

Lexie's eyes widened.

David snapped it open and took out the ring. The white-gold setting and tiny diamonds sparkled, refracting the light from overhead, but the blue teardrop sapphire in the middle shimmered like the captured Montana sky.

"Is that a Rock Creek sapphire?" she whispered.

"Yes," he said, slipping it on her finger. "To remind you of where you found a home for yourself and our daughter. And now, me. Thank you for making my dreams come true, Lexie. I love you."

Sarah tugged on his pant leg. "And me, Daddy?"

He picked her up. "Definitely you." He embraced both Sarah and Lexie at the same time. "Family hug."

"Family hug," Lexie echoed, still looking stunned. "I love you both."

As his parents watched, Sarah placed one hand on the back of each of David's and Lexie's heads, pushing them together until their noses bumped. "Now you gotta kiss. It's what mommas and daddies do."

David obliged his daughter, kissing Lexie tenderly.

Maybe being blinded by love wasn't so bad after all.

Sarah giggled. "And they lived happily ever after," she intoned. "Even if the daddy wasn't a king."

* * * *

You'll absolutely love the next novel in
A LITTLE SECRET *series.*
The SEAL's Baby *by Rogenna Brewer*
is out in March 2006!

Don't miss it!

SILHOUETTE® SuperROMANCE™

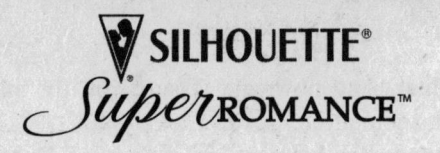

THE SEAL'S BABY by Rogenna Brewer
A Little Secret
Hannah Stanton, engineer and single mum, is suddenly called to active duty by the Navy. Now she has to leave her baby behind while she flies helicopters in support of the Navy SEAL team that includes the man who doesn't know he's her baby's father.

GETTING MARRIED AGAIN
by Melinda Curtis
9 Months Later
Jackson loves his job, but hates the fact that it takes him away from his family... That is his expanding family—his wife, Lexie, has just informed him that she's pregnant again. How can he prove to her that he'll be there for her this time...and forever?

HOME TO FAMILY by Ann Evans
Heart of the Rockies
Leslie Meadows has had anything but a perfect life. She loves her nursing job, but it's been hard taking care of her father all these years. Then life takes a turn for the better when her best friend, Matt D'Angelo, comes for a visit. Can Leslie convince him to stay?

THE SAINT by Kathleen O'Brien
The Heroes of Heyday
Everyone in Heyday loves Kieran McClintock—everyone except Claire Strickland that is. But when Kieran comes to see her, she succumbs to loneliness and grief and ends up in his arms. Six weeks later she discovers that her one night with Kieran has had major consequences.

On sale from 17th February 2006

Available at WHSmith, Tesco, ASDA, Borders, Eason, Sainsbury's and most bookshops

www.silhouette.co.uk